Praise for the Detective Gal

'Mind blowing'

'Keeps you on the edge of your seat'

'A great crime procedural series!'

'An amazing thriller from beginning to end'

'Couldn't ask for a better read'

'This series just keeps getting better. I was hooked from the first page'

'A five-star read, no question'

Born in Dublin, **JENNY O'BRIEN** moved to Wales and then Guernsey, where she tries to find time to both read and write in between working as a nurse and ferrying around three teenagers.

In her spare time she can be found frowning at her wonky cakes and even wonkier breads. You'll be pleased to note she won't be entering *Bake Off*. She's also an all-year-round sea swimmer.

Also by Jenny O'Brien

The Detective Gaby Darin series
Silent Cry
Darkest Night

The Stepsister

Fallen Angel

JENNY O'BRIEN

ONE PLACE. MANY STORIES

This novel is entirely a work of fiction. The names, characters and incidents portrayed in it are the work of the author's imagination. Any resemblance to actual persons, living or dead, events or localities is entirely coincidental.

HQ
An imprint of HarperCollins*Publishers* Ltd
1 London Bridge Street
London SE1 9GF

www.harpercollins.co.uk

HarperCollinsPublishers
1st Floor, Watermarque Building, Ringsend Road
Dublin 4, Ireland

This paperback edition 2021

This edition is published in Great Britain by
HQ, an imprint of HarperCollins*Publishers* Ltd 2021

Copyright © Jenny O'Brien 2020

Jenny O'Brien asserts the moral right to be
identified as the author of this work.
A catalogue record for this book is
available from the British Library.

ISBN: 9780008390204

MIX
Paper from
responsible sources
FSC™ C007454

This book is produced from independently certified FSC™ paper
to ensure responsible forest management.

For more information visit: www.harpercollins.co.uk/green

Printed and bound in Great Britain by
CPI Group (UK) Ltd, Croydon CR0 4YY

All rights reserved. No part of this publication may be reproduced,
stored in a retrieval system, or transmitted, in any form or by any means,
electronic, mechanical, photocopying, recording or otherwise,
without the prior permission of the publishers.

This book is sold subject to the condition that it shall not, by way of trade
or otherwise, be lent, re-sold, hired out or otherwise circulated without
the publisher's prior consent in any form of binding or cover other than
that in which it is published and without a similar condition including this
condition being imposed on the subsequent purchaser.

To Ady Sarchet, the Sea Donkey, who works tirelessly for Guernsey disabled swimmers.

Prologue

She lies on her back unsure of what the delay is. After all, she's not stupid. She's guessed what must be next. It's there in the gleam of his eye and the excited sheen on his forehead as he leans towards her, his hands rearranging the pale cotton around her body. She knows now that there's no hope. No knight to rescue the damsel in distress. No future in her golden prison of green.

The light morning breeze and weak early sunshine do nothing to warm her skin or assuage her fears. If anything, her fears escalate as she wonders how much more of this glorious day she'll manage to see. The rock underneath her shoulders and bottom is cold and hard, the musty nightdress unable to protect her tender skin or prevent the panic bubbling up underneath her fragile, pale beauty. It's there to see in her wide-eyed stare, the black of her pupil etched against the pale grey of her iris and the pulse in her throat dancing to its own frantic beat.

With her arms and legs unbound she knows she could run. There are lots of places to hide and, having visited the Great Orme regularly since childhood, she knows most of them. But it's not string or tape that bind her to what she suspects will be her final resting place. It's the words she can't forget in the dark thicket of her mind. Her throat constricts, her breath now a hollow rasp as his fingers start their inevitable journey across her flesh. If she runs someone else will die.

1

Chapter 1

Gaby

Wednesday 15 July, 2.10 p.m. St Asaph Police Station

Acting DI Gaby Darin was going to suppress the yawn with the back of her hand but decided not to bother. There was little point in hiding the truth. She was in one of the most exciting careers imaginable. Almost at the top of her game, if you like, with cases being flung at her from all corners as society dug deep and threw the worst kind of humanity in her direction. Yet here she was doing a cop's version of twiddling her thumbs: flicking through the stack of cold cases they had lurking in the storage room in the bowels of the station.

She hugged her new, grey, pin-striped jacket more firmly across her chest, bemoaning the fact that she hadn't had the foresight to wear one of her old suits. When the station had been remodelled, no expense had been spared on the glossy new reception and interview rooms. But the same couldn't be said for the, quite frankly, miserable storage facilities hidden from public view. Oh, there were computers, high-tech systems that could do everything

2

from trapping a perp with only part of a number plate via the ANPR tracking system, to searching international databases using state-of-the-art face-recognition software. But for that to happen records had to be electronic and the crimes she was looking through had all happened well before a desktop meant anything other than a surface to work off.

Pushing back from the table, she stood and stretched, her tight muscles rebelling against the last two hours of enforced inactivity, her eyes raking over the list of three murder victims' case numbers she'd scribbled down to examine in more detail. The problem was one of motivation. It was easy to be enthusiastic about a current case, a case where she'd built up a sense of rapport with the victim or, in the case of a murder, their relatives. But these . . . While all of them were serious cases that deserved to be solved, it was likely that there'd be few people left who remembered what had happened or even cared. She wanted something exciting. Something to get her teeth into while she still had the free time to make a difference. With summer well and truly here, who knew what crimes would claim her attention? But while things were quiet, she was determined to make inroads on the ever-growing pile of unsolved cases. For one thing it would keep her boss, Henry Sherlock, out of her hair. He was forever banging on about crime rates and how well the North Wales MIT was performing against the rest of the UK – a solved cold case would garner an additional boost to those rankings.

She returned the files to their relevant boxes and, picking up her notepad, headed for the door.

'Thank you, Colin,' she said, tossing the grey-haired archive officer a smile before signing out and walking up the stairs back to her office. She'd have a coffee and while she was drinking it, make a list for and against each of the cases shortlisted. It shouldn't be too difficult to narrow it down, she thought, her mind running over each one as she entered her office and threw her pad on the desk. But before she could head back into the incident room and

3

pour a drink from the coffee pot, Detective Owen Bates barged through the door, his hands full of newspaper cuttings which he unceremoniously spread across the desk with a flourish.

Folding her arms across her chest, she threw the tall, stocky Welshman a small smile. 'I take it you've decided to add to my list of potential cold cases, Owen?' Her gaze slid to the top article and the image of a young woman, a girl really, her hair swept back into an untidy ponytail. 'It had better be more interesting than the poor retired bank manager you were telling me about who pitched himself under that bus last month – poor sod.'

'There's no comparison. This one here,' he said, placing his hand flat against the top article, his customary smile missing, 'is a real humdinger of a case that, if rumours are to be believed, had old Stewart Tipping running around in circles.'

Gaby frowned, managing to hide her surprise. She'd worked with Owen now for nearly six months and had always found him to be the most mild-mannered of people. Nothing fazed him and, despite the often grizzly nature of their job, he was always the one to break the tension with the most inappropriate of jokes that only other members of the force could truly appreciate. So, there was something about this case that had piqued his interest, was there? Something that had made him gather a file full of tattered newspaper articles. Something that had pulled him so far out of his comfort zone as to remove any trace of humour from his face. Now, for the first time in what seemed like ages, she was interested.

She unfolded her arms, picked up the top newspaper article and started to read, her mouth saying the words out loud.

'The body of the missing Llandudno teenager has been found on the Great Orme. A spokesperson for the North Wales police department has said that the body has been identified as eighteen-year-old Angelica Brock, who went missing from her home in Llandudno in the early hours of Tuesday morning.'

She paused as she scanned the rest of the article, the words causing her lips to curl and her jaw to tighten. A well-known phrase streaked through her mind: *Be careful what you wish for.* She'd been bored out of her mind since her return from sick leave, so bored that she'd even pulled out her end-of-month report, something that was never started until the warnings from above became too threatening to ignore – usually halfway through the next month. She'd wanted a case to sink her teeth into but the disappearance of an innocent girl from her bedroom and subsequent discovery of her lifeless body in a well-known picnic spot, wasn't what she'd envisaged. Scrolling to the top of the page, she noted the date. 1995. Twenty-five years ago, which would have made Gaby only six. Far too young for her to have taken an interest in the news. But for Owen, born and bred in Llandudno, the case obviously meant something more than the facts spread out in front of her in all their messy tabloid glory.

'Go on then.'

'Ma'am?'

'Oh, cut the crap, Owen.' Her voice was edged with more razors than the average barbershop. 'You know very well I'm still only acting DI and, when we're alone it's Gaby or Gabriella. Even Miss Darin will suffice – but ma'am,' she added, the slight twang from her Liverpudlian accent hammering the M into submission, 'is not allowed – ever.'

'Gaby then,' he said, his expression still grim.

'Why this case now after all these years?' she said, her mind taking a walk through the other cold cases before switching back to Angelica Brock – there was no comparison. 'And if you reply with the "Why not?" that I can see you're about to, then you're a lesser man than I thought.'

'Because I knew her.'

5

Chapter 2

Gaby

Wednesday 15 July, 2.25 p.m. St Asaph Police Station

'You knew her,' Gaby repeated, plonking herself down in her chair and gesturing for him to do the same, only to stop, her hand tapping the rim of her empty mug. 'Coffee, please. It's only fair if you're going to land this in my lap that you fuel my caffeine addiction first.'

'I thought that was chocolate, Gabriella?' he said, casting her a wink before backing out of the room, his hands raised as if to ward off the inevitable snappy reply.

Gaby shook her head, her mind already on the case in front of her, her hands skimming through the articles for the most reliable report. After a morning of dealing with facts, the lurid headlines almost had her wishing she'd passed on the coffee, the smell of Asda's cheapest dry roast wafting through the door causing her nose to wrinkle and her stomach to flip.

'There you go. Extra strong, just the way you like it,' Owen said, making room for both mugs on the desk and pulling up a chair.

6

'So, tell me about Angelica Brock then. How did you know her?' She pushed her mug to one side. 'You'd have only been about . . .'

'Twelve, and I didn't know her, not well.'

She leant forward, propping her elbows on the desk, her chin balanced in her hands. 'Explain.'

'Well, we went to the same school but she was miles out of my league. She made head girl so we all knew of her.' Gaby watched him blink rapidly, before continuing. 'She was quiet. Studious even. You know the sort. Heading for a posh degree in some English university to study medicine, but nice with it. Her sister was in my class, not that I had much to do with her then being as she was only a girl,' he finished, managing a smirk of sorts.

'Of course you wouldn't.' Gaby returned his stare head on, well aware that his blasé attitude was only a ruse. There was more going on under the slight blush trailing a path underneath his cheeks, only partially covered by his beard. She had a pair of older brothers back in Liverpool. She knew what it was like with boys especially when the girls looked like Angelica Brock. Dropping her gaze, she examined the top photo. Angelica had that near white-blonde hair that always ratcheted up male heartbeats. But there was also an innocence about her, an innocence that would have been bound to attract the worst kind of individual. And with that thought, something curled deep inside, dragging Gaby straight to the dark place that resided in the corner of her mind.

All coppers had such a place. If they didn't, they wouldn't be able to survive even a week in the force. They certainly wouldn't have a home life and as for even considering having children . . . They had to compartmentalise the day-to-day horrors they came up against or face drowning in their poison of choice, be that alcohol, drugs or, in Gaby's case, chocolate.

'So, what can you add?' she said, pushing the pile of cuttings in his direction.

'What do you mean?'

7

'Come on, Owen. Give me more. Stewart Tipping is one of the best coppers around. If the case nearly broke him, what's to say it isn't going to be a complete dead end or, indeed, break me?'

He didn't answer at once, the flooring covering her office taking up more of his attention than the wood-effect laminate deserved.

'I don't know what else there is. Llandudno changed after that. It grew up if you like and yanked us kids along with it. Almost overnight, we weren't allowed out at night without being interrogated about where we were going and who with. Yes, Llandudno became a little safer, but it also became a little sadder. With her death, we lost a whole lot more than her, if that makes sense?' He lifted his head and, if Gaby didn't know any better, she'd think that his eyes were moist. 'I don't know what else to say.' He spread his hands again before twisting them and reaching for the now empty mugs. 'I was just a lad. It was only later, when I decided to go into the force that I searched up her case file or should that be files – there's boxes of them.' He tilted his head, aiming a smile in her direction. 'We all know what a stickler Stewart is for recordkeeping. She seemed so sweet and innocent when they found her, that beautiful hair billowing out like a pillow. Her pure white nightdress didn't help. It looked like she'd dropped off to sleep. I could see then why the press hit on the tagline of The Angel Murder. The force even adopted the moniker in the case title – Operation Angel.'

Operation Angel. Gaby let the phrase roll around her mind, her hands shuffling through the photos. This Angelica Brock wouldn't be the first pretty schoolgirl to meet a grizzly end and, sadly, she wouldn't be the last. Wherever beauty lay there was always ugliness lurking in the shadows. So, what made this different and, more importantly, what made her think that this might be a case she could solve? She'd be arrogant in thinking she was even half as good a detective as Stewart Tipping. Before going off sick, he'd had thirty years in the force and a conviction rate that was renowned throughout the North Wales network. If he

8

couldn't find the clue that would break the case wide open then there probably wasn't one to be found.

Pulling out her notepad, she scrolled through the list of the other crimes she'd jotted down earlier, before shutting it with a snap. She wanted to sink her teeth into a case that would occupy her mind and distract her thoughts. After the craziness of recent months, the idea of a cold case appealed. If truth be known, not that she'd admit it to anyone, she still suffered from exhaustion following her near-fatal stabbing during the previous case. A nice quiet mystery to work through while she continued to convalesce from her injuries would suit her nicely.

'Okay, Owen. Let's do this. Pop down to Colin in Archives and give him the heads up as to what files we'll need and, on the way back, you can make some fresh coffee. That one tasted as if a mouse had thrown up in it. And after, I'll treat you to lunch. Your usual sandwich from the canteen do?'

Chapter 3

Gaby

Thursday 16 July, 5 p.m. Old Colwyn

Stewart Tipping had once been a large, imposing figure. But the cancer had ripped through his body, stripping away the covering and leaving only the inner man under the disease-ravished flesh. His body was now skin attached to bone, his face shrunken to almost a death mask and his upright bearing now an old man's stoop. The changes wrought since Gaby had last seen him had her hiding her feelings behind her habitual bland countenance: Stewart wouldn't take kindly to even a flicker of compassion. After a brief smile for Sheila, his long-suffering wife, Gaby took the seat offered and got right down to business.

'I'm sorry it's been so long but . . .'

He waved her comment away, the veins standing proud on the back of his hand. 'While you're always welcome, I wouldn't expect you to keep popping in,' he said, reaching for his mug and cradling the pottery between his fingers. 'What can I help you with? I do take it that there is something?'

10

'How do you know that I haven't popped around for a chat?' she fired back, with an answering beam.

'Well, have you?'

She glanced down at her hands before replying, taking the time to choose her words carefully. She'd spent all day reading up on Operation Angel but examining dry-as-dust witness statements and file notes had done little to bring the case to life. The reason she'd swung past Stewart's bungalow in Old Colwyn was to get a first-hand feel for the crime, all those little thoughts and nuances that would need a truck-load of notebooks to fill, and she needed to do it in such a way as to not offend the man in front of her. Now she was here it was the sense of guilt that would keep her long past her original motive for visiting.

'No.' She raised her head, meeting his gaze square on. 'The reason I'm here is because of Angelica Brock.'

'Ah.'

There was a wealth of feeling in that one meaningless syllable. Stewart's expression remained unchanged but his tightening knuckles told their own story. She'd upset him – the very last thing she wanted but it couldn't be helped. Owen's knowledge of the case was coloured by the viewpoint of a twelve-year-old boy. He couldn't be the impartial partner she needed and everyone else had either retired or moved to other teams round the country. Dropping in on Stewart and Sheila on her way home was meant to be the easy option, But, by the sudden tension in the room, it felt like the wrong decision.

'My one big failure.'

What could she say that wasn't going to upset him any more than she was doing? After all, he was only stating the truth. All coppers had their fair share of failures. It was never just one that got away these days. With manpower pressures, they were hard pressed to keep on top of whatever came through the door let alone have the time to invest any energy into unsolved cases. Gaby sighed, thinking back to her own failings over the years.

11

The successes never featured. The families she'd helped. The lives she'd saved. No . . . She sighed again. She shouldn't have come but, now she was here, she owed this man complete honesty.

'I can't promise to have more success than you had, Stewart. But I've been reading over the files with Owen and I think it's something that deserves our attention.'

He ran his hand over his bald head, his gaze avoiding hers. 'Of all the cases I've ever worked on, it's the one that baffled the most. We did everything we could. Followed all the angles we could think of. Interviewed half of Llandudno in the process, but nothing. It had more blind ends than Hampton Court Maze. She disappeared from a first-floor bedroom and yet there were no clues. We didn't know if she had a secret assignation or if she'd been abducted. But if it was the latter, how was it managed without an accomplice or two? But there were no fingerprints left at the scene. No DNA on the body. The post-mortem was inconclusive as to the method of her death. All they could come up with was that her heart had stopped.' He leant forward in his chair, his hands gripped together. 'The truth is, all we had was the body of an eighteen-year-old. There were no indications of sexual activity and no evidence of force or bruising. Her blood alcohol level was pretty much zero as was the drugs screen. It's as if she climbed out of the window and made her way to the Great Orme before curling up and drifting off into a sleep that resulted in her death.'

Gaby took a deep sip of tea, made the way she liked it. She was hoping that he'd give her additional information. All the little extras that on their own didn't add up to squat but together might just have the makings of a case. But he wasn't telling her anything she didn't already know.

'What about the boyfriend? He had an alibi, I believe?' she said, placing her now empty mug back on the table.

'Yes, and, as the most obvious candidate, one we looked to break. But there was no evidence that he wasn't exactly what he

12

seemed, completely heartbroken,' he said with a sigh. 'Also that scenario would mean that she'd climbed out of the window to meet him without leaving any evidence, which is unlikely at best. There was no other way out of the house.'

'No other way.' Gaby frowned, her mind stepping back into the reports she'd read. Obviously, there were still a fair few box files to go through but . . . 'What about the front door, or indeed the back?'

'Not a chance. Their younger daughter, Katherine, suffered from an extreme form of sleepwalking – it's well documented in one of the files. The house was locked down at night, the keys kept under the mother's pillow. The only answer is that Angelica unbolted the window from the inside. Therefore, it follows that she must have known her murderer.' He rested his head against the blue fabric of his chair, his voice whisper soft. 'Believe me when I say that we examined this from every angle and came up with nothing. If it wasn't for her wearing that nightdress, we'd have been happy to pass it off as one of those things but . . .'

Gaby pulled out her notebook and, flicking through the pages, quickly found what she wanted. 'A long-sleeved, Victorian, pin-tucked nightdress? It did strike me as odd at the time.'

'Indeed.' He sent her a long glance before delivering his punch-line. 'Her mother insisted during interview that Angelica only ever wore pyjamas to bed and that she'd never seen the garment before in her life. And . . .' He paused, taking a deep swallow. 'Before you ask, yes, we did do a thorough search. But we quickly realised that the nightdress was handmade. We didn't have a chance.'

Gaby felt a tension headache start to build. Headaches weren't her thing, unless they were self-inflicted and, apart from the odd glass of wine with her evening meal, she rarely drank anymore. Since coming out of hospital she hadn't touched a drop. She blinked down at her pad, trying to work out what else to ask, her mind weaving back through the key points, even as she silently cursed Owen to hell and back for plonking this onto her lap.

13

The problem was that he knew her too well. As soon as she got excited about a case, she wouldn't let it rest until she'd exhausted every lead. But what would she be able to do when there were no leads? Operation Angel wasn't so much cold as absolutely polar.

'So we have an eighteen-year-old girl climbing out of a window to meet person or persons unknown, only to lie down in a ball and die of natural causes in borrowed nightwear. I don't get it!'

'Join the club. Like I said, if it wasn't for the nightwear side of things, we'd have passed it off as death by misadventure.' He threw his hands up in the air, letting them fall down on his thighs with a dull slap. 'It's as if the killer wanted us to know what he'd done.'

Gaby's eyes narrowed. 'What – like a serial killer?'

'Apart from there being no other murders either before or since carried out with anything like the same pattern. Believe me when I say that up until my illness, I continued to carry out a search where cause of death was unclear. There's been plenty of those but none where the medical examiner couldn't eventually come up with a reasonable explanation, and none of the women found were wearing someone else's nightie.'

'That's useful, thanks.'

She'd have to leave soon. She could see it in the way Stewart's shoulders had sunk further into his chest and in the shadows bruising his skin.

'I'll pop these into the kitchen and say hi to Sheila before I head off.' She collected the mugs, her mind still running over the case. 'I don't know what Bates is trying to do. There's no way I can bring anything more to the table apart from modern science but there's no DNA to throw at it.'

She watched him jerk forward, suddenly wide awake when seconds before she'd thought he was dropping off to sleep.

'I can't believe that he wouldn't have told you.'

'Told me what?'

'About Katherine, the sister. It's his wife, Gaby. It's Kate.'

14

Chapter 4

Gaby

Thursday 16 July, 7.15 p.m. St Asaph

'Why the hell didn't you tell me, Owen? I felt like a right wally,' Gaby said, as soon as the door had closed behind Kate's back.

She'd gone straight from Stewart's house to Owen's end-of-terrace situated around the corner from St Asaph's Town Hall. The neat two-bedroomed property might not have either the sea views or the gardens of her cottage but Kate's flair for design had turned it into a cosy retreat, perfect to come home to. It was little Pip's bedtime when she'd arrived, so she'd had to wait until Owen had gone to tuck him up for the night before coming out with the reason for her visit.

'Sorry about that but I wanted you to make the decision based on the worthiness of the case and not because of Kate,' he replied, sitting down in the chair opposite and stroking his beard, a clear sign that he was anxious or worried – quite possibly both.

'The one thing I don't understand,' Gaby continued, as if he hadn't spoken, 'is why you've never said a word. Not a peep in

15

all the time we've been working together. For your wife's sister to be murdered is quite a big thing, or isn't it that important?' She watched him open his mouth, only to snap it closed when he caught her look. 'No, don't speak. I don't think I could bear to hear an explanation now. It's all a bit too late.'

Gaby felt her anger build. As a child she'd had an explosive temper, which she'd learnt to manage. Now the pot was boiling to overflowing, pushing the lid aside and releasing a lava of emotion – she didn't know why. Owen wasn't just a colleague. He was a friend and, next to Amy, probably her best friend but that didn't mean that they lived in each other's pockets. She rarely saw him if it wasn't to do with a case and, while she'd met Kate a few times, she couldn't say she knew her that well. They were entitled to their secrets in the same way she was. So why did she feel as if he'd let her down?

Her attention shifted to the coffee table and the bowl full of assorted pebbles, all topped off with three featured stones emblazoned with the words love, hope and finally trust. The bowl was typical of Kate's sense of style, the beach theme running throughout the open-plan ground floor with its grey oak laminate flooring. The white walls were plain except for the large black-and-white photos of Pip, carefully displayed in driftwood frames. She frowned, her gaze shifting back to one stone in particular. She remembered Kate telling her the story of the pebbles the first time she'd visited on some work-related matter that had necessitated her dropping off some files. In the same way people collected champagne corks, Owen and Kate collected stones. Every time they went to the beach, they chose one to add to the bowl and, after a relationship that spanned over twenty years, they had many such bowls dotted along the windowsills.

She stood and, reaching for her keys, turned to face him. 'I'm not sure if I'm the right person to look into Angelica's disappearance. There needs to be complete trust between colleagues and the way I'm feeling—'

16

'It's not Owen's fault. It's mine.'

Gaby twisted her head to the door, colour staining her cheeks. The last thing she wanted was to upset Owen's wife, not least because she was eight months pregnant. Her eyes dropped to Kate's belly, straining against the pretty, pink, floral top. Where seconds before there was anger, now there was guilt – lots and lots of gut-curdling guilt.

'I'm sorry. I didn't mean to . . .'

'I'm sure you didn't,' Kate said, her tone taking the sting from her words. Turning to Owen, she added, 'Why not pop the kettle on, love, while Gaby and I have a little chat?'

Owen had jumped to his feet as soon as Kate had appeared. 'Are you sure you don't want me to stay?'

'There's no need. Why don't you nip up and check on Pip while you're at it? We'll be fine.'

As soon as Owen had pulled the door closed behind him, Kate walked to a hard-backed chair close to the fireplace, placing a hand on her lower back before sitting down.

'I wouldn't wish my body on anyone currently, including my worst enemy,' she said, frowning down at her swollen feet that she'd stretched out in front of her.

'I hope I don't fall into that category?'

'As if! If Owen is to be believed, there lies the heart of a pussycat under that front you put up.'

Gaby offered her a cautious smile, well aware that most of the team thought her a tough cookie and long might it continue. Having to suffer fools wasn't in her repertoire, and one way of ensuring the very best from the team was to keep them guessing as to what she was thinking. Only with Owen and Amy had she felt comfortable in revealing her soft centre – a decision she hoped she wasn't about to regret.

'All lies.' She returned her keys back to the coffee table, her attention now on Kate's white-blonde hair. She wondered why she hadn't spotted the similarities between the two women, but

17

then again she'd had no reason to suspect that Owen would have withheld such an important part of his life. 'I know this must be difficult for you—'

'Not as difficult as not knowing what happened that night. You don't have children yet, Gaby. When you do, you'll suddenly realise how precious they are. Oh, Pip can be the most maddening brat imaginable. He's mastered the skill of knowing when and how to be at his most annoying. But we wouldn't harm a hair on his head – he's part of us. Some piece of magic that's a reaffirmation of our life together. If something was to happen to him, I don't know what we'd do.' She placed her hand flat on her stomach, her jaw hardening. 'Angelica's death broke my parents in every way possible. They were never the same. It was as if someone took a shredder to their happiness. My dad couldn't take it in the end. He walked out leaving my mum to try and hold the fragments together – there isn't a glue invented that can mend a broken heart. The day Angelica disappeared was the day sadness invaded Mum's body and mind, leaving no room for any other emotion. She didn't even shed a tear when my dad died. The only time I ever see her happy is when she's with Pip, and then it's only fleeting.'

Gaby leant forward, her elbows resting on her knees. 'But finding out what happened to your sister won't change how she feels. In fact, dragging up the past might even make it worse.'

'Please believe me when I say that nothing could make it worse. We lost a lot more than my sister all those years ago,' she said, lifting her chin, her expression glacial. 'Now it's time to claw some of that back. Most people talk about the need for closure when something like this happens but that's not what I want. I'm not hoping for an ending here but a beginning – a beginning for Owen, Pip, my mother, the baby and me. My husband has faith in you, Gaby. He says that you're the very best of detectives. If anyone can help us it's you.'

The sound of Owen's heavy tread outside had her dragging her hand across her face and pasting a smile on her lips. 'He doesn't

18

like seeing me upset. So, it's only a few days until Amy and Tim's party,' she said, neatly changing the subject. 'I was amazed when I heard that they were getting engaged so soon.'

Taking her cue, Gaby sat back in her chair and crossed her legs, watching Owen enter with a handful of mugs.

'I have to say so were we,' she said, noting Owen's look of concern. Dropping her gaze, her attention focused again on the bowl of pebbles and that one pebble in particular – any last trace of annoyance disappearing under the heavy weight of remorse. She knew more than most the devastation the loss of a child could bring to a family and for Kate to trust her with trying to find out the truth was something she should have considered. 'I don't know how Amy has managed to arrange it all so quickly. I only heard a few days ago that he'd popped the question.'

'I'm only pleased he did,' Kate said, patting her bump. 'Otherwise I probably wouldn't have been able to attend. At least no one will miss me in the photos – it's not often you get to see a whale at a party.' She put her hand up, pushing the heavy weight of her hair away from her forehead. 'Owen has it easy. All he has to do is pop on a pair of clean jeans and one of his trendier shirts.'

'Don't I know it,' Gaby moaned. 'Amy's insisting on me wearing a dress to the dance. There isn't even time to diet.'

'There's a lot worse things than worrying about your weight.' Kate glanced at her. 'Have you decided yet whether you'll reopen the case?'

'It's never been closed, Kate. Serious crimes just get shifted down the pile as newer cases get dumped on top. As long as you realise the damage that opening old wounds can cause?'

'There's only so much healing that can occur without knowing what happened. All I ask is that you go easy on Mum. She's lost far more than you can ever imagine.'

19

Chapter 5

Gaby

Friday 17 July, 9 a.m. St Asaph Police Station

'Right then, ladies. The enforced holiday's well and truly over.'

Gaby threw a thick file down on the table, trying to hide a grin at the state of her team. Jax Williams was still knotting his tie while Malachy Devine's tie hadn't even got that far. It was draped around his neck, the red and pink stripes complementing the bleary look he was rocking this morning. She scrolled down to his freshly shaved cheeks before turning to Owen, who looked, for once, every day of his thirty-seven years. While he'd brought it upon himself with his eagerness to bring Angelica's murder to her attention, she could still spare some sympathy for what he must be going through right now. He'd never said anything outright, but Gaby had long suspected that his wife wasn't happy with the long hours he put in. Reopening her sister's case would only increase that pressure. Whether she would have acted the same way as Owen had, if their positions had been reversed, was a difficult question and one she wasn't prepared to dwell on.

20

Being a matter-of-fact sort of person, she always relegated such introspections to the same drawer as crystal balls. But a part of her, quite a large part, knew that she'd never have given up until she'd found out what had happened.

Moving on, she pulled a frown at the empty chair beside him. It was unusual for Marie Morgan to be late for anything and she hadn't mentioned a word about an appointment yesterday. She was probably held up by something unavoidable. But, even so, Gaby made a mental note to have a chat with her later. It didn't matter that Gaby was still only acting DI. Her job was important. The most important thing. It was the rest of her life that was falling around her ears, along with her cottage. She grimaced at the thought of the house she'd bought within weeks of joining the North Wales MIT. While the fabric of the building was sound, the Seventies-style décor and antiquated plumbing was something she was learning to live with. She certainly didn't have the money to do much about it.

She shook her head and the image disappeared, her fingers now reaching for the file. Work was the one part that she was succeeding in. Having staff she could trust in the pressure-filled field of crime fighting was essential to that success. Her colleagues mattered even if it meant she'd probably have to fit in a one-to-one with Marie around the other one hundred things she'd already planned for her day. With a sigh, she opened the cardboard wallet and pulled out the first item – a post-mortem shot. It was the next photo that she couldn't bear to focus on, the one where Angelica was still alive and about to embark on the rest of her life.

Her words came easily but she still took a moment to send a compassionate smile in Owen's direction before sharing them.

'As you're all aware, the place has been quieter than a morgue since my return, so Bates and I felt that we should liven it up a bit.'

She watched in amusement at the sight of Malachy rolling his eyes in the direction of Jax and paused a moment for some pithy response. But, for once, they both remained silent. Managing

21

the two of them was a little like overseeing a kindergarten. They both had a lot to learn, something made more difficult by their failing to realise how much. Of the two, Malachy was by far the cockier. He pushed the boundaries of their relationship most days and it was only by counting to ten that she managed to rein in her temper. She just hoped that when the time came for him to crawl up the ladder, he'd have an arrogant so-and-so slouching against the bottom rung ready to trip him up.

'I know having a bit of a breather to catch up on paperwork is great but only up to a point and sitting on my bum isn't how I want to spend my day.' She placed a photo on each of their desks. 'I don't know whether either of you have heard of Operation Angel but, while we have time on our hands, I'd like us to see what we can turn up.'

Returning to the table, she picked up the next photo along with a single sheet of paper. 'I've put together the main points of the investigation. But, in short, twenty-five years ago, Angelica, aged eighteen, disappeared from her first-floor bedroom, via the window, only later to be found halfway up the Great Orme. We have no method of murder and no motive but she ended up dead all the same. This wasn't a rape gone wrong. There was no sign of sexual intercourse having taken place and, with her hymen still intact, Miss Brock was a virgin. The crux is the white nightdress she was wearing,' she added, picking up the post-mortem photo and holding it up. 'Where did it come from? Not as easy as it looks, lads, because the original team quickly discovered that it's handmade.' She glanced across at Jax, her lips twitching. 'Being the nice boss that I am, I'm going to leave the nightie trek to Marie. Instead I'd like you to go through the files with a fine-toothed comb and see what gives – a nice little desk job for you this time, Jax, instead of all that dog walking in the last investigation.'

'Yes, ma'am.'

She flicked her head towards Malachy. 'I'd like you to track down the boyfriend, Mal. A Leo Hazeldine. He shouldn't be that

22

difficult to trace. I hear he had a bulletproof alibi. He's obviously still going to be in the frame so see what you can do.' She checked her watch. 'We'll meet back here at four to discuss what's next.'

A noise from the back of the room had her lifting her head. But her smile of welcome froze at the sight of Marie Morgan's tentative approach.

Marie was one of the most confident women she knew. Tall and with sweeping blonde locks, she'd look equally good walking down a catwalk as she would in an old sack and Gaby wasn't the only person to ask what had attracted her to a career in law enforcement. But the woman slipping behind her desk wasn't the Marie Morgan she knew. Instead of hair draping her shoulders, she'd pulled it back into a greasy ponytail, the style emphasising the thin slash of her cheekbones. Gaby was used to seeing her with a light dusting of make-up, nothing heavy but enough to make her eyes seem bluer and her lips brighter. Today she'd left her skin bare, which only accentuated the tiny lines radiating from her lips. The clothes were the same; the suit was one Gaby had seen her wear many times but today it appeared different, crumpled – almost as if she'd slept in it. There was something wrong with Marie – something very wrong – and the plans she'd made for her day suddenly disappeared as a more important concern pushed them down today's to-do list.

'Good to see you, Marie. I'll fill you in on our next case in a moment.'

Turning her back, she deliberately focused on Owen, conscious that all three men had equal looks of concern stamped across their faces, something that shouldn't have surprised her but did. It also pleased her, not that they'd have noticed from the set of her mouth.

'The only bit left in our *search and find* operation, Owen, is the autopsy results. I've tracked down the pathologist, a Dr Herbert Tomlinson, but he passed away last year. So, I'd like you to catch up with Dr Mulholland ASAP and ask him to review the case notes.'

23

Owen's expression switched from serious to cheeky in an instant. 'I'm not sure I'm the right person for the job, if you don't mind me saying . . . ma'am. I'm sure Dr Mulholland would much prefer to discuss it with you rather than me.'

Gaby should have been expecting that, and her anger flared at the oversight. She'd been waiting for him to mention Rusty Mulholland for days now, ever since the large bunch of flowers that had been left for her on her return to work following her six weeks' enforced sick leave.

'I'll be happy to ram that "ma'am" down your neck, if you're not careful,' she said, her hands now entrenched on her hips.

But Owen, who was used to her mercurial moods, simply shrugged his shoulders before strolling to the door with his hands in his pockets as if he didn't have a care in the world. Pausing, he tilted his head towards Malachy and Jax. 'Come on, you two, let's grab a coffee and leave the girlies to their chit-chat.'

Gaby watched them go, well aware that Owen was doing her a favour in emptying the room and yet still livid at the way he'd undermined her with that dig about Dr Mulholland. Okay, so Rusty wasn't a problem that appeared to be going away anytime soon, the only saving grace being the lack of cases requiring the skills of North Wales' top forensic pathologist. She'd bump into him one of these days and she still had no idea as to how she was going to play it, her mind skipping across to Amy and her engagement party later. For her to invite him was bad enough but to then proceed to tell her that the only reason that she had was to bang both their heads together was both unwarranted and devious. She hoped that she'd be able to use her recent injury as a good enough excuse for sloping off early.

Settling back in her chair, she rested both elbows on the desk, mindful that Marie was doing a fair job at avoiding her gaze.

'Sorry I'm late. The traffic was terrible.'

If Marie had told the truth, whatever that might have been, Gaby would have been happy to let it go with a silent promise

24

to keep a closer eye on how she was doing. But to lie so blatantly had her sitting up and concentrating on what she'd thought was going to be a pretty routine conversation.

One of the first things she'd done on accepting the temporary post of acting DI was to go through her team's staff files. For instance, she knew that Jax Williams still lived with his parents although the gossip around the office was that he was hoping to move in with his new girlfriend. Malachy was more of a mystery. He lived by himself and, certainly at work, kept to himself. If she'd had to guess at a member of her team telling her porkies, she'd have guessed at it being him.

Marie was different again. Newly separated, she'd only moved out of the marital home a few weeks ago and was now living in a room in Glascoed Road, only a ten-minute walk from the station. Amy, the font of all things gossipy, had told her that Marie's husband had moved some bimbo into the house and, as he'd owned it previously, she didn't have a leg to stand on. Rumour had it that she was finding it difficult to manage on her income and was trying to cut every corner imaginable, which included selling her car.

'Indeed, especially Rhos-on-Sea way,' Gaby said, the implication that she'd still managed to get to the station on time clearly hitting the mark by the colour flooding across Marie's cheeks. 'You look a little flustered, if you don't mind me saying. Everything okay with the job? None of the men annoying you?'

'As if. Owen is a pussycat as is Jax. While Mal . . . well, he's fine too. A little different but certainly not a threat.'

Gaby raised her brows at her unusual choice of words. If Mal wasn't a threat did that mean someone else was?

'Well, if it's not work?'

'I'm fine, really. I promise I won't be late again if that's what's worrying you.' Marie raised her hand to her head, grimacing at the feel of her hair. 'The truth is I overslept.'

She didn't look as if she'd overslept. If Gaby had to guess, she'd say she hadn't slept in weeks. But it wasn't up to her to question Marie further unless it was affecting her performance and, up until this morning, she'd always been the first one in the office, and the last one to leave. More questions could be viewed as harassment. All Gaby could do was keep her eyes and ears open as well as her office door.

'Right, back to work then but, you do know that if you ever need my help with anything, either inside or outside of the job, all you have to do is ask?' She waited for the sight of her nod before continuing, stretching out a hand and placing the photo of Angelica on the desk between them. 'You see this nightdress—?'

26

Chapter 6

Owen

Friday 17 July, 11.30 a.m. St Asaph Hospital

Owen bounded through the doors of the pathology department, a locked document wallet under one arm. After a quick coffee with Malachy and Jax, where he heard more than necessary about Jax's new girlfriend and little or nothing about Mal, he'd headed back to his desk to make an appointment with Rusty. He had no idea what forensic pathologists actually did when they weren't either on the scene of a crime or performing autopsies. But after finally managing to wheedle an appointment out of his frosty PA, he now knew that whatever Rusty did, it certainly took up most of his time.

'Good to see you, Owen.' Rusty rose to his feet and shook hands before placing his balled-up fist in the small of his back and bracing his shoulders. 'If I have to read another report, I'll go mad,' he said, inclining his head in the direction of his laptop and the open Excel programme with an array of columns packed with figures. 'So, tea or coffee?'

'Coffee, if it's not too much bother?'

27

'No bother at all. I'm delighted that you've decided to lighten my day with your presence.'

'Well, I'm not sure about that.' Owen broke the grey, plastic security tag on the case, removed a red file and placed it on the desk, the photo of Angelica plonked dead centre.

Kettle on and mugs assembled, Rusty joined him.

'May I?'

'That's why I'm here.' Owen stepped back, wandered over to the window and pulled back the vertical blinds to glance out at the bright, cloudless sky before turning back to him. 'Her name was Angelica Brock. I don't know whether you've ever heard of Operation Angel, or The Angel Murder, as it was coined? It was quite a while ago – 1995 to be exact.'

'The Angel Murder? Hmm.' Rusty squinted down at the photo, his eyes alert behind his black-framed glasses. '1995. I would have been sixteen and going into my Leaving Cert year in Dublin but there's something . . . something to do with a nightdress?'

'Yes, that's it exactly. It could have been all very innocent excepting she went to bed in her PJs and was found wearing that,' Owen said, nodding at the photo and swallowing hard. 'The thing is, with the North Wales MIT being so quiet, we've decided to look into one of the old ones gathering dust.' He sat down on the spare chair and lifted his chin. 'I knew her, you see. She was my wife's sister.'

'Ah.'

Owen watched him place the photo back on the desk and continue with the drinks, the silence in the room only broken by the sound of metal chinking against pottery. Rusty only spoke again when he'd placed the mugs down and eased himself into the swivel chair opposite, the frame creaking slightly under his six-foot-two frame.

'So, why do you think it wasn't solved then? I take it that it's something you'd have investigated when you joined the force? It's certainly something I'd have done in your position.'

Owen felt his cheeks heat under the weight of Rusty's blue-eyed stare because, of course, he was right. Almost the first thing he'd done when he joined was to run a search on the Police National Computer, or PNC, only to learn that electronic crime records didn't stretch back as far as the 1990s. It was all very well working for the police but checking out records he didn't have clearance for wasn't as easy as all that. He'd quickly discovered that the subject of Angelica's death was something that wasn't discussed and it wasn't a topic of conversation he'd ever start for fear that he wouldn't know how to finish it. Kate, for all her serene exterior and practical approach, had never gotten over the loss of her big sister. It lingered in the far corner of her mind, always slightly out of reach. But when the opportunity came for him to suggest revisiting the murder, initially he didn't jump at the chance. There were too many things to consider, top of the list being what it would do to Kate if they were unsuccessful. To broach the subject had been difficult. One of the most difficult things he'd had to do and something he'd been regretting ever since. He had no idea what would happen to them as a couple if they failed to find her sister's murderer second time round.

'The force takes a dim view of coppers going *off piste*,' he finally said, avoiding the question. 'Apart from the nightdress, there was no evidence that she was even murdered. No witnesses and no DNA to speak of. Also no evidence of sexual intercourse, consensual or otherwise.'

'Mmm. People seem hung up on DNA these days, don't you think? They tend to forget that we still managed to solve crimes before all these profiling techniques kicked in. Oh, I agree that it's vital in modern-day policing but not if it's at the expense of the other elements in a crime fighter's toolbox like our eyes, ears, touch and smell.' He picked up the top folder and started removing the photographs, setting them out on the desk in a snowstorm of gore. 'Detective work has always been 95 per cent common sense and we ignore that at our peril. So there weren't

29

any obvious clues. So what? Your colleagues still identified that a crime had been committed?'

'Yes but lack of evidence means that I'm not sure why I'm here. Yes, I want it solved but for very selfish reasons. If I'm honest, I think far too much time has passed and if it wasn't for Gaby sending me to you—'

'How is Gabriella, Owen?' Rusty interrupted, pulling out the autopsy report and quickly scanning to the conclusion.

'Good. She still gets the odd twinge but, apart from that, raring to go. The office is far too quiet for her liking.'

'Well, it will be. Provides too much time for thought. She was very lucky, very lucky indeed.' He raised his head, changing the subject. 'So, explain the crime scene to me.'

'Angelica was found in the Happy Valley, which is . . .'

'I know where it is. The place with the bandstand, halfway up the Great Orme. Carry on, I'm listening,' he said, now holding a sketch of the crime scene.

'There's a stone circle. It looks old, ancient even, but it's a relatively recent addition, placed there sometime in the 1960s. She was found on the slab in the middle by a dog walker. She couldn't have been there long. Only a few hours or so. Her parents had barely raised the alarm before she was discovered.'

'And she was positioned like this?' He tapped the edge of the photo with his finger.

'Yes, curled up into a ball, one hand under her cheek as if she'd dropped off to sleep.'

'Mmm, I would suggest that's relevant. She didn't *just* drop off to sleep, did she? She was placed in the foetal position post-mortem. The question you need to ask is why?'

It was Owen's turn to say, 'Go on,' his notebook open on his knee. The notebook was more of a prop than anything but he added a line about her position all the same.

'I'm afraid at this juncture that I don't have a huge lot to add,' Rusty said, leafing through the report from the CSI team.

30

'Her toxicology screen showed no traces of drugs or alcohol.' He paused, studying the list of samples they'd collected. 'I take it you'll be sending the nightdress and any other articles of clothing or jewellery found on the victim back to the CSIs for further analysis? With advances in touch DNA techniques, if the killer has left any skin traces, they should be able to find them. The absence of any physical evidence makes it unlikely but you never know.' He shuffled the papers into a neat pile. 'I'll revisit the samples collected at the time and, if they haven't degraded, I'll see if I can run some additional tests. I'd like to keep these, if I may?' He picked up the photo again. 'Pretty girl. Distinctive hair.'

'Yes. Very. Kate's very like her,' Owen said, careful not to stare at the picture. It brought back a host of memories, most of them unhappy. He couldn't remember the time now before Angelica's death. He'd give anything for it not to have happened. The next best thing would be ensuring that her killer was caught.

31

Chapter 7

Gaby

Friday 17 July, 11.30 a.m. St Asaph

'You've got to be kidding me!'

Meeting up with Amy at St Asaph's bridal shop was as good enough a reason as any for Gaby slipping out of the office after the briefing and taking what must be the earliest lunch break in living memory. Now, faced with the reality of Amy's quirky dress sense, she wished she hadn't bothered. Okay so it wasn't the pink meringue she'd feared but it was still pink, an old-rose shade that was apparently an excellent colour-choice with her second-generation Italian complexion. Gaby turned sideways but it wasn't any better, her gaze fixed on her balloon-glass silhouette instead of the hourglass figure she craved. If she'd had to conjure up the worst possible thing to wear, ever, it would be this . . . this disaster in front of her.

The dress was lovely, beautiful even. The fragile lace bodice was intricate and finished with wide chiffon sleeves that fastened at the wrist with little pearl buttons. The skirt, in the same pink chiffon, was a dream. No, it wasn't the dress that was the disaster – far from it. There was no getting over the fact that she was a big girl. She was always on a diet and therefore always hungry. In the last six months she'd managed to shed the couple of stone she'd put on in South Wales but she still had a good stone and a half before she reached her goal weight.

Amy stood from where she'd been grovelling on the floor helping the saleswoman to pin up the hem. 'I think you're beautiful, Gaby. That colour brings out the warmth of your skin and as for your figure – so you're not skinny. You're not even thin but who's to say what the perfect body must look like? You're fit and healthy and there's nothing wrong with your figure that isn't in your mind. It's like one of those voluptuous Rubenesque paintings. And anyway, with the wedding not until the end of August you'll have plenty of time to lose a few pounds if you want.'

In Gaby's book, voluptuous was another word for fat. But one glance at Amy's expression and she decided there and then to go along with any and all of her fairy-tale plans. No one knew more than her just how close Amy had come to never walking down the aisle and the terror they'd shared in that isolated farmhouse, situated on the very edge of Snowdonia. She'd swallow any ideas of a tailored dark dress in perhaps a dark blue or even navy and go along with every romantic notion in her best friend's head. It was only for one day, half a day considering that the wedding wasn't until noon.

'And your hair,' Amy continued. 'I think down, with a few tiny flowers weaved through the top to complement your bouquet.' She threw her a grin, which transformed her features. 'Now, as for shoes. I was thinking of . . .'

Gaby zoned out, her mind drifting back to the case. She had no worries as to how Mal and Jax were getting on, and determinedly avoided any thoughts of Rusty. It was Marie she was worried about. For Angelica's murder to be solved required total commitment from all the team. To expect the sustained period of quiet

33

to carry on for longer than a few days would be foolhardy. Their workload could escalate in a heartbeat and there was no way that their DCI, Henry Sherlock, would allow them to waste precious resources on something that, on paper, looked like a dead end. No, they had to come up with something new pretty smartish or he'd pull rank and direct their skills elsewhere. It was all about crime stats. Numbers and not names. It didn't matter that there was still a family struggling with the aftermath of the hand dealt them. Gaby scowled. If she ever started to think of her job solely in terms of success rates, she'd know it was time to hang up her badge. There was Owen, too, to consider, she remembered, her scowl deepening. With Kate so heavily pregnant he'd be torn between the case and his home life. She'd have to make sure that she found the time from somewhere to support him . . .

'You're not listening to a word I've been saying,' Amy interrupted, holding up a pair of delightful pink courts with copper flowers pinned along the side. 'I thought these would be perfect but if you're not interested . . .?'

'It's not that,' Gaby said, forcing herself to focus on the flimsy shoes. 'They're lovely. Perfect even.' She slid off her plain flat black pumps before sliding her feet into them, trying not to grimace at the pull on the back of her calves. She loved shoes with a passion but long days on her feet and a non-existent social life meant she could hardly remember a time when she'd worn anything with more than a one-inch heel.

She glanced behind her to make sure that the shop assistant was out of hearing range. 'I'm a little worried about Marie. What were you saying again about her husband?'

She watched Amy relax. Arranging a wedding was stressful at the best of times but to plan it from start to finish in less than six weeks must be viewed as herculean. Marrying someone whose parents owned a hotel with a garden big enough for a marquee helped. It was the other million things left to organise that had caused her friend to lose her normally sunny demeanour. She

34

hoped the engagement party tonight would go some way to wiping away the trauma of the last few weeks.

'I thought I'd upset you with me wanting everything to be perfect.' Amy hugged her briefly. 'I'm really not surprised Marie's gone off the rails. Her husband did the dirty on her in the worst way possible. You're not to share this, all right, but she confided that they'd been trying for a baby. There apparently was some difficulty. She didn't go into any details but I suspect that's only out of loyalty to her husband. Within weeks of receiving the test results he told her he'd found someone else.' She bent down, picked up the shoes and returned them to their box, placing it beside the slim-heeled trifles she'd chosen to compliment her dress. 'I think what broke her was that the new woman has kids already. A couple of toddlers – a readymade family if you like. After ten years of being together, five of them married, Marie got to walk out of her home with pretty much the clothes on her back and little else.'

'The absolute bastard!'

'Exactly. I've told Tim if they ever come into the restaurant to refuse to serve them.' She waited for Gaby to hand her the dress before placing it back on the hanger and hanging it up beside her wedding dress. 'Do you think it would be wrong of me to whisper something into the ears of the "boys in blue"? I'm sure there's any number of traffic violations . . .'

'Amy Potter, I can't believe you're even thinking such a thing,' Gaby said, her grin belying her words. 'While retribution might be gratifying, it also might backfire if he suspects that she's involved.'

'What else can he do? He's stolen everything from her. Her past, her present and now her future. She's mid-thirties and desperate to start a family.' Amy walked towards the next rail and started removing evening dresses by the handful.

'But if I'm reading between the lines, he's not a man that can give them to her,' Gaby said, her fingers now on her buttons.

'You can stop right there,' Amy tut-tutted, pointing to the pile

35

of clothes now draped over the back of the gilt-framed chair. 'If you think I'm letting you wear trousers to my engagement party, you're sorely mistaken. Now, what about this?' She held up a long navy-blue dress with a full skirt and beaded neckline. 'It's your size and you won't be showing even a smidgeon of leg, much to the disappointment of Dr Mulholland I might add.'

Gaby ignored the dig, instead starting to unbutton her blouse again. She'd first seen that determined look of Amy's when they'd worked together in Swansea and had learnt the hard way that it was best to give in to her vagaries. It made life a whole lot easier.

Chapter 8

Gaby

Friday 17 July, 2.30 p.m. St Asaph Police Station

Gaby spent the next few hours with Jax in the archives, trying to piece together the investigation. It helped that she'd had the benefit of working alongside Stewart Tipping before he'd been forced to take sick leave. He was meticulous in his recordkeeping, every piece of evidence methodically referenced and cross-referenced. Every interview transcript annotated with further questions and additional leads to follow. Every thought he'd had, he'd recorded for posterity in one of the many notebooks that were kept alongside the reams of information. And these notebooks were where she started, leaving Jax to plough through the family and friend interviews.

There were fifteen books in total, spanning the initial six months following the discovery of Angelica's body. Each one was numbered, each entry timed, dated and initialled with Stewart's lazy scrawl. She could imagine his expression, the frown punctuating his brow as the puzzle changed from something solvable to

37

the Rubik's Cube of all cases. Just like the infuriating cube, stuffed in the back of her sideboard, the case was easy to solve if only she knew how. But there was no YouTube channel dedicated to guiding each twist and turn. She was on her own with only her smarts and her team keeping her from the fear of failure. But in this instance, she wouldn't only be letting Angelica's family down, she remembered, her mind switching to Owen and how hard it must be for him.

'Fancy a top-up, ma'am?' Jax asked, starting to collect the mugs.

'No. You stay there – you got the last lot.' She stood and flexed her shoulders, feeling every one of her thirty-one years. While painstaking research was all part and parcel of her day-to-day job, she'd much prefer being out and about than stuck in the same position for hours on end. With the mugs in her hand, she made her way to the door, shooting a smile at the archive officer on the way. 'Fancy a coffee, Colin?'

'Two sugars,' he replied with a toothy grin. 'How's it going?'

'It's not. Too many trees and not a chainsaw in sight.'

'I know that feeling.' He scratched his head and, into the suddenly awkward silence, said, 'If you don't mind me saying, the lads never knew why they didn't pin it on the boyfriend. It seemed obvious to almost everyone except Tipping.'

'Really?' She eyed him briefly before picking up his mug and dangling it between her fingers. She didn't know Colin Wynne well, but rumour had it that he was soon to retire. 'I take it you were based here back then?'

'Sure was. Started in 1985. I was on the beat those days and part of the team scouring the Happy Valley after she'd been found. Poor *dwt*. It upset us all to see her like that. To think that someone could steal her from right under the nose of her parents.'

Gaby rested her hip against the edge of his desk. She couldn't stay standing for long without a sharp twinge in her side to remind her of her recent injury. 'So, you all thought they should have fingered the boyfriend for the murder?'

38

'Yup. He was clever. Didn't leave any clues or anything but then he was heading off to veterinary college – he'd have known about stuff like that.'

'But apart from suspecting him, there was no real evidence, was there and he did have a bulletproof alibi?'

'Hmm. We never gave any credence to that. As we all know, alibis can be bought.'

'Indeed they can. Any idea why he'd risk it though?'

'Perhaps he couldn't help himself.' He paused, all trace of his grin long gone. 'The way she was positioned, I'd forgotten all about that until that young lad there reminded me earlier,' he said, his attention now on Jax. 'Perhaps he went on to kill again. There's something here, something I've read and recently too . . .' He tapped the side of his head with his index finger. 'It'll come back to me. When it does, I'll give you a bell.'

Gaby nodded before heading to the door. There were a fair few detectives she knew that would discount the views of their uniformed colleagues but she wasn't one of them. Just because they'd decided on a different career path didn't mean that they didn't have a wealth of information and experience to offer. They were the detectives' eyes and ears and as such they had much more of a feel for what was going on than a detective ever could. He'd given her lots to think about. One of the first things she was going to do on her return was to check out how far Jax had got with the interview transcripts. It all seemed a little too convenient for the boyfriend to still be in the frame but stranger things had happened.

Chapter 9

Gaby

Friday 17 July, 4 p.m. St Asaph Police Station

'Right, quiet, everyone. We have a lot to get through and I want to leave on time for once what with Amy's party later.'

Once she'd secured their attention, Gaby strolled across to the whiteboard, taking a moment to stare at the photo of Angelica that she'd pinned dead centre. It was her way of connecting with a case. Her way of hardwiring her brain to remember why she'd undertaken a career in law enforcement. Through the killer's actions, Angelica Brock had missed out on what most people took for granted. A career. A secure home and future. A partner and possibly even kids. A chance to make mistakes and learn by them. It was up to Gaby to restore the balance. It was twenty-five years too late for Angelica but not for her family. Justice needed to be done. She only hoped that she was the right person to serve it.

Alongside the photo, she'd bullet-pointed some key information – top of the list being their main piece of evidence: the nightdress.

'Right, Marie, what have you got for us?'

40

'I managed to track the garment down in the evidence room, ma'am,' she said, passing around some photos. 'I also decided to take numerous pictures before sending it up to the CSIs as it's unlikely we'll be getting it back anytime soon. But I'm afraid this isn't going to be as easy as it looks. If I'm honest I don't think it's going to help us unless there's some previously undiscovered DNA that turns up.' She paused, picking up the top photo and holding the image up for the team to see. 'The main problem is that the nightdress is handmade so it's impossible to trace it back to the manufacturer. Not only that but the style is based on a very common design. You see the pin-tucking around the yoke in the centre and here, the tiny mother-of-pearl buttons down the front,' she said, tapping on the photo with her fingernail. 'I could show you a hundred websites now selling nearly the exact garment. Oh, the fabric wouldn't be the percale cotton I suspect this one is made of, probably some polyester mix, but the style is so common that I wouldn't be surprised to see it being sold in branches of Primark. The fabric isn't going to help us either. I'm guessing that, like the nightdress, it's sold by the hundred-weight in material shops the length and breadth of the UK. I could probably track down the pattern used in the design but I think that it would be a complete waste of time. The thread used to sew it together is going to be mass produced. The sewing machine one of thousands. The stitching is regular so it's not as if we could trace it back to the machine used if it still existed after all this time.'

'I'm pleased DI Darin chose you instead of me,' Jax said in amazement. 'I wouldn't know where to start. I thought a yoke was something only found inside an egg?'

'It's the thingamabob that sits over the shoulders and falls to the front. At least I know that!' Gaby said, silently congratulating herself on dragging up that little piece of information from her school sewing lessons. She also congratulated herself on her choice of Marie for the job. She'd known instinctively that, with her

41

fashion sense, she'd be the ideal person to move this forward but that wasn't the main driver behind her decision. Marie needed something in her life, something to sink herself into that wasn't related to her marriage. However, it looked like she'd need a lot more than luck on her side to remove the nightdress from where it was currently lurking – on the very top of the dead-end pile.

'So, there's nothing to investigate apart from what Jason and the rest of the CSIs might find under their microscope? That's disappointing.'

'Well, I wouldn't go as far as to say that. The buttons interest me. I'm not sure how much you know about buttons but some are quite unique. The mother-of-pearl ones used are of a particularly high quality. These days many are made of resin but, in this case, I think that they're the real McCoy. Having said that, to high-end shirt makers, they're two a penny so probably not that unusual. Jason might be lucky and find some DNA for us. It's also possible that the killer removed his gloves to fasten them being as they're small and quite fiddly.' She leant back in her chair, crossing one leg over the other. 'I'm not done yet though. There's a button company that might be able to help. With your permission I'd like to get a few high-resolution photos from the CSIs and email them over?'

'By all means. Thank you, Marie. Right then, Jax and I have spent most of the day with Colin in the archives. We're not here to criticise DI Tipping's investigation but certain things have come to the forefront that need looking into.' Picking up a red marker, she proceeded to write the name Leo Hazeldine in capital letters. 'As you can see, Angelica's boyfriend is top of the list just as he was all those years ago.' She recapped the pen, placing it on the desk before raising her head and scanning the room, her gaze resting on each of them in turn. 'The picture I'm getting of Angelica is that she was a diligent straight-A student who had to work for everything she got. Her father was unemployed. Her mother, a childminder, managed to hold the family together by the skin of her teeth. There wasn't the time or the money for much fun in Angelica's life. That was all meant to come later until some bastard got there first. She had a summer job behind the bar at the Penrhyn Yacht Club and that's where she met Leo.' She walked to the nearest chair and took a seat, waving a hand for Jax to take over.

'Leo Hazeldine, aged nineteen at the time.' Jax stood and turned to survey the rest of the team. 'He was interviewed on numerous occasions by DI Tipping and on each one managed to convince everyone that he was the distraught boyfriend. They'd been dating six months, ever since she'd turned eighteen and got the job behind the bar.' He dropped back into his chair before saying, 'He acted the way one would expect even down to being adamant that they hadn't had intercourse, but honest enough to admit that they'd come close a couple of times.'

'And the bulletproof alibi?' Owen interrupted. 'Exactly how bulletproof is it?'

'Pretty much K-K-Kevlar,' he stuttered. 'He'd travelled early that morning to a residential placement on a farm in Blaenau Ffestiniog. Although he'd passed his test, he didn't have a car so instead he took the train. The people he was with all supported his statement that he'd gone to bed at midnight and was up at the crack of dawn in the milking shed.'

'Mmm. And how far is Blaenau from here? A little less than an hour so not out of the realms of possibility,' Owen added, answering his own question, his mouth twisting.

'But not without transport and he didn't have any. And, before you ask, the train doesn't run overnight now – it certainly didn't then. I-I-I have already checked.'

'Thank you, Jax. Good work,' Gaby said, firing Owen a quick glare that said *cool it* in all the languages possible. She was protective of all her officers but particularly Jax. She'd spent the last few months nurturing him so that putting voice to his thoughts wasn't the nail-biting experience it had been when she'd first met

43

him. It would only take a few more interruptions like that for his stutter to return. 'So, in effect, unless we can find an accomplice that ferried him to and from Llandudno, he can't be in the frame.' She transferred her attention back to the whiteboard and the photo of a narrow-faced young man with pale blonde hair and an intense expression. He was good-looking in a Hollywood leading-man sort of way, not her type but she could imagine what other women might see in him. Angelica, with her fresh innocent beauty, complemented if anything by the starched white of her nightdress, seemed the type to be taken in by his dreamboat looks . . . although it wasn't her nightdress, was it?

'I still have some problems with how she managed to get from a first-floor window to halfway up the Great Orme without even a scratch or a bruise. Willing suspension of belief isn't something, as a crime officer, I can sign up to so we have to try and find an alternative scenario that fits.' Raising her head, she was met by a sea of blank faces. 'Okay we'll leave that part for now but if anyone has any bright ideas, they know which door to come knocking on.' She flicked her eyes towards Malachy. 'Last but not least, Mal. You were tasked with locating Hazeldine. How did you get on?'

'I didn't, ma'am,' he said, tightening the knot of his tie, his long fingers lingering on the smooth silk fabric before dropping to rest on his solid thighs. 'I assumed that as a vet he'd be relatively easy to trace. They all belong to professional bodies and what have you but in Hazeldine's case it's all a bit of a disaster. He went to university as planned but, after failing his first year, he dropped out. Picking up the odd job here and there, he wasn't exactly on the breadline but not far off. I followed him via his social security contributions across to Australia but, at some point he went completely off radar – I'm not sure what happened. No job. No passport records. A complete blank. We don't know who his father is, that part of the birth certificate was left blank, but I've managed to locate his mother. She's living in Wrexham. As an only child, there's not really anyone else to talk to now. I'm going

44

to have to do a bit more digging before I come up with anything conclusive. The Penrhyn Yacht Club might be somewhere to start as it's where he met Angelica. There might be a steward or something that remembers them both.'

'Okay, good plan. Remember we only have a finite time on this so let's target the easy wins. The nightdress. The boyfriend. I don't really want to harass Angelica's family yet.'

'I'm afraid it's too late for that,' Owen interrupted.

'Too late? I don't get you.'

Owen stood, his hands in his pockets, in a stance that she recognised. For all his laidback demeanour and jokey ways, Owen was a deeply complex individual. There'd been that time a few months ago at the start of their last investigation when she'd thought he was going to give up the police force altogether. Now she knew about his background, she wasn't a bit surprised. She'd have been more surprised if he'd come out of his childhood unscathed by the events of twenty-five years ago. Twelve was a difficult age at the best of times and she suspected, by the way he'd talked about Angelica that his feelings were still mixed up. She'd been such a beautiful girl that quite a few hearts would have fluttered in her presence. Gaby watched him square his shoulders and launch into what felt like a pre-prepared speech.

'I need to say that it's no coincidence that we're now investigating this murder. I asked the DI if it was something that we could focus on.' He coughed into his hand, his voice so low Gaby had to lean forward to catch his words. 'My wife, Kate, and Angelica were sisters. Her abduction and subsequent death have coloured most of our lives – it's time to draw a line under all that. Last night Kate decided that her mother had to know about us reopening the investigation.' He spread his hands. 'There was nothing I could do to stop her but actually I think that it was the right thing. If she'd heard from anyone else, like the media for instance – and we all know how news seems to leak out of this place like a dripping tap – anyway it's done. We went round

45

and spoke to her mother about what it might mean with regards to press interest and to reinforce that opening the case was no guarantee of success.'

Gaby was pleased that Malachy, Jax and Marie remained silent. It was probably more due to having no idea of what to say but, whatever the reason, she welcomed their restraint. There weren't enough words in the world to comfort the suddenly stern-looking Welshman. While she wouldn't go so far as to admit that coppers were *blasé* about crime, it was something that rarely touched them personally. It wasn't their partner, parents, children, their loved ones affected. Most days they could still brush off the trials and tribulations of the job as soon as their front door closed behind them and, by the time their dinner was in the oven, their mind had closed to all but the minutiae of life.

'No problem, Owen, and, as you say, probably wise under the circumstances. Did Mrs Brock have anything to say that we should know about?'

He ran his finger under his collar, unbuttoning the top button as if the neck was suddenly too tight. 'Not a great deal. We didn't talk about the investigation as such but . . .'

'But?' she prompted, aware of his sudden discomfort.

'She did say that Hazeldine had visited her sometime after. She couldn't remember when exactly.'

'And?'

'And she didn't think that he could be guilty.'

'And that would be because . . .?' she said, her voice now tinged with frustration.

'That would be because she was pretty sure he was gay, ma'am.'

The silence extended a beat. 'Unless I'm missing something, and please tell me if I am,' Gaby said, staring around the room, 'Hazeldine's sexual orientation has no relation to whether he's guilty or not.'

46

Chapter 10

Gaby

Friday 17 July, 8 p.m. The Imperial Hotel, Llandudno

'Would you like to dance?'

Gaby glanced up at Dr Rusty Mulholland, an automatic 'no' forming on her lips. She'd spent the last hour being twirled and sometimes dragged around the room. An hour didn't seem that long in the scheme of things, but she'd only returned to work a couple of weeks ago after an extended period of sick leave. An hour was more than enough for her still recovering body. Twisting her head, she could see Amy and Tim wrapped around each other on the dancefloor. Amy, her best friend and someone she felt very close to throttling. She'd forced Gaby to truss herself up like a chicken in the frock from hell and as for her shoes . . . While the four-inch courts matched her navy sparkly dress to perfection, they were the worst form of torture known to man. Long gone were the days when she could slip on a pair of her favourite heels and dance until dawn. The only good thing about it was that she wouldn't have to put up with the pain for much longer.

47

She'd already pre-warned Amy and Tim that she was planning on sloping off early and, with the way the dancefloor was filling up, no one was going to miss her . . .

Her thoughts froze, her focus shifting from Amy and back to Rusty and the red-haired boy standing behind him. His son. She'd heard rumours that his ex-wife had dumped him with full custody but the station overflowed with grapevine gossip, most of which was from dubious sources. She'd ignored it all in a half-hearted attempt to deflect her team's unwarranted interest in her love life but the one thing she couldn't ignore was the woe-begotten expression etched onto the boy's face. He wanted to be here just as much as she did and, by the looks of things, his dad was determined to drag out the evening right to the end.

Hiding her annoyance, she slipped her feet back into her shoes, and stood, her attention flickering between man and boy. She wasn't in the mood for social niceties but there was something about the downturn of the boy's lips and the droop of his head that struck a chord. She remembered, like it was yesterday, how it had felt growing up in Liverpool to parents that spoke English in a funny accent. Being different was a red flag to the bullies and some sixth sense told her that this child's life was full of such flags, her eyes once again drawn to his hair.

'Hello there,' she said, ignoring Rusty's question as if he'd never voiced it. 'I'm Gaby, one of your dad's colleagues.'

'This is Conor,' Rusty interrupted, guiding the boy forward.

She crouched, hoping and praying that the seams of her dress were up to it. 'Well, Conor, what do you think of parties then? At your age I'd have been bored to tears.'

'It's okay,' he said, dropping his gaze.

'Only okay?'

'Well, a bit boring if I'm honest but . . .'

'No buts. I can imagine there's a computer game with your name on it. What is it these days, *Minecraft*? *Fortnite*?'

'*Rocket League*.'

48

'*Rocket League*,' she said, her brow furrowing. 'That's a new one on me but, I'm sure it's much more exciting than being stuck with a pile of adults. So, how long do you think your dad will make you stay, do you reckon?' she continued, struggling to ignore the sudden glare sent in her direction.

'Oh, not long, Gabriella. I promised him we'd leave straight after the last duty dance so, the sooner you agree the better,' Rusty answered, holding out his hand, his lips a thin line. 'Five minutes, Conor,' he added, tilting his head in the direction of her recently vacated chair.

Gaby found herself being led onto the dancefloor and manoeu-vred into his arms before she could even start working on a suitably cutting response. She didn't want to dance with Rusty and, obviously he felt the same way if his comment about duty dances was anything to go by. She ground her teeth at the way he'd managed to outsmart her. It was almost as difficult to bear as the feel of his arms around her back and the warmth of his breath against her ear. She didn't want this with him or indeed with any man, she told herself, despite the slight hitch in her breathing and a feeling akin to liquid silver hijacking her veins. After the disastrous experience she'd had with Leigh Clark back in Cardiff, she couldn't afford to drop her guard; one slip and Rusty would crawl through the narrow space between her ribs and set up basecamp.

She stiffened her spine in an act of self-preservation. It had taken her months and a transfer to a different part of Wales to recover from the damage Leigh had wrought. She couldn't allow herself to go through all that again no matter what her body was telling her.

Lifting her head, she stared up at him, aware of the way he towered over her. 'Look, Rusty, there's nowhere in either of our contracts that says we have to be anything other than professional and duty dances went out with the last century.'

'When did I say that this was a duty?'

49

She opened her mouth only to close it with a snap. 'Just now when you . . .'

He shook his head. 'I was talking about Sherlock's wife. Dancing with you is a pleasure.'

'Oh please!' She tried to pull away but he only strengthened his hold, his muscles bunching under her fingertips. 'Everyone's staring.'

'No, they're not and even if they are, so what? It's not as if we're doing anything we shouldn't. It's only a dance, Gabriella, and I wouldn't have been forced to take such a drastic step if you hadn't been avoiding me.'

'Avoiding you? What do you mean avoiding you? There's been no reason to be in touch. Our patch has been the quietest I've ever known. No unexplained deaths. Nothing that needs your particular skillset. We've even had time to delve into some of the old cold cases that never get a look-in. Thank you, by the way, for meeting up with Owen. He found your comments very useful. As soon as you have any—'

'You know that's not what I meant,' he interrupted. 'There's a time to talk about work and this isn't it. So, when are you going to relent and agree to go out for a drink?'

'Out for a drink?' she repeated, unable to break away from the intensity of his stare. She must have missed something – huge swathes of conversation – because, as far as she was concerned, he hadn't even broached the subject of a date apart from that one time . . . She squeezed her lids together, forcing her mind not to explore the recent past. She'd be lying to herself if she didn't realise that on some level he wanted to progress their relationship from professional into something more meaningful just as she was determined not to let him. She slammed the door on any thoughts of a happy ever after. Her brain for some reason was determined to ignore all the preliminaries of the dating ritual, instead jumping straight in at a couple of kids and maybe an animal or two, even as she

50

tried not to relish in the feel of his fingers playing with the ends of her hair. He was clever, this Dr Rusty Mulholland, but she was far from stupid . . .

An hour later found them sitting around a table in McDonald's.

'When I invited you out for a drink, I was thinking of a little country pub,' Rusty said, handing out bags of chips and cups of Coke, his gaze roaming over her navy chiffon dress. 'You do realise that we're the only ones here not wearing jeans, don't you?'

'Well, it did seem like an ideal opportunity and Conor's happy, aren't you?' she replied, trying to hide a laugh at the way his son was tucking into his burger. 'Didn't he eat before coming out then?'

'He ate everything on his plate and half of mine. A growth spurt, or so he tells me.' Rusty ruffled his son's hair, much to his annoyance. 'Are you sure you don't want anything?' he added, gesturing to the chips in front of him.

'No, I'm good. I can't breathe as it is, any more food and I'm likely to have an indecency order slapped on me which, apart from scaring the children, wouldn't do anything for my CV,' she said on a laugh.

'If it's any consolation I think you look great, well worth the effort. I especially like your hair; I've never seen it any way other than tied back off your face.'

She resisted the temptation to put her hand to the carefully blow-dried style that Amy had insisted on helping her with, suddenly at a loss. If Rusty Mulholland stayed like this, she wouldn't be able to come up with one solitary reason for not accepting if he asked her out again. But she knew deep down that he wouldn't. As soon as they were back on a case, he'd return to the rudest, most arrogant man she'd ever had the misfortune to meet and the very last man she'd ever agree to date. She damped down a sigh, silently bemoaning that he couldn't be more like Owen. Despite everything going on in their lives, Owen and Kate

51

had one of the strongest marriages and, with the birth of their daughter imminent, he'd hurried away after only one dance, his arm firmly around his wife. That's what she wanted from a relationship and if she couldn't have it then she'd go without.

'Thank you, not the most practical of hairstyles when out on a case . . .' she started, only to stop at the sound of her mobile. It took a few seconds of searching in her evening bag before finding it. One glance and she pushed away from the table, hurrying to the door, the phone held to her ear.

'Darin speaking.'

Chapter 11

Gaby

Friday 17 July, 9 p.m. McDonald's

Heading back inside, Gaby was surprised to find Rusty looking incongruous with her beaded bag clutched in his hand, encouraging Conor to hurry up.

'There's no need for you to rush. I can always grab a taxi.' She took her bag, dropped her phone inside and snapped it closed.

'Not dressed like that you can't. I'll drop you off home to get changed and then . . . I take it there's a case?' he said, immediately taking charge of the situation. He picked up the tray and deposited the empty cartons in the bin. 'I didn't think you'd be on call?'

'I'm not, but with half the station at Amy's do I told them to contact me if anything unusual turned up,' she said, walking to the door. 'After all, I'm the one who's had the last six weeks off.'

'Off sick following a serious injury, or had you forgotten?'

Reaching the car, she tilted her head, throwing a speaking glance at his son.

'Oh, don't mind Conor, he can't hear a thing with his earphones in,' he said, opening the door for her and waiting while she swivelled her legs in before slamming it shut and walking around to the driver's side.

'Okay then. Actually it's not a bad idea you coming along. There's a good possibility you'll be needed unless you've managed to get someone to cover your shift?'

'Ha, as if. They never manage to cover my shifts, Gabriella, unless I'm on holiday and even then they still sometimes contact me. What about Owen? Surely he could have stepped in?'

'Owen had to prop up the MIT team in my absence and is therefore well overdue the long weekend he's currently on. He's off until Tuesday and I don't expect to see him one second before then.' She fastened her seatbelt and, turning in her seat, decided to take him at his word about Conor. 'There's been a gas explosion. One fatality. Probably routine but who knows at this stage.'

Ardwyn House must have once been a glorious property. Situated at the foot of the Little Orme, almost opposite the Craigside Inn in what was viewed to be one of the most sought-after areas in Llandudno, it was glorious no longer. Its windows were blown. Its once butter-cream exterior coated in ash. Its roof and one wall partially collapsed. A glimmer of rose-patterned wallpaper was partly visible in the stream of light cast by industrial floodlights.

Rusty slid his car to a halt on a yellow line behind the second fire engine, turned off the ignition and twisted in his seat. 'You okay to stay in the car, Conor? We won't be long.'

They walked to the CSI van in silence, which changed as soon as they reached the back door – open to reveal neatly stacked clear plastic boxes full of equipment.

'Let's get one thing clear, Gabriella. You're not going inside. It's far too dangerous.' Rusty grabbed her arm, his look fierce.

She stepped back, pulling out of his grasp. While she'd been happy for him to take the lead in McDonald's and more than thankful that he'd offered to drop her home so that she could get changed out of her fancy clothes, enough was enough. It had taken her a long while to earn the respect of her team and being prepared to go into any situation without any obvious qualms was all part of that. The fact that the blackened building filled her with a dread that stretched from her hastily bundled-up hair right down to the tips of her Reeboks was not the point.

'The structural engineer has declared it safe and, as this is my gig—'

'—and, as I keep having to remind you, you're only just back to work after what was a pretty horrendous injury. You might as well save your breath because there is no way I or any of the team, and that includes Craig, over there,' he said, nodding in the direction of the fire scene investigator, 'will let you set foot anywhere near. And anyway, what good will it do, hmm? I have to go in to see where the body is and then, believe me, I'm out of there too.'

Gaby shifted her gaze to the partially demolished house. She knew he was right but that didn't make it any easier to accept. It was attitudes like his that could easily have them whispering about how she was losing her touch.

'If you're doing this because of some sense of misplaced chivalry because I'm a woman . . .?'

He flung his head back with a crack of laughter. 'You never give up, do you? I'd act the same way with man, woman or child,' he said, climbing into the bio-hazard suit handed to him and adding overshoes, gloves and mask. 'Why put yourself in unnecessary danger when you don't have to? I, on the other hand do need to see what happened. It will make trying to piece the puzzle together a whole lot easier when I have the body back in the lab. Why don't you go and speak to Craig to find out the background? I promise I won't be any longer than I have to be.' He turned his back and went to talk to one of the firemen, laughing again when he was handed a hard hat

55

to wear, which he rammed down on top of his head. Within seconds he was being led inside.

Gaby watched until he was out of sight before slowly making her way across to the first of the fire engines and where Craig was holding on to the lead of the latest addition to the team, Penny, a gorgeous, chocolate-brown Labrador.

'How's she settling in?' Gaby crouched down, putting her fist out for the dog to sniff.

'Worth her weight in gold, Gaby.' He crossed his arms across his chest, the lead dangling from between his fingers. 'If I'm truthful I didn't think using a dog to detect things like fire accelerants would work but she led me straight to what remained of the wall in the kitchen and where the cooker should have been.'

'What? An electrical fire?'

'Nope. A gas explosion. Probably forgotten that she'd turned the oven on.'

'Is it safe . . . for the men?'

'Safe enough. Don't you be worrying about the doc. He's a man with nine lives – the luck of the Irish.'

Ignoring his smirk, she said, 'So, what can you tell me about what happened?'

'Called in at seven o'clock or thereabouts by the next-door neighbour. Thought it was a bomb at first.' He lifted his hand to scratch the side of his nose, leaving a trail of soot across his cheek. 'The funny thing is that the deceased, a Mary Butterworth, shouldn't have been left alone. She had some sort of brain cancer. The neighbour says that it's a huge tragedy. Needs constant supervision. Can't even wash and dress herself anymore. The daughter's been pulling her hair out since her dad died, trying to find some home to take her. She's been coping with the help of a live-in carer until the finances for a home are sorted, but for some reason she gave the woman the night off. That's the daughter there.' He tilted his head in the direction of a thin, blonde woman huddled in a black padded jacket. 'Avril Eustace. She says she only popped

56

out for half an hour to pick up some milk. But half an hour is all it took.'

Gaby's eyes narrowed, trying to remember where she'd seen the woman before. 'You say she recently lost her dad?'

'That's right. Remember that bloke that fell under the bus outside Marks and Spencer last month?'

'Of course.'

All unexplained deaths had to be investigated much to the annoyance of the team. In the normal run of events they usually had more work than they could cope with without the added annoyance of having to trail around nursing homes and the like to probe into deaths that were clearly either expected or accidental, as in the case of Tony Butterworth. She'd still been on sick leave when it had happened, which was probably the reason she'd had difficulty in remembering the daughter, Avril. She'd only caught a fleeting glimpse in reception when she'd popped in to see DCI Sherlock a couple of weeks ago to confirm her return date; not enough for her to have left more than a passing impression of the woman.

Turning away, she looked around the sea of faces, searching. 'Is her husband here?'

'Away on business. Due back tomorrow. There's a neighbour who's taken her under her wing.'

'Thank you.' She offered him a brief smile, concentrating now on the building ahead and any sign of Rusty. She'd have to meet with the daughter at some point but that could wait. The evening, which had started out on such a high note, was quickly turning into a disaster. If only he'd . . .

'All done.' Rusty placed a hand on her shoulder, almost causing her to jump out of her skin. 'Can you leave or . . .? I'd like to follow the ambulance but firstly I need to sort out Conor.'

'You can drop us both off at mine, that is if he won't object? It's on your way.'

'Far from objecting, he'll be over the moon. It's that or the

57

childminder and she's got four of her own already.' He squeezed her shoulder before removing his hand and tucking it back in his pocket. 'It's really very good of you.'

'Don't read anything into it,' she said, stepping away and walking back to the car. 'It's the sensible solution.'

'Of course it is.'

Chapter 12

Gaby

Saturday 18 July, 12.05 a.m. Rhos-on-Sea

The knock when it came had her jerking awake from the snooze she'd drifted into after taking Conor upstairs and tucking him into bed until his dad came back. After the excitement of the day, culminating in being dragged to a gas explosion, he'd been dropping on his feet.

She slipped her feet into her slippers and padded across the lounge to the tiny hall, remembering to engage the security chain before pulling the door open. It only took a quick glance at his drooping shoulders and ashen features, visible in the dim light cast from the hall lamp, to immediately feel guilty at the couple of hours she'd spent curled up on the sofa reading. Not the end to the evening that either of them had been expecting. She unhooked the chain and, pulling the door open, gestured for him to follow her back into the lounge and the tiny kitchen beyond where she flicked on the kettle.

'Cup of tea all right or do you fancy something stronger?'

59

'I still have to drive home so tea would be lovely.'

'Take a seat in the lounge. Conor was falling asleep so I tucked him up in bed. I'll bring your drink out in a sec.'

But instead of retreating, he propped his shoulder against the wall, his gaze wandering over the drab yellow-pine cabinets and dark brown tiles. She didn't need him to comment on what a state it was in. The whole house needed a huge injection of TLC but, with little money and even less spare time, she only used the place as somewhere to eat, sleep and charge her mobile. She barely noticed how dreadful the place looked until she brought someone back and, as the only people she ever invited over were either family or Amy and Tim, it was never an issue – until now.

She handed him a mug, picked up her own and walked back into the lounge, waving a hand at the chair opposite, resolutely turning her attention to her drink. She could apologise about the state of her home but she wasn't going to.

'So, do you think it was accidental or . . .?'

He rested his head back against the chair. 'Do you know this is the first time you and I have been alone properly without half the station being in shouting distance, and the only thing you can think of is work!'

'We're not alone. Conor's upstairs.'

'You know what I mean, Gabriella.' He shook his head as if trying to dislodge some unsavoury thought or other. When he spoke again it was all business. 'I haven't performed the autopsy yet. But I've checked her medical records and it's pretty much as the daughter says. Mrs Butterworth was diagnosed with a malignant meningioma last year. They operated but, as with some of these brain tumours, it caused more damage in the long run. Her life expectancy wasn't good but that's not the main thing. She needed to be supervised pretty much constantly. Leaving her alone, like the daughter did, was risky at best.'

Gaby put her drink on the battle-scarred coffee table before answering. 'So the likelihood is that it was an unfortunate accident

60

that could have been avoided if the daughter hadn't popped out,' she said finally, thinking back to the way Avril Eustace had looked standing by the police car earlier. She didn't appear to be strong to begin with. Something like this could really tip her over the edge particularly as the blame fell clearly with her. The reality was if she hadn't left her, her mother would still be alive.

She pulled her cardigan securely around her, trying not to waste time thinking about what she'd have done in the same situation. In instances such as this there was no right or wrong answer, only a tragedy where everyone was the loser. Mary Butterworth had paid the ultimate price with her life but it would be left to her daughter to pick up the bill. Oh, the likes of Amy Potter would be able to offer a wealth of support but nothing could change the facts. The only good thing to come out of it was that they could continue concentrating on Operation Angel without having to puzzle out who would want to murder someone whose death card was clearly marked with the stamp of a terminal disease. Leaving Angelica's murderer to go free, even after all this time, wasn't something Gaby was prepared to let happen.

'Please don't take this the wrong way but I'd like you to continue helping out with the cold case. I know it's not a priority after so many years and, with the paucity of clues, there's probably little hope but I want us, for Owen and Kate's sake, to do our best.'

'Well, I'm not sure there's much I'll be able to add. After I've re-examined the samples there's not a lot for me to do.' He clasped his hands behind his head. 'Have you had any ideas yourself?'

'Nope, not a scooby. But, to be honest, there hasn't been time to give it more than a cursory look.' She bit down on her lower lip hard. 'I can't be blasé about it especially not on the back of the explosion, which has been a huge reminder of what can come through the door at any minute. Having to tell Owen that we've had to shelve his sister-in-law's murder due to lack of manpower is a very real threat,' she continued, shivering despite the warm sultry night. 'It's all very well getting the team to reopen the case,

61

much more difficult to mentally shut it especially when we've barely wiped the dust off the files.'

'But no one could blame you for that, certainly not a professional like Owen.'

'Can't he just. No one would be to blame, Rusty, but common sense doesn't come into it when there's personal involvement in something like this. All these years he's been silently waiting for the ideal opportunity to present itself. You know Tipping. He wouldn't dream of reopening a case unless there was a sniff of new evidence. So Owen bided his time. It's only now with Stewart being off and the station quiet that he's pounced into action.' She slipped off her slippers, tucking her feet underneath her. 'Oh well, talking about it isn't going to change anything. At least we've been given a respite with Mary Butterworth's death. For form's sake, I'll get someone to double check through the husband's file but it will only be a cursory glance. So, you've no ideas then as to how Angelica could have ended up dead?' she asked, neatly changing the subject. 'If it wasn't for that blasted nightdress being left, we'd have passed it off as death by misadventure but . . .'

'An interesting point.' He sat up, his hands now resting on his legs. 'I'm no profiler but you may be onto something with that nightdress.'

'How do you figure that? Trophy-taking is well documented but for a perp to leave something with the victim . . . I don't buy it, I'm afraid, and neither would any criminal. Rational thought must lead them to assume that anything left with or on the victim would also be a sewer pit of evidence.'

'Just because it's never been done is no reason to close your mind off to the possibility, Gabriella. The one thing you're forgetting is that neither of us are criminal profilers or indeed criminals. Who knows what goes through the mind of a murderer when they take something from their victim to drool over? An item of jewellery. A photograph. A lock of hair. A body part. What's so different about leaving something with them – something precious. Something that has a wealth of meaning but only to the murderer. You said that DI Tipping couldn't find any leads on the nightdress, perhaps because of its age.' Flicking his cuff back, he checked the time before standing. 'Okay so he didn't have Google's electronic brain to help, but I'm betting that the nightdress isn't going to be that easy to trace.'

Gaby followed him into the hall, her mind still full of the case. 'What? You're thinking of some kind of family heirloom?'

'Exactly. And who's to say that this wasn't the first act of many? Twenty-five years is a very long time. Something for you to think about.' He picked up his jacket from the newel post. 'Anyway, it's getting late. What about we continue this conversation another time? I've taken up far too much of your hospitality as it is. Thank you once again for looking after Conor.'

'My pleasure,' she replied automatically. 'When I was living in Liverpool, I babysat for my brother's two boys all the time. I miss that.'

She went past him up the stairs and beckoned for him to follow, reluctant to continue the conversation now it had turned onto personal matters.

The landing was tiny, barely enough space for one let alone two. The only upside was that when she eventually got around to decorating, it wouldn't take more than half an hour to slap on a fresh coat of paint. She swiftly pushed open the door on the right and hurried over to the other side of the room, her attention now on Conor. Her bedroom was in the same state as the rest of the house and she was reluctant to be privy to Rusty's expression. After working with him since nearly the start of the year she was well aware of his biting comments and disparaging glances but that didn't mean she had to see them directed towards her own personal space.

The room was large. The flooring was the original bare boards but in desperate need of a varnish. The curtains had come with the house, the previous owner's love of dark brown prevailing,

63

but at least they kept the light out. Her bed was the one note of luxury, if you could call a white metal-framed Victorian bedstead, which she'd picked up at the local auction rooms for a song, a luxury. She'd dressed it with cheap linens in different shades of blues and greys, the overall effect calming and tranquil. In the future she hoped to peel back the 1970s brown floral wallpaper and get new doors for the yellow-pine, built-in wardrobes but for now it would have to do.

Conor was asleep, the picture of innocence tucked under her duvet, his thumb resolutely stuck in his mouth.

'It seems such a shame to disturb him, doesn't it?'

'Then by the looks of things you'd have nowhere to sleep?' he said, with a lift of his brow.

'No, well. I'm still trying to put the house to rights. A guest bedroom is on the list somewhere.'

'You don't have to explain, Gabriella.' He gently scooped Conor up, secured his head against his shoulder and stepped towards her, his expression intense. 'You have a beautiful home; the rest will follow as and when. There's nothing to be ashamed of. We all had to start out somewhere.' Bending his head, he placed a brief kiss against her cheek before making his way down the stairs and out of the house, the door banging closed behind him.

She lingered on the top stair, her feelings in disarray. It suddenly felt as if she was missing something. She didn't know what.

64

Chapter 13

Gaby

Saturday 18 July, 9 a.m. Rhos-on-Sea

Gaby couldn't sleep. She'd spent the first half of the night trying and failing to find the comfy spot on her pillow and the second half staring at her wood-clad ceiling trying not to think about Rusty Mulholland. Daybreak found her spooning porridge into her mouth in between sipping tea from her favourite mug and bemoaning the fact that she hadn't opted for a nine-to-five job. For once it would be nice to leave work and let the day's trials and tribulations fall off her shoulders like apples off a tree instead of spending every waking moment, and a fair few sleeping ones, ruminating over a case as she had last night.

After washing the couple of dishes, she grabbed her bag and keys and headed out to the car. With nothing planned and the conversation with Kate running like a movie in the back of her head, she'd much rather waste the morning at the office delving into Angelica's murder than moping around home looking for jobs to do. She didn't spare a thought for the pile of ironing

65

waiting to be tackled on her return or the promise she'd made to herself in the small hours to redecorate sooner rather than later. The lounge, with its tongue and groove panelling, was a complete joke but one she'd managed to turn a blind eye to until yesterday and the look of astonishment she'd caught on Rusty's face. There wasn't a lot she could do about the panelling but attacking it with sandpaper closely followed by a couple of coats of emulsion couldn't be that difficult, surely.

An hour later and she was walking into her office, a takeout coffee in one hand while she carefully shut the door with the other, in the hope that no one would actually realise what she was up to. There was no rule forbidding her from going into the station on her day off, far from it. The force would be in a much worse state if it wasn't for the dedication of its employees. No, the only fear was the interruptions that would come if anyone bothered to check. But with Clancy on duty in reception, she knew she was safe. For some reason the large serious Welshman had decided that she needed protecting, if not from herself then anyone who came close enough to cause her harm. She took his fatherly attitude in the way it was meant and ignored the teasing from the other officers about favouritism amongst the ranks. Whatever they thought, Clancy was a good man and had continued to treat her like the daughter he'd never had. Taking five minutes out of her day to have a laugh and a joke with the fifty-year-old was something she would continue to do despite the side swiping comments.

Slipping her laptop from her large shoulder bag and placing it in the centre of the desk only took seconds. It had long been her belief that a woman couldn't have a large enough bag or too many shoes. As she'd grown older the bags had changed from brightly coloured patchwork to finely tooled leather, her one extravagance. Her shoes, on the other hand, were now chosen for comfort over fashion, although the leather slip-ons were in the same cherry-red as both her bag and over-blouse. Not that she

66

spared a thought for either her bag or her shoes. She was here to work and, if there was still time, to stop off at the nearest DIY store for paint on the way home.

Gaby sat in her chair, but instead of opening up her laptop, she picked up her drink. Anyone walking past the office door and peering through the small square window that punctured the wood would perhaps wonder what she was up to. With her hands cradling her cup, her attention wasn't on her open computer screen or the notepad in front of her. There were lots of things she could be doing. Lots of searches and background checks she could make. Lots of instructions she could jot down for the 9 a.m. meeting she had scheduled for Monday morning. But Gaby Darin wasn't doing any of those things. She wasn't writing. She wasn't typing. She wasn't even taking a sip from her rapidly cooling coffee and the one thing she hated above all else was a lukewarm drink. No, Gaby Darin was thinking. Her mind was following an all-too-familiar path as she tried to put herself in the footsteps of the victim. Now, she wasn't sitting in her first-floor office with views out across the car park. She wasn't dressed in her comfy jeans with the elasticated waist, her hair tied back in its signature plait. Now, instead of bright sunshine seeping in through the partly closed blinds it was dark, that pitch dark that only comes in the early hours when the air is colder and the world is at its most silent.

She's lying in bed but something wakes her. A sound? A tapping at her window? There's no need to be scared. There's no need for her pulse to race and her heart to thump. This is Llandudno after all. She waits a moment thinking that she's misheard but there it is again. A bird at the window. No. More likely a stone? Climbing out of bed, she doesn't bother with slippers. She doesn't even bother to right the duvet; she'll be sliding back in underneath its warmth soon enough. She's at the window and, sweeping the curtain aside, peers out, taking a moment for her eyes to adjust to the change in light. Looking down, she sees something. No. She sees someone. She sees someone that makes her unbolt her window and ease it open.

67

Gaby blinked, her long unadorned lashes sweeping closed before opening again.

She sees someone that makes her forget all about her warm bed and the lure of sleep. Words and phrases flash through her mind, jumbled and confused but with one common thread. Something's happened. I need to see you. It's urgent. Only you can help. Please. I'm desperate.

She climbs down and makes her way across the drive to the waiting car. She's not scared. Not now she recognises the person. They wouldn't harm her. It's only later that things change – that the fear escalates, causing her mouth to dry and her throat to close. She's too scared to even scream. She's placed her trust in someone who doesn't deserve it . . .

Gaby placed her untouched cup back on her desk. It had served its purpose and was now destined to go the same way countless other coffees had gone – down the sink. Pulling her notebook towards her, she flicked back a few pages to where she'd noted a comment made by Colin Wynne, the archives officer. '*The lads never knew why they didn't pin it on the boyfriend. It seemed obvious to almost everyone except Tipping.*'

With her pen between her fingers, she tapped the point on her pad, creating a fine series of dots under the word boyfriend. The obvious answer. Angelica had known her assailant – a boyfriend in need would fit that scenario perfectly. Leo Hazeldine was meant to be a good hour or more's drive away and without a car but that wasn't an alibi, nothing like. So what if he was in Blaenau Ffestiniog at midnight and up at five. That would still leave five hours – more than enough time for a round trip followed by a little case of abduction and murder. He wouldn't be the first teen to go without a night's sleep and he sure as hell wouldn't be the last – sleep wouldn't even have come into the equation.

There were still unanswered questions, motive being the most obvious. He was her boyfriend so why the need to abduct her? A question that was impossible to answer without Leo Hazeldine sitting in front of her. Gaby brushed aside the thought that he might have been gay purely because it was unsubstantiated. It wasn't something that the investigating team had hit on and all the reports indicated that their relationship had been full-on. Okay, so Angelica had still been a virgin but that in no way explained the untouched nature of her body.

Gaby flipped to a new page and started jotting down notes that needed to be followed up on. A list of meaningless words that would have had Stewart Tipping cringe. Detectives' notebooks were admissible as evidence but with Gaby's unique shorthand and sloppy handwriting, the only one ever able to understand what she'd written was her. But there were things she needed to find out and wasting time on neatening her handwriting wouldn't change the outcome no matter how many rollickings she received about her illegible scrawl. That didn't make her entries any less important. She still needed to know how the duvet on Angelica's bed had been left – flung back or arranged neatly? Had the bed even been slept in? Gaby also wanted to ask about any pebbles that might have been found under the window. It would take one stone with skin cells attached for the whole case to be put to bed in an instant. But back in 1995 that advance in DNA science had yet to be discovered.

She threw down her pen, pushed away from the desk and made her way across to the other side of the room. With her hand on the string, she adjusted the blind before glancing down into the car park, noting the empty spaces with barely a flicker of a frown. Sherlock and Owen would be home playing happy families while Jax would probably be somewhere canoodling with his girlfriend. She couldn't even begin to guess at what Malachy was up to but it sure as hell wouldn't be anything to do with work. While poor Marie . . . She turned away, embarrassed by the direction of her thoughts. Marie had it all. Stunning looks and an enviable figure to match and yet her husband had still gone and done the dirty on her. The reality was that there was

69

no hope for normal people like Gaby to have a perfect life, with tragedy waiting, silent and heartbreaking, around the corner. Okay so Marie was young enough to find someone else and start again but she'd still have the scars. She'd still find it difficult to recapture that level of trust. She'd always wonder at what kind of life she could have had if her husband hadn't strayed. And what about Angelica? Angelica must have been viewed in the same light as Marie by her then counterparts. Young, beautiful and intelligent. The golden girl with the perfect life mapped out. Could that have been the motive?

Gaby moved back to the desk but this time she pulled her laptop nearer. She'd seen jealousy in action during her previous case in St David's, an all-encompassing jealousy that had ruined more than one life. But she wasn't so sure that jealousy would have been the reason for Angelica's murder. Just because there'd been no physical evidence didn't mean that she hadn't been murdered and, in her bones, Gaby knew that this was to be the case. Now she had to prove it. Typing in her password brought her thoughts full circle back to Rusty Mulholland and his throwaway comment about trophies being a possible reason as to why the nightdress had been left. At the time she hadn't given it much credence. That had come later in the small hours when she'd taken his comment out of the place she'd tucked it. The truth was she was no expert on profiling but she couldn't discount his expertise either. Wales wasn't long on serial killers; she could only drag two up from her memory banks and both were locked up with no hope of parole. What were the odds on there being a third?

The idea that Angelica's murder could have been the first of several had Gaby pause because, however unlikely, now it was something she'd have to follow up on. Instead of logging on to the police network, she turned to a fresh page of her notebook and stared, tapping the end of her pencil against her teeth. Offender profiling was something that had long interested her and last year's week-long course she'd attended at the Centre for Investigative

70

Psychology at Liverpool University had only cemented this interest. But it was a relatively new phenomenon in addition to a rapidly expanding science. During her preliminary look at Operation Angel there'd been no question that it wasn't exactly what it seemed – an isolated case – but what if they were wrong? What if it had been the start of something? She'd learnt as a rookie that criminals changed over time, altering their *modus operandi* to fit their shifting circumstances and increasing confidence when they weren't caught. What if that was the case here and no one had spotted it until now? She bit the end of her pencil, the bitter taste of lead causing her to wipe her mouth against the back of her hand, all the while considering her options. She didn't have any. Without evidence, all she had were thoughts and suppositions. So, what elements of the Angelica inquiry were unique, she puzzled, her pencil hovering over the paper before speed writing with all the finesse of a spider who'd just cut his toenails in the inkpot.

Any crimes committed from 1990 to the present day where the perpetrator leaves a token instead of collecting a trophy.

That was more than enough to be going on with. She quickly logged the query into the police database. She'd either get far too many to narrow down or zilch. She had no idea which.

The programme, an intuitive system, worked on keywords and, as with anything electronic at the station, it wasn't known for its speed. Instead of staring at the little egg timer in the top left corner, she stood and stretched before collecting her mug and heading out into the corridor to the drinks machine at one end, which served what passed for coffee on a good day and grey slop the rest of the time. During the week she either made her own or headed down to the incident room cafetière, which was meant to be kept full. The last time she'd found it empty she'd thrown so many toys out of her pram that Sherlock had hurried out of his office to see who'd dropped the baby. But this was meant to be her day off so she wasn't about to start messing about making coffee. Her plan hadn't changed. To spend as little

71

time as possible on the case before reclaiming as much of what was left of her weekend as possible.

Back at her desk she spent a moment checking for any messages. But apart from one from her mother telling her she'd Skype her later – which caused her to frown – and a second from Amy telling her she was trying to eradicate the hangover from hell with a full fry-up – which removed it – her phone was resolutely silent. She placed it back in her bag, out of temptation's way and returned her attention to her laptop and the result of her search, her frown returning with a vengeance.

In truth, she'd been expecting the second option – zilch – because the parameters she'd set were pretty narrow. She'd never in all her years on the force come across the concept of a perpetrator leaving a token but, by the look of the 193 results, she'd been wrong. Nearly 200 instances where a criminal had left something meaningful with their victim. How completely bizarre.

Within minutes she was sitting back behind her desk, a yellow highlighter in her hand and a print-out in front of her as she started working through the list, deleting anything that couldn't be relevant. By the time she'd finished she realised that she should have narrowed the search parameters further, her father's words ringing in her ears. *One learns by experience* wasn't the most helpful of phrases as she read through the sixty-one references left. Policework was all about the organisation of material into some sort of a pattern that made sense and for that she needed Excel, her least favourite of all programmes. With a shrug, she launched a new document and started filling in the fields, trying not to read too much into the information in front of her. An incident in Scotland where the rapist wrapped the victim in his coat before giving her money for the bus fare home wasn't really what she was looking for but she included it all the same. She knew all too well that she didn't have either the manpower or skillset to follow this trail without the agreement from Sherlock for extra staff in addition to the input from a criminal profiler.

72

With a quick glance at her watch, she resisted minimising the document until all the cases had been added. There was no point in doing only half a job when she could do it all now. While the Butterworth case was a lucky escape there were bound to be more crimes pushed in her team's direction especially with the summer influx of visitors swelling North Wales' population like a tidal wave.

When she'd finished, she sat back and drained her mug in one before shifting it to the edge of the desk. She knew she was using delaying tactics and with good reason. Did she really want to read about the exorbitant level of crime in her patch? It was bad enough having to deal with the day-to-day incidents when they landed on her desk but to be confronted with an uncompromising truth that included the victim's name, age and the crime against them was a little too close for comfort when she appreciated as well as the chief superintendent just how many would never get solved.

Lifting her head, she finally concentrated on the screen, her jaw clenching at the figures in front of her. For someone who didn't really know what they were doing before she'd started, she'd created a list of sixty-one crimes set in the UK that might possibly be relevant to the case. While she could probably spend some of her Monday working on the list, in between all the meetings she had scheduled, the reality was she needed help. But the only person that she could think of who had the specialist knowledge she required, was Professor Angus Ford. Probably the last man, after Leigh Clark, that she should be thinking of contacting.

73

Chapter 14

Gaby

Monday 20 July, 11.50 a.m. St Asaph Police Station

'That was some party on Friday. Hope the hangover's gone?' Gaby said, bumping into Amy on the way back to her office, her hands full of files.

'Only just. Tim and I were on family duties yesterday. Welsh roast lamb with all the trimmings and champagne on tap.'

'Lucky you.' Gaby managed a smile, thinking of her solitary walk along Rhos-on-Sea beach followed by an afternoon sanding down the panelling in the lounge.

'No, not lucky me at all. I'd much rather have been doing what you were doing. All Tim's mother did was bang on about the wedding. Bridezilla has nothing on her behaviour. She now wants ... No, she now *demands* that both Tim's sisters are bridesmaids and that all four of her grandchildren are either flower girls or pageboys. I tell you, if it wasn't for the fact that I'd be upsetting my parents, I'd drag Tim to the nearest registry office for a quickie ceremony and spend the money on the honeymoon instead.'

74

Gaby only managed to bite back her laughter at the expense of her bottom lip. 'How about we meet for lunch later and you can tell me all about it? But first I need your help. You probably heard about the explosion on Friday night in Llandudno? I have the daughter and husband coming in shortly to talk things through.' She grabbed her arm, squeezing it gently. 'The woman has lost both parents in little over a month. It's not going to be the easiest of interviews so I want all the help I can get.'

Avril Eustace was exactly how she remembered her. A thin, pale mouse of a girl with insipid, dishwasher-blonde hair dragged back into an elastic band, a few wispy strands framing cheeks with less colour than the bowl of porridge oats that Gaby had eaten earlier. She appeared distraught and in need of comfort, but by the dour expression stamped on her husband's face, Gaby was convinced that Avril wasn't going to get it. The thought lingered while she directed them to interview room one – the largest and often used for purposes such as this – a thought she determinedly put aside. Being invited into a police station for whatever purpose wouldn't be on anyone's bucket list. There was an exhaustive number of reasons for his displeasure stretching from an unpaid parking fine to missing the sport on the television. In fact, there was no reason to think that he was anything other than a supportive husband who was doing his best in what must be viewed as a very difficult situation.

The door closed with a click while Gaby waved them into their chairs, standing back so that Amy could slip past her into the free seat closest to the wall.

'Thank you once again for coming down to the station. I know that this must be difficult for you.'

'Then why do it?' Samuel Eustace interrupted. 'My wife is beside herself with grief and yet here we are, dancing to the copper's tune, when she should be back home trying to sort out the funeral.'

'Mr Eustace, while this is a formality, there are certain questions that still need to be asked.'

75

'Really? My wife has lost both her parents and yet you insist on dragging her in here?'

'That's not quite right though, is it, Mr Eustace?' Amy said, her melodious Welsh accent soothing to the ear. 'You might remember that we did offer to visit you in your own home.'

'Oh that's right. Put it back on me,' he said, unwilling to be soothed, his elbows now propped up on the table. 'I do at least have a say in who I invite to my house and it doesn't include members of the local police constabulary, Officer.'

Gaby looked at his eyes, gleaming under heavy lids, and came to the sudden realisation that the husband was enjoying this. Her stomach twisted at the thought, her focus now on Avril and where she was mangling a tissue between her hands. But feeling sympathy for his wife wouldn't get her anywhere. She removed her notebook from her jacket pocket and flipped it open, her pencil gripped lightly between iron-stiff fingers.

'To get back to the issue at hand so that you and your husband don't have to spend too long here – while I know it's painful, I'd like you to run through what happened with your father?'

'I don't think that I—' Avril started, only to be interrupted.

'As you can see, my wife is in no fit state to answer any of your questions. Perhaps in a few days.'

'No, I . . .' Avril Eustace swallowed hard, her knuckles bone white under a translucent layer of skin. 'I want to get it over with now otherwise it will be hanging over us. Please, Samuel.' She laid a tentative hand on his arm before picking up her tissue and wiping her face. 'Carry on, Detective.'

Gaby noted Samuel Eustace's resigned expression with a frown. He was good-looking with his carefully arranged, brushed-back brown hair and square jaw with a deep cleft. Dressed in a smart two-piece suit with pink shirt and old school tie, it was his attitude that let him down. Men like him always made her feel uncomfortable not least because of the way his attention flickered more than was necessary to her boobs. He was the type that women flocked

76

to and not just for his looks. He oozed charm and if he was the faithful type Gaby would eat the whole box of chocolate eclairs that someone had left at reception. If her day continued on its current trajectory, she might eat them anyway, she mused, resisting the urge to fold her arms across her chest. It would be a whole lot worse if Samuel Eustace realised that he was getting to her. She shifted her attention to his wife. Gaby didn't want to make life any more difficult for Avril but she very much feared that it was far too late for that.

'Your father was involved in an accident along Mostyn Street on the 26th June,' she said, her voice soft. 'The bus driver said in his statement that he saw him step out between a couple of cars but that it was too late by the time he jammed on the brakes. When we met with you afterwards you said that your father might have been depressed, something corroborated by his GP. In light of what's happened to your mother, is there anything else you'd like to add to your statement?'

'No, not really. It was very hard for him. You see, he loved my mother so much. They met when they were teenagers and had been together ever since. Her illness devastated him and, if I'm being honest, I wasn't surprised when I heard.' She pressed her tissue back to her face with both hands, almost hiding behind their protective barrier.

Gaby gave her a cautious look of encouragement. 'I believe you were in your parents' house minding your mother when it happened?'

'Yes. She couldn't be left for long and Dad wanted to nip to the bank. Being a sole carer is draining. I tried to help out when I could.'

'I'm sure. Are you okay to carry on with the interview?' Gaby asked, pushing a fresh box of tissues nearer to her. She only carried on at the sight of Avril's brief nod. 'If you need me to stop at any time just say. So moving forward to Friday night. Can you tell me what happened in the few hours leading up to your mum's accident?'

Avril sniffed, reaching for another tissue and balling it up in her hand. 'There's not much to tell. We'd employed carers to help

77

while we planned what to do.' She threw a swift glance at Samuel. 'It wasn't too bad. I used to visit in the morning and again in the afternoon to check up on things and of course to spend some time with Mum. On Friday, with Samuel away, I wasn't bothered about having to rush so I decided to let the carer have the evening off and spend the night in my old room for old times' sake.'

'Go on. You're doing fine.'

'There's not a lot to tell other than the fact that I killed her . . .' she said, her voice dissolving into tears, the wad of tissues pressed back against her eyes. 'I killed the kindest, most gentle mother I could have ever wished for.'

'Avril, you don't know what you're saying . . .' Samuel interrupted, his gaze skimming the top of her head and focusing on Gaby. 'Don't listen to her. Surely you realise that she's not talking sense?' He stood suddenly, pushing the chair so far that it rocked on its back legs while it made up its mind whether or not to fall backwards. 'Come on, it's time we left before you say any more. I told you we shouldn't have come.'

'Mr Eustace, this won't take long. You need to calm down. Getting angry isn't going to help matters,' Amy said, trying to take charge of the rapidly deteriorating situation.

'Who's going to make me?' He wrenched his wife's arm and dragged her out of the chair, kicking it out of the way in the process. 'You people are unreal, treating us like this.'

'Really? You think that your behaviour is acceptable under any circumstances?' Gaby reached her hand for the panic button with a sigh.

It was a matter of personal honour that she'd yet to press the red call bell despite the taunts by Owen and the team. There was no shame in calling for help and Clancy, again on duty behind the front desk, was always keen to remind her that he'd be right there if she was ever in need of assistance. It was the sight of Avril visibly cowering as she struggled to prise her husband's bruiseworthy grip from her arm that removed any sense of bravado

78

from Gaby's bones and stubbornness from her soul. She'd come across many types over the years. The criminal world seemed to be overflowing with arrogant tosspots but the man in front of her topped the lot. Anger pulsed from every pore as he continued to half drag, half lift his wife towards the door, and Gaby being a full head shorter made a mockery of all the self-defence courses she'd gone on over the years. Samuel Eustace was a man who obviously thought second and acted first. Something he was about to regret.

Within seconds the corridor was flooded with the stamping of what sounded like a thousand footsteps trampling down the corridor no doubt at the detriment of Sherlock's brand-new flooring. The door burst open, Clancy in front closely followed by four other officers, batons at the ready and Gaby didn't even try to hide the quirk of her lips that wiped clean any trace of the fear she'd been desperately trying to hide. She'd be the first to admit that she wasn't hero material – she must have missed that lesson. She'd also have been horrified to learn about the email winging its way to head office with her name at the top. The National Bravery Awards of England and Wales were the police's way of honouring the special kind of courage displayed by some of their officers. Gaby's recent actions where she'd saved Amy's life and been nearly fatally injured in the process had Sherlock almost drooling with pride. To Gaby's mind, she'd only been doing her job.

'Having a little problem, Detective Inspector Darin?' Clancy said, his beefy arms folded across his broad expanse of chest, his mouth compressed into a thin line.

Gaby stepped aside, shifting to let him through the door. 'Thank you, Officer Parkyn. I'm fine but Mrs Eustace is in need of some assistance.'

'Is that right, ma'am? Sir, I suggest you release your wife's arm and return to your seat until your conversation is finished.'

Samuel, with a quick look of dislike in Gaby's direction, did exactly that, choosing to pick up the overturned chair on the way. Only when his wife was sitting beside him did Gaby continue, secure in the knowledge that Clancy had decided to stay for the rest of the interview.

'Your neighbour said that you'd popped out to the garage for milk, which is only down the road? Is that correct?'

'I thought I'd only be gone a few minutes but the garage next to the hotel was closed early so I nipped to Asda. I wasn't long but obviously long enough. When I returned . . .' She bent her head, reaching back under her sleeve for her tissues.

'Thank you.' Gaby forced herself to focus on Samuel. If looks could kill, she'd be a dead woman and she was increasingly thankful for Clancy's reassuring presence behind her. 'Mr Eustace, I believe you were away. On business or pleasure?'

'Business. I'm an IFA,' he said, the smirk back.

Gaby frowned a second before her forehead cleared. While she wasn't in the bracket for an independent financial adviser it was a term she'd come across. 'Whereabouts were you staying?'

'Manchester. I left on Friday morning, stayed in a Premier Inn, returning Saturday morning as soon as I heard. I was meant to stay until Sunday but . . .' He spread his hands.

'A little unusual to be working at the weekend?'

'Not at all. My clients are very wealthy, Detective. Managing their investment portfolio isn't something they would choose to do in the office. Weekends are my busiest time.'

Gaby stared at him, liking him a little less with each passing second. She knew the interview was over. They'd answered all of her questions and, until she got feedback from the crime scene and autopsy, there was no need to keep them. She pushed back her chair, reaching into her jacket pocket to the small pile of business cards she slipped in each morning. 'Mrs Eustace, if you think of anything else please give me a ring. I'll be in touch if I have anything further.'

With a brief nod to Amy, Gaby escorted the Eustaces to the entrance before hurrying across to greet Owen who was standing by reception with Pip in his arms and Kate by his side.

80

'Here to take my right-hand man off for lunch, Kate? Don't hurry back. He's almost out of any candle left to burn.'

'You're telling me. I see him less now than before we were married!'

Owen managed a thin smile but Gaby could see that he had more things on his mind than conversing with her. So instead of keeping them talking she waved them out the door, her attention caught by the sight of the Eustaces climbing into their car.

Lunch was in a small sandwich bar, a five-minute drive from the station and a firm favourite with the locals. The homemade ham and salad-filled rolls together with their soft drinks and chocolate cookies were a huge improvement on the yogurt and banana Gaby had planned to eat at her desk with her pad in front of her as she made notes for the afternoon catch-up meeting.

'So, not the easiest of half-hours,' Amy said, glancing around to check that no one was within hearing distance.

'You're telling me. If I'd known the husband was going to kick off like that, I'd have asked Owen to sit in. In fact, that's not a bad idea,' Gaby added, removing the cellophane from her roll and adding extra mayonnaise. 'There's still the autopsy findings before we can close the case. If I get him to finish off the paperwork it will at least keep his mind off what we're up to.'

'I don't think he'll be that easy to palm off.'

'No. Neither do I but he'll have little choice. Sherlock will go spare if he realises a member of the victim's family is part of an active investigation.' She took a sip of her ice-cold diet lemonade, a little groan of contentment escaping as the liquid almost evaporated in her mouth. She only spoke again when the glass was empty. 'The husband might respond better to a man.'

'Well, he certainly couldn't be any worse. I hate know-it-all bullies like that. I wouldn't put it past him to knock her about.'

'No, well, not a lot we can do about that unless she comes forward,' she said, placing the glass down on the table. 'Now what are we going to do about your mother-in-law? Isn't it the mother

81

of the bride that's meant to be a pain in the bum?'

'My mum's a sweetheart as you very well know and even if she wasn't, I wouldn't let her interfere. But Tim's mother is a different kettle of fish. He admits himself that she's got exacting standards.'

'But surely if you're paying for the wedding . . .?'

'We wouldn't have it any other way but she's still insistent on adding to the expense any way she can.' Amy bit into her roll and swallowed. 'The thing is she's doing us a huge favour as it is with having the marquee in the hotel grounds. She's even going to help with the catering side of things too. I don't feel I can refuse her when on the one hand she's going out of her way to help but . . .'

'But it's still your and Tim's wedding? A once-in-a-lifetime event unless you're planning on Tim being the first in a long line of grooms,' she said, trying not to laugh at Amy's pained expression.

'As if!' She dropped her half-finished roll onto her plate and picked up her cookie. 'But what can I do?'

'You can compromise, my love. Is it that much of a hardship having a couple of extra bridesmaids? That would only be three so about average I would have thought and getting them to buy their own dresses is pretty standard these days. The same goes for the kids. Don't you think it would look quite sweet having a procession of little people cluttering up the aisle?'

'I suppose you're right.'

'You know I am. There's no point in sweating the small stuff and, remember, a few years down the line she's going to be on the top of your list of free babysitters. If you alienate her—'

'Now hold on a minute.'

Back in her office, Gaby slipped behind her desk, her mind returning to the phone call she was about to make to Professor Angus Ford and the reason she hadn't been able to finish her lunch much to the amusement of Amy who'd been quite happy to eat her cookie for her.

82

She remembered meeting him on that profiling course she'd been pressganged to attend. Not that she'd minded. A week of living with her parents and catching up with her two brothers and little nephews was like a gift. It had felt more like a holiday than the reality of an intensive series of university-based lectures with homework and reading material to catch up on every night. She'd been in her element.

As men went, Angus Ford wasn't the handsomest, or the tallest, she recalled, her brow creased into little lines. But there was something about him that had her riveted to every word of his hour lecture on 'Suspect prioritisation and offence linking'. She'd nearly fallen off the end of the bench when he'd strolled up to her at the end of the lecture and questioned her interest in the topic. She hadn't had the guts to tell him that it was part of her annual CPD and that the week-long course was more important for the hours she could add to her professional development plan than the actual content.

By the end of the week she'd fully appreciated the work that went into offender profiling, a field that was starting to become a bit of an obsession if the number of books she'd bought on the subject was anything to go by. She'd also realised that Angus Ford was as determined to shift their relationship from professional to personal just as she was determined not to let him. While she liked him as a man, the sort of short-term liaison that he was looking for wasn't on her radar no matter how hard he pressed.

With a purse of her lips, she stretched out a hand and picked up her mobile, scrolling down to his number. She had a job to do – only that.

'Ah, Gaby, when are you coming to see us again? I have a bottle of Barolo with your name on it.'

'I'd rather hoped you'd come to us this time, Angus. We have a problem on our hands that's right up your street.'

'Really! Do tell, dear lady.'

She could imagine him sitting behind his desk, his frameless glasses pushed onto his forehead, his chin propped on his hands.

83

He was forty-nine, looked ten years younger and had the best manners she'd ever come across.

'What would you say to a serial killer possibly working out of Wales for the last twenty-five years?'

'Go on.'

'Well, there's not a lot more to tell, if I'm honest. I'm investigating a cold case. You might remember the murder of Angelica Brock back in the mid-Nineties?'

'Nightdress?'

Gaby grinned, her thoughts veering towards Rusty who'd apparently made the exact same observation to Owen. 'Exactly. No suspects. No evidence. No defensive wounds on the victim's body. No clues. I've picked this up again and done a preliminary exercise to see if I can link it to any other cases,' she said, her phone cradled to her ear as she pulled up the Excel spreadsheet on her laptop. 'I've come up with sixty-one.'

'Only sixty-one.' His laugh rang out.

'I know. Too many, huh.'

'Sadly, it isn't too many if the killer is prolific,' he said, all trace of his earlier laughter gone. 'I take it that most of the other cases you found didn't take place in Wales? You'll know better than me the red tape that cross county working takes up.'

'You're way ahead of me. As I don't have anything definite yet . . .'

'Just a hunch that you want me to help investigate?'

She let out a sigh of relief. 'Exactly.'

'Okay, ping over what you've got so far and I'll take a look. At the very least I'll be able to tell you if any patterns emerge. But, in the meantime, you do need to run it by your SIO.'

'I know I do,' Gaby said, sighing for a second time at the difficult conversation ahead of her with Henry Sherlock.

'And, Gaby?'

'Yes?'

'You still owe me that drink.'

84

Chapter 15

Gaby

Monday 20 July, 3.30 p.m. St Asaph Police Station

Visiting Inspector Sherlock always had Gaby feeling as if she was back at school and ordered to see Mr Duffy, not that she'd ever been called to the headmaster's office. No, she'd been one of the good ones. One of the class swots and, as such, she'd managed to avoid one of his 'letting me down' talks.

She stood in front of the chief's desk, her hands neatly linked in front of her new M&S grey trouser suit, her low-heeled shoes polished to within an inch of their life, and waited – her attention fixed on the wall above his head while she endeavoured to read the titles of his books sideways. She managed to get to five before he indicated with a tilt of his head for her to take a seat.

Gaby sank down into the chair and waited. The DCI never did anything in a hurry. She often wondered how he managed to achieve anything like the successes they had. He reminded her of a retired brigadier with his upright bearing and square shoulders that displayed his uniform better than any shop mannequin. But

85

the smart-as-paint uniform was for show as was the benign smile. Behind his wire-framed glasses lay a pair of sharp blue eyes that rarely missed a thing. His desk might be clear of everything apart from one open folder and the usual laptop and phone but that didn't mean that he didn't take an active interest in every case currently on their books.

'Thank you for dropping in, Gaby. Your team has been busy,' he said, glancing down at the folder open on his desk. 'I hear that the explosion along Colwyn Road looks to be an unfortunate accident?'

'Yes indeed, very unfortunate. I'm still waiting for the autopsy results but at the moment there's nothing to indicate otherwise. When DS Bates returns tomorrow, I'll ask him to go through the motions before completing the paperwork.'

He placed his elbows on the desk, his plain gold watch peeping out from his cuff.

'And what about the cold case you've been working on?'

Gaby swallowed. 'I'm exploring the possibility that Angelica Brock's death might be connected to other similar murders. We just need to dig a bit further to forge the link.' Sherlock remained silent, a silence which she chose to fill. 'I've spoken to Professor Ford in Liverpool and he's prepared to offer his assistance.'

'And what exactly is this link?'

'In the case of Angelica Brock she was dressed in a nightdress that didn't belong to her so I thought, what if it meant something – something special to the murderer?' she said, leaning forward in her chair. 'And if he or she left something with the first victim, what about subsequent ones? Did you know that over the last thirty years alone there's nearly 200 incidents where some item has been left with the victim as opposed to being removed?'

'No and, quite frankly, I don't care.' He placed both hands flat on the desk and glared. 'The reason why criminals take trophies has been well documented. Don't you think that the same would be true if the opposite were the case? The force hasn't the time,

86

manpower or money to waste on this sort of nonsense. Give me something substantial to work with and I'll be more than happy to throw everything we've got on this. But if I take this to the chief superintendent, he'll send me away with a flea in my ear not to mention a kick up my backside.'

'Right, everyone, settle down.' Gaby strolled into the incident room and perched on the edge of the table up front. 'I've come from a meeting with Sherlock. We need to provide substantial new evidence on the case before he's prepared to support it.'

'There's a surprise,' Malachy said, tilting back in his chair.

'Yes, well, Mal. I wish I had your foresight – it would have saved me half an hour I can ill afford.'

Gaby still hadn't quite made up her mind about Malachy Devine. He was very quick to crack a joke, usually at someone else's expense, but she couldn't fault either his work ethic or intelligence. She'd have preferred if he'd dress down for the job instead of the designer suits and double cuffs he sported. It didn't do anything for office morale when the rest of the lads bought their clothes from whichever chain store was the cheapest. Her gaze shifted to Jax Williams' ill-fitting brown suit even as she made a mental note to ask Owen how Devine could afford designer clobber on an annual salary of £21,000.

'The good news is that there's not a lot any of us can do until Dr Mulholland comes back with the autopsy findings and the CSIs have finished over at Ardwyn House. The likelihood is that the explosion was an unfortunate accident but we do need all of those nasty little boxes ticked off before we can set the case aside. Right, back to Angelica's murder. Any news on the buttons, Marie?'

'The CSIs have done an amazing job with the photos. I'm about to email them across.'

'Sounds promising. Keep me posted,' she said, pleased that Marie was looking and sounding a little more like her old self. 'What about you, Mal? Any luck in locating the boyfriend?'

87

'Not as yet, ma'am but I'm getting there,' he said, firing her a quick glance. 'As we already know, he flunked university, failing his exams at the end of the first year. After that he travelled around a bit, picking up odd jobs from sheep shearer in Melbourne to stable hand in Adelaide. He appears to have disappeared into thin air after that but I'm still searching.'

'Okay. What about a criminal record?'

'I'm just coming to that. There was an incident when he was at university. A fight outside a bar. By all accounts he didn't start it but he left the man who did with lifechanging injuries.'

'So he has a temper. Interesting. What about family? There was something about a mother in Wrexham?'

'Yes, she's living in a care home. I'm assuming it's a single-mum scenario.'

'Don't assume anything, Mal. Check then recheck,' she said before turning to Jax. 'What have you got for me?'

'There's boxes of s-s-stuff to get through,' he stuttered, fumbling through his notebook. 'I started with the interviews, her parents and then her sister. The father was unemployed at the time, the mother holding things together. They said that they were both at home, thus conveniently providing each other an alibi. The first thing they knew she was missing was when she failed to turn off her six o'clock alarm. Kate, the daughter, was interviewed by a police social worker. Being younger she went to bed at nine and didn't hear anything until her mother woke her up with the news that her sister's bed was empty. I've started going through the interviews with Angelica's school friends. There's also her work mates at Penrhyn Yacht Club, where she waitressed Saturday lunchtimes and for the odd evening function that I need to go through. I'm s-s-sorry. I'll have more later.'

'No need to apologise, Jax. I chose you because you have an eye for detail. Anything odd, however stupid it sounds, let me know at once. It's not that we're here to criticise the original team. You know as well as I do that sometimes it's impossible

88

to see something that's right in front of you. Not only that but there's new ways of looking at things now. New technologies and computer software, which leads me on to the next point. There's something that's been puzzling me,' she added with a frown. 'I'm toying with the idea of someone perhaps signalling for Angelica to let them in. See if you can check with the list from the original CSI team about anything found on the ground below. I know ladder marks have already been mentioned. But also pebbles thrown at the window. I know they found footprints that didn't lead anywhere at the time but they might now. It's probably worth digging them out and sending them off to be checked against the National Footwear Reference Collection.'

Gaby made her way to the whiteboards that extended the whole length of the room and the photos she'd stuck up earlier. The first was of Angelica taken on Llandudno beach with the wind in her hair and a huge beam that transformed her serious face into a thing of beauty. The second, a photo she barely glanced at, showed Angelica curled up in that nightdress, the backdrop of Llandudno pier and the beach beyond stretching out in the distance. Picking up a marker she pulled off the cap and started to add a quick list in her best handwriting, bracketing a detective's name beside each item she wanted checking. At least she knew now what had to be done. That any of it would make a blind bit of difference was something not worth worrying about at this stage. Owen would be back tomorrow and add his usual reasoned ha'penneth to the mix, she reminded herself, worrying her bottom lip with her teeth. That he wasn't going to be happy about being side-lined was an understatement.

Chapter 16

Marie

Monday 20 July, 6 p.m. St Asaph Police Station

Marie felt more at home at the station than she did in her bedsit. It was warmer for one thing and with free coffee on tap, cheaper too. The only thing it lacked was food and somewhere comfortable to rest her head. But neither of those things were relevant, not anymore. Both her appetite and her ability to sleep had deserted her along with her husband.

Standing at the printer, she loaded the carefully chosen photos before typing in her work email and scanning the pictures to her Outlook. Security at the station was tight and all emails had to be encrypted. Long gone were the days when she used to fax experts for their opinion, which was all very well. Management had no idea how time consuming it was ensuring data protection rules weren't compromised. The reality was that simple information transfers were now far from simple.

She headed back to her desk, taking a sip of herbal tea, her fingers clinging to the last vestiges of warmth from her chipped

90

mug with a picture of a deerstalker on the front. While the calendar was tripping its way merrily through the months, and the sun was still streaming in through the windows despite the lateness of the hour, she couldn't seem to warm up no matter how hard she tried.

Her lips curled at the direction of her thoughts. Summer was the very last thing she wanted to think about, not now. She'd had such great plans – plans that up to a few weeks ago had included arranging a romantic four-day minibreak in Amsterdam to celebrate Ivo's fortieth. Presents had been bought and, following careful wrapping, hidden in her usual spot at the back of the cupboard under the stairs – gifts that she could have returned and exchanged for cash but she'd never given them a thought when he'd dropped his bombshell. Now he'd be celebrating with his new family, while she'd be spending the day alone thinking of what might have been. Even if she'd had the inclination to go on the minibreak by herself, she didn't have either the money or strength to travel that far. After their climactic final confrontation she'd stuffed her clothes and laptop into the back of her car and walked out of the house without a backward glance.

Logging on to the system, she double-checked the business name scrawled on the top Post-it note. It was the first time she'd heard of The Button Queen but, after a brief chat with the owner on the phone earlier, she was convinced that if anyone could help them find out about the buttons, it would be her. The truth was the unique fastenings were a long shot but, with nothing else to go on, it was the only shot she had of actively contributing to the case.

Within seconds she'd opened a new email, drafted a few words, attached the photos and clicked send – the last task of the day. Under normal circumstances she'd now be busily folding her laptop shut and gathering her phone and bag in preparation for slipping her light jacket on and heading home – that is if she had a home to go back to. Instead she folded her hands across her lap and stared into space, at a total loss. There was no what comes next, no turning the page and starting again. The mental, emotional and financial battering she'd had over recent weeks meant that she'd lost the ability to move forward. No. Not lost. Ivo had stolen it from under her, she remembered, tears building.

Marie Morgan wasn't a weakling. She worked in a tough job, populated by far more men than women. But she'd earned her colleagues' respect the hard way. She never shirked away from the less salubrious of tasks and was often the last to leave the office. But Ivo's actions had floored her. He'd removed every rung from her confidence ladder and blocked off every avenue open. Only the dregs of a woman remained.

She lifted her hand and wiped her damp cheeks with her fingers, trying to find the enthusiasm to walk home, not that the one room could in any way ever warrant that term. But with no money in their joint bank account it was all she could afford until she was able to save up for the deposit on a flat.

The fall of footsteps and the push of the door had her picking up her bag in a hurry, her head averted.

'Oh hello. What are you still doing here? Stupid me. I was halfway home before I remembered I'd left my mobile on charge.' Malachy strolled across the room, unplugged his phone from the wall and, checking for messages, slipped it in the pocket of his brown leather coat. He paused by her desk, watching as she plucked her jacket from behind her chair and slipped her arms in place.

'Oh, this and that. I had those photos to send to that button specialist.'

'Rather you than me. Although I don't think finding the boyfriend is going to be a barrel of laughs. A dead-end case if you ask me. Excuse the pun.'

'You're probably right,' she said, cursing under her breath that it had to be him of all people to find her in such a state. If it had been Jax, he'd have rushed in and collected his phone before

92

rushing out again, a few brief words on his lips, all delivered with a shy smile. Gaby Darin would have been upfront, checking if she was okay, while Owen probably would have been all embarrassed and chosen to ignore the clear evidence of her tears. But Malachy was different. He kept himself to himself and didn't mix with the rest of the team outside of the job. Like Gaby, he'd transferred to the area but that's where any similarity ended. While the acting DI was what she'd term a career cop, the jury was still out on why Malachy had chosen a future in law enforcement. Unlike the rest of them, he hadn't started at the bottom as a police constable. Instead, he'd entered the profession via the post-degree national detective programme.

'Well, that's me.' She tucked her bag and her laptop under her arm and headed for the door. 'I'll see you tomorrow.'

'What about now? I'm heading out for a drink. You're very welcome to join me. No fun drinking by myself.'

She shook her head. 'I couldn't, but thanks all the same.' She continued walking down the corridor only to pause at his next words.

'Why not?'

'Excuse me?' She turned towards him, unsure whether she'd heard him correctly.

'I asked why not? Unless you have plans, I think it's a great idea. It's not as if I have anything else to do. We might as well do bugger all together.'

Marie stared at him open-mouthed, unsure of quite what to say. With the virulent nature of the station grapevine, it was likely that he'd heard about her marital troubles. But did that mean he was looking for more than a drink? The way she was feeling towards men currently, she'd sooner top herself. The only thing stopping her from taking her own life was the determination to make it as difficult as possible for her husband. He'd had it all his own way up to now. That had to stop if it was the last thing she did. It very well might be.

93

Malachy must have read her mind, his expression changing from his usual one of habitual brooding to apologetic in an instant. 'Please don't think that there's an ulterior motive other than I hate drinking alone. For some reason women seem to hit on me as soon as I walk into a bar,' he added, clicking his fingers. 'I don't know what it is, but it can get wearing especially when all I want is a pint.'

'Really!' she exploded, her first laugh in weeks causing her lips to lift. 'God's gift, hey?' She scrolled down from the top of his wavy black hair, handsome features and leather jacket only pausing when she reached his brown boots. He looked good in a bad boy sort of way, but the jury was still out on whether she could trust him. However, all that was immaterial. With her lack of funds until payday she could barely afford to buy the bread and soup she needed to sustain her let alone throw cash away on alcohol.

'Mal, I appreciate the offer but I can't take you up on it,' she said, deciding that honesty was the best policy. 'I'm completely strapped for cash until the end of the month and . . .'

'If that's all you're worried about . . .' He stretched out a hand, cupping her elbow. 'You can call it an IOU if you like although I'm perfectly comfortable with buying a mate a few drinks. Look on it as protection money and think of all those poor women you're going to disappoint this evening.'

The Salt Inn was only a five-minute walk from the station but not a place Marie had ever visited before with her husband. Living on the outskirts of St Asaph they had been part of an active dinner party set, rarely venturing outside the homes of their friends except for the odd drink. Although now she had more time to think of it, they weren't really her friends at all. Ivo would have been horrified if she'd invited one of her colleagues around to their five-bedroomed house, situated on Upper Denbigh Road. She'd never asked but he'd made it very clear from the start of their relationship that having a wife working in law enforcement

94

was a huge embarrassment. The plan had always been for her to give up when the kids arrived. Or, at least, that had been his plan.

Now confronted with the bright, modern interior of the trendy bistro, she suddenly realised that there was a life outside of her broken marriage. It wasn't a life she was ready to live yet but it was there waiting in the wings for when she was ready. A part of her – no, that wasn't true – most of her, still hoped that Ivo would come to his senses. But she knew that he wouldn't. Their relationship was over the second he realised that, for whatever reason, she couldn't give him children. He'd said it wasn't personal, which hurt the most. What part of breaking up a relationship that had spanned ten years, wasn't personal?

'Come on, there's a table over there in the corner. What are you having?'

'A G&T, no ice or lemon please.'

She chose the sofa buttressing the wall and picked up the menu card for something to look at. Her mobile was silent just as it had been for days and it wasn't as if she could afford to do any online shopping.

'Here you go.'

He flopped down on the seat opposite and chinked glasses before taking a long sip from his beer. 'God, I needed that.'

'And me, thank you.' She took a small sip, relishing the flavour of Bombay Sapphire floating over her tongue. 'So, anyone try to pick you up then?' she said, managing to force a grin.

He leant forward, close enough for her to smell the slight trace of his woody aftershave. 'It was dicey there for a second until I pointed you out. You're a very attractive woman, if you don't mind me saying, Marie, and with fantastic dress sense. That husband of yours must be a complete fool.'

Her grin withered, only to be replaced by a blush. She thought she was well past the age of such youthful signs of embarrassment but obviously not if the heat storming across her cheeks was anything to go by.

95

'Thank you. But I'm sure you don't want to talk about my problems.'

'Well, what else is there to talk about?' He chuckled, the sound unexpected from someone she'd pigeon-holed as the serious type. 'We can't very well discuss the case. I'm happy to be used as a sounding board. I'm also a good listener unless you'd prefer to discuss it with one of your girlfriends?'

Which one? Ivo had done a great job of isolating her from everyone he didn't think fit his corporate lawyer image. At the time it hadn't mattered but now . . . now she was in a wilderness of her own making with no map or compass to guide her way. If she'd only stood up to him – he'd probably have walked out sooner. The sudden realisation that she'd wasted over a quarter of her life on a man that wasn't worth it had the colour leaching from her skin and the strength from her fingers.

'Hey, go easy.' Before she knew it, Malachy had joined her on the sofa, rescuing her drink and placing it back on the table.

'I'm sorry. Maybe coming out wasn't such a good idea.'

'I disagree, and what's more I'm going to feed you too,' he said, glancing at the menu briefly before standing. 'Two burgers and fries coming up unless you have any objections?'

It took about five minutes for him to return, his hands full of refills. But instead of taking the seat opposite like before, he sat beside her, bending his mouth to her ear.

'Don't look now but you're the topic of a very heated conversation between that couple seated the other side of the room.' He tilted his head, flicking a glance across the expanse of floor. 'He's about five-seven, stocky build and seems extremely pissed off. She's nothing to look at, not a patch on you if that helps. Ah.' He slid his arm behind her back. 'He's coming this way. Play along – darling.'

'Marie, what the hell do you think you're doing?'

'The same as you, old chap,' Malachy drawled, deliberately staring over his shoulder at the table the man had just come from and the woman staring back. 'And you are?'

96

'Her husband.'

'Really? I had heard you'd separated or is having two women on the go permitted where you come from?'

'Why, you little . . .'

Malachy slipped his hand out from behind Marie's back, squeezing her shoulder before standing to his full height, which was a good head taller.

'You were saying, old chap?'

'Marie, get your tosspot of a lover off my back. I need to speak to you. Now!'

'Well, she doesn't want to speak to you,' Malachy said, retaking his seat and wrapping both of his arms around her. 'Don't worry, darling. He'll soon get the message and if he doesn't, I'll get him thrown out. He's already caught the manager's attention.'

Marie and Malachy both watched as Ivo stormed back the way he'd come, only staying long enough to throw money on the table and bark orders at his partner.

'Oh God, I think I'm going to be sick.'

'No you're not. Here.' He picked up her drink, placed it in her hands and watched while she finished the glass. 'There, is that better?'

'Yes.' She rested her head back and closed her eyes, completely drained. 'I don't know what to say to you. Thank you seems somewhat lacking. I owe you one.'

'You don't owe me anything, sweetheart. Come on now. Chin up,' he said, placing a couple of napkins in her hand before shifting to the seat opposite and glancing over his shoulder. 'It looks like our meal is arriving and I'd hate for the waitress to think that I'm anything other than a respectable member of the public. She might throw me out and that would be a waste of a perfectly good burger.'

97

Chapter 17

Gaby

Monday 20 July, 6.50 p.m. Rhos-on-Sea

Dressed in her warmest pyjamas and fluffy pink dressing gown, Gaby settled on the sofa and booted up her laptop, all thoughts of tea pushed aside until much later. She'd decided that she really did need to add some paint to the sanded panels in the lounge, which necessitated an economy drive. So instead of her usual ready meal to look forward to, she'd popped into Lidl on the way home and picked up the makings of a stir fry. There was also a bulky carrier bag, emblazoned with the logo of a well-known DIY store, in the corner of the lounge, which she determinedly ignored. She'd also taken a diversion to drop into B&Q on the way past and was now the proud owner of an assortment of brushes and three tins of matt paint in varying shades of buttermilk.

Gaby didn't waste any time in thinking about what her team were up to while she waited for her computer to load. It was difficult in a station the size of St Asaph to avoid hearing the odd throwaway comment about how lonely they viewed her existence.

98

She'd even heard a whisper that there was more to life than work, but she couldn't seem to puzzle out how she was going to achieve the balance her colleagues seemed to have mastered.

Instead of allowing her maudlin thoughts to spoil her evening, she flipped open the lid of her briefcase and pulled the top sheet of paper towards her, determined to continue investigating Angelica's murder. While Henry Sherlock had annoyed her with his flat refusal to even consider her suggestion about the leaving of trophies, it hadn't been a surprise. He'd need evidence and she was determined to find it even if it was at the expense of her free time.

All crimes were assigned a unique reference number and it was these eight digits she typed into the system. The programme then subdivided into sections, each one drilling down into the specifics of the case. Gaby didn't read the reports in detail. Any one case generated more paperwork than a forest full of trees and she simply didn't have the time to go into the depth she felt each case deserved. Instead she focused on the age of the victim, the location of the crime and the brief synopsis that followed . . .

It didn't take her long to realise the emotional rollercoaster ride her self-imposed task would take her on. Gorgeous women, some of them little more than girls, who'd had their lives ruined, and in the most extreme cases stolen, by the hand of pure evil. Far too many crimes, still not solved even after the passage of months and sometimes years. Gaby was a copper for a reason and, to her mind, tougher than most of the women she came across. She'd seen more in the last thirteen years than most people in a lifetime. But scrolling through the reams of cases had her pause every so often and heave air into her lungs. She wasn't a watering pot, far from it. The last time she'd cried had been when she'd lain injured and near death in that Caernarfon farmhouse. Now her throat pricked at the crimes she had no reason to be delving into. Oh there was no law against a detective conducting research – they did it all the time in an effort to crack a case. But she had no proof that Angelica's murder was anything but an isolated incident, only her copper's instinct, which must be viewed at best as an inexact science. It had let her down too many times in the past to be viewed with anything but suspicion.

She was halfway to nowhere and thinking of giving up on the idea of trophy leaving when a knock on the door had her jumping with fright. The clock on the mantlepiece was a surprise. She'd been so wrapped up in her notes that she hadn't realised that it was approaching nine.

'Sorry about the time but I had to pick Conor up from Judo and thought I'd stop by to say thank you for Friday.'

Gaby stepped back to let them into the hall, silently cursing her choice of loungewear. Not that she wasn't perfectly respectable but she'd rather not have been caught wearing her dressing gown and matching fuchsia-pink pompom slippers. She followed them into the lounge, breaking into a smile when Conor presented her with a small posy of freesias.

'Oh, you shouldn't have. They're beautiful. I'll just go and put them in water.' She waved a hand at the two throw-covered armchairs. 'Make yourself comfortable. I'll only be a minute.'

Back in the kitchen she let out a sigh of relief. He wouldn't be here long, not with Conor in tow. She only hoped he wasn't going to make a habit of dropping in on the off-chance. She opened the cupboard under the sink, pulled out an earthenware jar that doubled up as a vase and, arranging the flowers, carried them into the lounge.

'Would you like a drink? I have tea, coffee or juice. Or there's some wine?'

'A tea would be grand and juice for Conor but only if it's not too much trouble?'

'None at all.' She spent a moment tidying her papers together, placing them in her briefcase and flipping the lid of her laptop closed before heading back into the kitchen, thankful of the interruption if she was honest. She'd wasted the whole of the

100

afternoon and most of her evening and all she'd come up with was the distinct impression that she was getting nowhere fast.

'At least you're in the sort of job where you can take your work home.'

Gaby glanced up from where she was placing mugs and a plate of biscuits on a tray to find him lounging against the door. 'Excuse me?'

'You know,' he said, taking the tray from her, his eyes twinkling behind his glasses. 'It's not an option open to a forensic pathologist.'

She gave an embarrassed laugh as she followed him into the lounge. 'If I didn't work from home, I'd probably never solve anything. As it is, it looks like I won't be solving this one either.'

'The case that Owen came to see me about?' he asked, settling in his chair.

'Yes. I was trying to be clever but obviously not.' She dragged a hand through her hair, which was still slightly damp from her shower. She couldn't quite believe that they were having a comfortable chat over a cuppa when, up until recently, they'd spent most of their time deflecting and inflicting verbal blows.

He rested his head back, his left ankle on his right knee while Conor had his head down, playing on his phone, earbuds in place.

'He seems a nice lad?' she finally said, reaching for her drink.

'He is. Obviously he takes after his mother,' he added, with a glimmer of his old spark back.

She quirked her mouth. 'Obviously. So he's . . . you've . . .?'

'Got full custody? Yes, for my sins. But it's good to have him around.'

'But difficult to juggle when holding down a demanding job such as yours, I'm guessing?'

'No more difficult than being a single mum, Gabriella.'

'No, I suppose not.' She eyed him over the rim of her mug, trying to think of what else to say in the verbal wasteland the conversation was heading. But she didn't have to wait long for him to break the silence.

101

He leant forward, lowering his voice. 'If there's anything you'd like to run past me. I'm pretty sure Conor can't hear a thing with those things in his ears but, to be on the safe side, don't be specific.'

What could she say other than, like Owen, she was starting to fixate on Angelica's murder even though the statistics were against her? The likelihood of a cold case being solved after all this time was minimal. Those infrequent reports in the news about criminals being caught years after the event were of lottery-winning rarity and there was no reason to suppose that this murder would be any different – if it was murder. The evidence on that issue was sketchy at best and perhaps something he could help her with . . .

'Have you had a chance to read the original medical report yet? I'm still not sure what happened to her and if I had a clearer idea of what I'm working with . . .' She patted to the laptop beside her. 'In all the cases I've been looking at there's been, without exception, a definitive cause attributed. But, in Angelica's it's unexplained. Maybe I'm being thick, it certainly feels like it, but I'm not exactly sure what an unexplained death means in relation to the case?'

'Exactly that, I'm afraid. The pathologist couldn't come up with a reasonable account for why her heart had stopped,' he said, his voice a mere whisper while he gathered up the mugs. 'I'll help you with the washing up.'

He continued as soon as the kitchen door had closed behind him. 'I think I might have an explanation but it's not one you're going to necessarily like.' He placed the mugs in the sink, his attention now on the makings of Gaby's meal sitting on the side. 'You should have said you hadn't eaten?'

'It's no bother. I often eat late anyway. I'm more interested in what you were saying. You can leave those, by the way.'

He propped against the wall, folding his arms across his chest. 'I think that Angelica Brock died of fright.'

Gaby frowned, her opinion of Rusty's competence suddenly dipping to an all-time low. While she'd been ambivalent about him as a man, she'd always thought that he was one of the best pathologists she'd ever come across – certainly on a par with Percival Pounder who was acclaimed in the field. 'You what? Get over. How the hell could she die of fright?'

'Very easily. I can see by your look that you're far from convinced, Gabriella, but it's the only explanation that makes sense.'

'But hearts don't stop for no reason.'

'True on the face of it but let's examine the facts. We know that her heart stopped which means that she went into cardiac arrest. But, the pathologist, while conducting a thorough autopsy, couldn't come up with a definitive reason for that. Most people who arrest have either an underlying heart condition or, in the case of children and young adults, either a congenital heart defect or a reason that makes sense like electrocution for example. Here you have a young girl whose only medical highlight is that she suffered from asthma. She was removed from her house and driven to one of the most secluded parts of Llandudno. It would have been totally deserted at that time of night. It's also obvious what she thought was going to happen and she would have been scared stiff because of it. Her body would have filled with adrenaline, in preparation for a fight or flight scenario, which would cause her heart to race further thus expediating the problem.' He shifted his position, opening the door a crack to check on Conor before shutting it again. 'He hasn't even noticed we've left the room.'

'I didn't expect him to. My nephews are exactly the same,' she said, her frown deepening. 'I still don't understand. There were no defence wounds or injuries on the body. No bruising from restraints and the report said no chemicals or alcohol in her system. So my question is, if this adrenaline causes this fight or flight response why did she do neither?'

'I think the simple answer is she couldn't. He – I take it a man is in the frame for her murder?'

'It's more likely. She was a tall girl and, while slim, it would

103

have taken quite a bit of effort to get her up there. I'm thinking she went willingly at the start but she would have known something was up pretty quickly.'

'So the question for you is why didn't she either try to flee or fight? Could he have had some kind of hold on her, do you think? Something that meant in the end she sacrificed herself.'

An image appeared in Gaby's mind of the broad flat stone in the centre of the rocks. Perhaps Rusty was onto something.

'And then he left her after she died? I don't get it, I'm afraid. Usually there's a sexual motive, isn't there? But no. He dressed her in someone else's nightdress and then left.' She shook her head. 'What the hell am I missing?'

It was his turn to frown. 'The one thing that does surprise me is the fact that there haven't been any similar crimes of the type. Someone who's gone that far wouldn't stop at an isolated case and certainly not if they were thwarted by her inopportune death.'

'Rusty, what do you think I've been doing, twiddling my thumbs? I've spent the evening trying to forge a link when there isn't a chain in sight. It was obviously a well-planned crime. I've searched the national database to find a similar MO but there's nothing. I've ploughed through nearly thirty of the sixty or so crimes committed where items have been left with the victim. In four of the incidences the rapist left behind the coat that he'd laid the women on, presumably forgetting it in his haste to get away – in all four cases he was easily apprehended. In two others he gave them money to get a taxi home. In none did he dress them in items of clothing that probably belonged to his granny.'

'But as we both know, Gabriella, unlike leopards, criminals do change their spots. Murderers and rapists don't usually start out with the big crimes. Fred West was a petty thief while the Yorkshire Ripper's first crime was stealing tyres. So maybe you've approached it from the wrong angle and' – he held up both his hands, palms facing outwards – 'before you have a go, I'm trying to help, not put obstacles in your way.'

104

'I know and I do appreciate it. I just don't know where we go from here.' She wondered whether she should mention having contacted Angus Ford, but for some reason decided against it. 'Owen is back tomorrow, which will be a great help.'

'Indeed.' With his hand on the doorknob, Rusty continued. 'With regards to the second matter, I'll have the report to you first thing but there's nothing outstanding. Mary Butterworth's post-mortem results confirm both her original diagnosis of brain tumour and poor prognosis. Death was as a direct result of the explosion and not the fire that tore through the house after.'

'You're sure that she couldn't have been dead already? You know, the explosion used to disguise evidence of her murder,' Gaby said half-heartedly, not really thinking that her death was anything but a tragic accident.

His eyes widened. 'You crack me up with your conspiracy theories, Gabriella. People are allowed to suffer mishaps on occasion, and no. In this case I'm one hundred per cent certain that the explosion was the cause of death. Okay, so she didn't have any soot in either her windpipe or gullet, or large levels of carboxyhaemoglobin in her blood stream, two factors that would indicate smoke inhalation. But the evidence of being decapitated by a baking tray is pretty much indisputable.'

105

Chapter 18

Gaby

Tuesday 21 July, 8.50 a.m. Gaby's Office

'So, what kind of weekend did you have, Owen?'

'Bloody lovely. Kate's parents had Pip for a couple of nights so we chilled at home instead of being dragged here and there. What about yourself? I heard about the explosion. You could have called me, you know. I'd have been happy to—'

'I know you would but I owe you too many uninterrupted weekends as it is. Mine was fine up until the dancing started – it went downhill pretty fast after that,' Gaby said, sitting back in her chair, her feet resting on the bar underneath. 'I'm glad you're here early. I wanted to have a word about Angelica's murder.' She studied him briefly, noting the circles bracketing his eyes and tense strain around his mouth. This was a difficult time for him, she wasn't about to make it any easier. 'I went to see Sherlock.' She noted his mutinous look and quickly added, 'So, I'm going to be overseeing Angelica's investigation while I'd like you to take charge of the one involving the gas explosion in Llandudno. To be fair

106

it shouldn't take you more than a day to finish the paperwork and then we'll have another think.'

'But ma'am—'

'No buts, Owen – and it's Gaby, as I'm sick of reminding you. You know as well as I do that officers can't be involved with crimes that involve family members, even distant ones like Angelica. We can't have the truth distorted by heavy emotion.'

She watched myriad expressions flit across his face until she got the one she was hoping for – reluctant acceptance. She didn't expect him to be happy, only to respect her decision and her reason for making it.

'Now back to the Butterworths. Rusty promised that he'd send me the autopsy results first thing but, in short, Mary Butterworth, age forty-three, died in a gas explosion on Friday. The thing is – remember that man who stepped in front of a bus along Mostyn Street when I was still on sick leave? That was Tony Butterworth, her husband. All the evidence is that it's an unfortunate coincidence but we need to do the legwork in case we're missing something.'

Gaby logged on to her Outlook before continuing, squinting down at her emails. She hadn't slept well last night, a habit that was starting to catch up with her. The light in the office was a little too bright. The tea not quite strong enough. The idea of skiving off for a day in bed with the curtains closed on the edge of her mind.

'Good. Here it is,' she said to herself, noting the time of the email with a frown. While Rusty might be a doctor, he obviously didn't follow his own advice if the middle of the night message was anything to go by. Not that he'd said much, she noted, skimming the briefest of sentences. Dr Mulholland was a complete enigma and one she didn't have the time to think about, her mind dragging her back to the dancefloor and the way he'd twirled her around the room, her skirt billowing around her legs. So why was she doing exactly that, her frown deepening. She cleared her throat, supressing any thoughts of the eminent physician.

107

Instead she set up a new encrypted email, chose Owen from her list of favourites and pressed send before clicking open the attachment – aware that Owen was glued to his phone waiting for the message to appear.

It didn't take her long to read through the summary, which Rusty always pinned to the top. The twenty-three-page document would be read later when she'd go to the trouble of highlighting anything she either didn't understand – something that happened regularly with this type of medical report – or wanted to clarify with the rest of the team.

'It has all the elements of an accident,' Owen said, interrupting her reading. 'She was in the advanced stages of terminal cancer with a very poor short-term prognosis.'

'Yes. Exactly. So it shouldn't take too long to tie up any loose ends that need tying.'

'I'll get right on it.'

She slid a buff-coloured folder across the desk towards him. 'Here's the transcript from my prelim meeting with the daughter and son-in-law, which should give you a good start.'

'What did you make of them?'

'I haven't quite made up my mind about that. The daughter was a mess but that's understandable in the circumstances, having lost both her parents. The husband appears flamboyant, for want of a better word, but I don't want to influence you with my views.' she said, choosing her words carefully. 'You'll see as you read the report what I mean. He was away on business when it happened so perhaps that's the place to start for elimination purposes. The bad news is that I've checked and Tony Butterworth has already been cremated. We have all the eye-witness accounts and I've asked for his medical notes from the incident but there's not a lot to go on.' She unlocked her top drawer and removed a second buff-coloured folder, which she passed to him. 'I think it might be easier for you to concentrate on the wife's death and work backwards. With a bit of luck you'll have it wrapped up in a neat little ribbon of explanation by teatime.'

108

Chapter 19

Marie

Tuesday 21 July, 9.05 a.m. Incident Room

Marie worked through her emails. She clicked open the one from The Button Queen only to grimace at the contents. Newport was the other side of Wales and nearly a four-hour drive, but the message said that it was both important and urgent to speak to her in person. It wouldn't have been that much of a problem if she'd still had a car but it was one of the first things to go simply because she'd needed the money to live on. For her husband to empty their joint account in the knowledge that she didn't have a penny to her name was the glue needed to cement the pieces of her heart back together. The fractures remained.

It wasn't only the lack of a car or the thought of the drive bothering her. After all, it was easy enough to borrow one of the pool vehicles available. It was more the time involved away from her desk when the rest of the team were drowning in work since the reopening of Angelica's murder – DI Darin would have a fit if she asked her.

'Morning, Marie, looking forward to another day in the office?' Malachy said, strolling across the room and plonking himself down in his chair, his Burberry raincoat replacing yesterday's leather one.

'You sound exactly like that bloke from *The Chase*.'

'But taller and far more handsome?' He ran a hand across his black hair, his brown eyes twinkling.

'Whatever! And, to answer your question, no. They want me to go to Newport, so not really.'

'Who exactly are *they*?'

'Those button people. God only knows how long it will take me to get there.'

'It's a bloody shame you don't still have your car.'

'There's nothing I can do about that now,' she snapped, reluctant to get into a personal conversation with him, especially after what he'd witnessed in the restaurant. That was something she wanted to forget as quickly as possible.

He pulled out his mobile and started searching Google Maps. 'What about we go together? I still have that interview in Wrexham which is on the way,' he said, waving the screen in front of her.

While it made sense to take him up on his offer, she didn't really want to spend the day in his company. It was probably immaterial anyway – Darin was bound to say no.

'I'm not sure what the DI will think?'

'Well, there's no time like the present,' he said, making his way across the room to where Gaby and Owen were walking through the door.

Marie watched him interrupt their conversation with a ready smile planted on his lips. Within minutes he was back.

'Right then, that's sorted. We don't have to return back to the office until tomorrow.'

'How the hell did you manage that?' she whispered, shoving her arms into the sleeves of her jacket.

'With my usual charm and magnetic personality.'

110

Marie raised her brows but managed to suppress the words on her tongue, her attention on the body language going on between Gaby and Owen. He was obviously in a temper if the folded arms and grim look were anything to go by, and it didn't need more than a couple of brain cells to know why. Suddenly a day in Mal's company was the preferred option.

It was only a thirty-minute drive to Wrexham, the largest town in North Wales. But with Malachy behind the wheel of his Jaguar F Type the miles flew by. They managed to make the care home in just under forty minutes, which had included a fifteen-minute stop for petrol and a coffee in one of the service stations along the A483.

Malachy picked up his keys and notepad from where he'd placed them in the cubbyhole before turning to her. 'You might as well come in instead of sitting here.'

Marie didn't need to be asked twice. Leo Hazeldine's whereabouts was starting to be an irritant she couldn't ignore. Disappearing like that was suspicious at best and had all the hallmarks of someone who was running away from their past but did that include murder? She slipped her legs out of the car, deep in thought, the feel of bright sunshine against her skin causing her to drop her sunglasses in place from where they'd been perched on top of her head. It was a travesty to spend most of the day cooped up in a tin can even if it was the poshest vehicle she'd ever been in.

The care home was situated at the end of a tortuous narrow track, which opened up to reveal a large expanse of lawn bordered by terracotta pots bursting with bedding plants in a startling array of yellows and reds. The building resembled a boutique hotel with its large windows and immaculate, white painted exterior, a feeling that carried on inside the light reception area. It was manned by a middle-aged woman who was keen to be of help.

They soon found themselves following her into an overly warm

111

bed-sitting room that looked as if it had come straight out of the pages of *Country Life* with its Regency striped wallpaper and swagged curtains. The walls were lined with large gilt-framed photographs that Marie wished she had the guts to examine, the only thing stopping her the gimlet gaze of the room's only occupant.

Elise Hazeldine was a rotund bottle-blonde with sharp eyes and thin lips. Marie was pretty sure that the visit would be a waste of time so, instead of taking part, she sat back in her chair and pulled out her phone.

'Thank you again for agreeing to see us, Mrs Hazeldine,' Malachy said. 'I know you've already been interviewed about your son but—'

'But you still think he's guilty of that poor girl's death despite never finding a shred of proof against him.'

'I didn't say that—'

'There's no reason to. Why else would you have bothered to drop in,' she bit out, reaching behind her back to readjust her cushion before returning her gnarled hand to rest across her large rolling stomach. 'While my body might have let me down, there's nothing wrong with my brain,' she continued, staring down at her heavily bandaged legs. 'Leo is a good boy despite the run-around you lot gave him. Why can't you get it into your thick heads that he loved Angelica? Her death devastated him. You could say that more than one person died that night in Llandudno because my boy was never the same after.'

'We understand that but there's still the unanswered question of what happened and Leo, as much as anyone, must surely want to know. Where is your son, Mrs Hazeldine?'

'I was wondering when you'd get to the crux of the matter and, thank God, I won't be lying when I say that I have no idea.'

'What about his father?'

Marie lifted her head in time to catch the gamut of expressions chasing across Elise Hazeldine's face and silently applauded Malachy for hitting such a sweet nerve.

'There is no father,' she said, almost spitting out the words. 'He was little more than a sperm donor – I wouldn't even be able to tell you his name now,' she elaborated, her tone taking on a cautious note.

'But you have been married?'

'Leo was already a little boy by then and, as the relationship didn't last the course, I can't see that it's relevant. My ex-husband is now dead and good riddance.'

'And there's no siblings or close friends that you can think of that might know of Leo's whereabouts?'

'Officer, as I'm sure you know, Leo is an only child and, as he's been living in Australia for years, I have no idea who he hangs out with, if anyone.'

Within minutes they were back in the sweltering heat of the car.

'Well, that went well – not!' Malachy slammed the door behind him before slamming his hands down against the steering wheel. 'Darin's not going to be pleased.'

'Inspector Darin to you and me, Mal, and what exactly did you expect, hmm? That she'd roll over and give up all her secrets? That's not going to happen. I might not be a mother,' she said, a catch in her throat, 'but no parent is going to rat on their child, no matter how difficult their relationship might be.'

'So in effect I've driven halfway across Wales to sit in a bedroom smelling of piss . . .'

'It wasn't that bad and the smell probably came from those bandages as opposed to her bladder.'

'Whatever!' He crunched the gears into first and put his foot down, leaving a trail of gravel behind.

'You're in a strop and all for nothing.'

'For nothing,' he said between clenched teeth. 'I'm only hanging on by a thread at work and you're saying it's nothing. Darin hates my guts. You see the way she treats me when she's as nice as pie to the rest of you. I'll have you know this case means something. It could be my big break . . .'

113

'Break into where, Mal? Because, from where I'm looking, you're doing fine.'

'Not into. Out of.'

'Excuse me? Out of where?'

'Out from under my mother's eye, if you must know.'

Marie threw back her head and laughed. Malachy Devine, one of the smoothest operators she'd ever met, not only had a mother, but one he didn't want to upset. 'You're killing me, you really are. And DI Darin doesn't hate you by the way. I don't think she's capable of hatred. Okay, so she's firm but then you have to admit that you do have a tendency to wind her up.'

'Are you so sure about her not disliking me?' he said, flicking on the indicator and turning off the A483.

The laughter died in her throat as suddenly as it had started. She'd never have pegged Malachy as the self-doubting type but all the indications were that she'd misunderstood his behaviour as arrogance when all he sounded like was an insecure little boy. And if she'd misread his behaviour what were the odds that everyone else at the station had, including Darin? She went to pat his leg only to still her hand and lift it to push her hair back instead. No point in fuelling any wrong ideas but now that she was aware of how he felt, she'd try and do something about it.

Chapter 20

Marie

Tuesday 21 July, 2 p.m. Newport

The Button Queen's warehouse in Newport wasn't what Marie had been expecting. In truth, she didn't know what to expect but the shop flanked with dwarf conifers on either side of the door certainly wasn't it.

Malachy pulled up opposite and waited while she clambered out and made her way to the front door before zooming off into the distance. She'd already invited him to sit in on the meeting but he had other ideas, which she was pretty sure involved coffee and cake in one of the cafés they'd passed while they tried to negotiate the unfamiliar town. She hitched her bag up her shoulder, bemoaning the lack of caffeine not to mention cake. She wasn't sure how much help buttons could actually be to the inquiry, and the coffee Malachy had bought her at that service station seemed a very long time ago. But the shop window looked interesting with their array of buttons and, if nothing else, she might treat herself to a few to liven up her wardrobe. It would be a long time before she'd be able to afford anything larger.

115

The shop was empty apart from a slim, attractive brunette arranging metal buttons by their various sizes into Perspex trays. It didn't take long for her to stop what she was doing and offer to put the kettle on, introducing herself as Kat, one of the owners.

'Come in the back. I've been at this all morning and I could do with a break.'

The rear of the shop opened into a small kitchenette with a table and a couple of chairs, which they were soon sitting around with mugs of steaming coffee.

'Right then.' Kat wiped her hands on the side of her jeans and opened the first in the pile of books she'd placed in the centre. 'Your buttons have certainly been causing a storm at the shop,' she said, thumbing through the pages before stopping and twisting the book in Marie's direction.

'How come? Mother of pearl aren't that unusual, surely?' Marie pulled the book a little closer and stared down at what appeared to be a replica of the buttons on the nightdress.

'You're right, of course,' Kat said, closing the book with a snap and choosing a second, which she'd bookmarked with a yellow Post-it note. 'Have a look at that a mo while I get the original photos you sent.' She was back within seconds, laying four blown-up images on the table in front of her. 'The buttons appear a little different, I'll grant you. We enlarged each one further to see the detailing.'

'Which is something I should have thought to do.'

'Don't worry about it. Those of us in the know,' she said with a wink, 'know only too well that the devil is always in the detail.' She pushed the photos over, one by one, her red-tipped finger tapping on the last button. 'Do you notice anything different about this one?'

Marie squinted at the A4 enlargement, frown lines wrinkling her normally smooth brow. 'It's different, isn't it? How come I didn't spot that?'

'Probably you wouldn't unless you'd been looking.' Kat sat back, her elbows on the table, a smile breaking. 'Remember you

116

sent me photos of all four buttons, which were still attached to the original garment, so easy to miss.'

But an elementary mistake all the same, Marie thought, mentally berating herself for the simple rookie error, her attention trained on the picture of the final button. It was the same shape and the same size as the other three and not a bad colour match. It was also the top button and therefore partially concealed with the lace detailing so not that noticeable. But that wasn't the point. She'd missed the difference as had every copper on the case, past and present.

'So why would someone add an odd button?' she finally asked, picking up her mug and staring at Kat, her fingers laced through the handle.

'Why do any of us add a button to a garment? She lost it and at a guess didn't have another one the same size and shape so chose this one as the best match. Up until the last twenty or so years it was commonplace for the woman of the house to keep a stash of spare buttons. Before the Internet and the growth of the throwaway society we now live in, getting a spare one to match would have necessitated a trip to the local haberdashery store but with no guarantee that a suitable replacement would be found. It's a good habit to get into and, of course, the most likely reason for her choosing this specific button,' she continued, the building excitement clear in her voice.

Marie's gaze sharpened, her mug now back on the table. 'You sound as if it's something special?'

'If it's what I think it is then it's one of a kind and might solve your little puzzle for you.' She laughed, pushing a packet of biscuits in her direction. 'You should see your expression, Detective, but I mean every word. Have you ever heard of a memorial button?'

'You look like the cat that's fallen headfirst into a carton of cream,' Malachy said, completing a U-turn and heading back towards the A449, his foot on the accelerator.

'That obvious, huh?'

117

'Go on then. Spill. What's the exciting news in the world of buttons?'

'If you're going to be sarcastic . . .'

'Moi? Sarcastic? When have I ever been . . . oh, all right then.' He glanced at her before turning his attention back to the road ahead. 'I'll admit that I was born with a cynical outlook on life – you'll understand why if you ever get to meet my mother.'

'You mentioned her earlier. But I'm not sure where you got the idea from that I'm ever going to meet her.' Marie twisted in her seat, her mouth gaping to reveal even white teeth. 'It's not as if this is a date or anything. We're colleagues, something I was hoping I wouldn't have to remind you about. You need to stop playing games, Mal. I do need to get back to the office and quickly. The button thing, which you so quickly dismissed, could actually break the case wide open and I for one want to be right there when it does.'

She shifted, turning away to stare out of the passenger window, more annoyed than she cared to admit. It would be a very long time before she invested any degree of trust in a man either in or outside of the workplace. Malachy trying to manipulate the boundaries of their relationship when he knew what her husband was like, was low even for him. She pulled the collar of her jacket around her and folded her arms across her chest. She was tired, fed up and, despite three biscuits, ravenous. But not only that. While she was disappointed with the man by her side, she was more disappointed in allowing herself to get dragged into the situation. All in all, it would have been easier for her to borrow a car from the station or even take the train. It might have taken nearly twice as long but feeling obligated was something she could do without.

'Look, I'm sorry. All right. Let's wipe the slate clean and start again,' Malachy said into the growing silence. He indicated and, shifting lane, headed towards the exit. 'It's not that far to Shrewsbury. Let's stop off and I'll buy you a sandwich – we can discuss what you've found. I'd also like some advice on that interview with Elise Hazeldine. I'm pretty sure she's hiding something.'

Chapter 21

Owen

Tuesday 21 July, 2 p.m. Incident Room

DS Owen Bates wasn't having a good day. It had started with an argument with Kate at the breakfast table and had steadily gone downhill. To be excluded from Angelica's inquiry was the last straw as far as he was concerned.

On returning to his desk, the first thing he did was to switch on his laptop and search for the resignation letter that had been lurking on his C Drive. Originally penned in anger over some long forgotten slight, the letter had sat there for months waiting for a final decision on his part. Kate was in favour of him having a complete career change but then she'd had more than enough of the police invading her life. As she'd said only this morning, she didn't need to be reminded at every juncture about her sister's murder. When he'd joined the police at the tender age of eighteen, his job had been a huge sticking point. But with the new baby imminent, she'd given him an ultimatum and he really couldn't blame her. He'd missed enough of his son's important milestones

119

to know that the police force was a way of life in addition to a career choice.

He stroked his beard, the cursor hovering over the print button, still undecided as to what to do. He couldn't deny the number of occasions that he'd put his job over his marriage. There'd been countless times too numerous to remember let alone mention. Missed anniversaries and birthdays. Even spoilt Christmases. His marriage was currently the underdog in his scales of life and he knew that he had to do something to change that. He'd loved Kate since he was fifteen and he still couldn't quite believe that someone like her would go out with someone like him. But he loved his job with a passion that far exceeded his wage packet. To give it up now when they were so close to nailing Angelica's murderer . . . well, it was the only thing that stopped him from printing the letter off. Instead he turned to his notebook and the neat list of witnesses who'd been present when Tony Butterworth had walked out under that bus, his decision made. He'd promise Kate that as soon as they caught Angelica's killer he'd quit. That and a commitment to make it home on time for once should pacify her for now, he thought, picking up his mobile and sending her a quick text. If the weather remained nice there might be enough sun to sit in the garden for an hour or so after work. He couldn't remember the last time he'd been home in time for anything apart from a hasty meal and an hour or so in front of the TV before bed. That was about to change.

The bus driver of the number five was a short, skinny man of indeterminate age with a sharp chin and a gelled comb-over, which had Owen turning his head in an effort to hide his smirk. He showed him into an interview room on the first floor of Llandudno's police station, invited him to take a seat and offered him a drink. Derek Hughes wasn't under suspicion of anything other than being in the wrong place at the wrong time, and a cup of coffee might be the thing to settle his anxious look and unsteady hands: while he wasn't guilty of any crime it was clear that he was suffering from some form of extreme anxiety as a result.

After Owen had placed a couple of mugs on the table, he took the seat opposite and began. 'Thank you for coming in this afternoon, Mr Hughes. I just wanted to run over again what happened when Mr Butterworth stepped out in front of the bus. And, to reiterate, there's no concern on our part that you didn't do everything in your power to avert the disaster. The skid marks on the road and statements from the passengers on the bus all indicate that you did everything possible.'

He didn't mention the string of invectives that the passengers had heard stream out of Mr Hughes' mouth when he realised what had happened, or the off-duty policeman's eye-witness account. Gaby had wanted him to check and that's what he was doing.

'There's not a lot to tell. I'd driven into Lower Mostyn Street coming from Craig-y-Don direction,' he said, pulling at the sleeve of his jumper and where the cuff was starting to fray. 'I had to stop at the zebra-crossing by Subways and then again at the traffic lights by the Victorian Centre – you know – the ones outside M&S. I'd just started up again when I saw something flicker in the corner of my vision. A man running from behind the tree outside the library. I weren't going fast. Only about five or ten mile.' He picked up his mug, cradling it between clenched fists, his eyelids scrunched tight briefly before flashing open to meet Owen's stare. 'I tried to stop. I slammed my foot down on that pedal so hard it nearly went through the ruddy floor. He came out of nowhere.' He placed the mug back down on the table, again with two hands. 'I'll never forget the expression on his face for as long as I live. It were a living nightmare.'

'In what way?' Owen asked, hunching his shoulders forward. 'If he came out of nowhere, how did you have the time to notice how he looked?'

'It was in the . . . just before . . . when I . . . when he . . .' He

121

shut his eyes again briefly only to snap them open. 'He looked completely terrified. If I didn't know any better, I'd say that he was the very last man who wanted to throw himself under ten ton of metal. Something scared the life out of him and it wasn't the bus.'

The weather was dry but the bitter wind, blowing off the Irish Sea, made Owen stuff his hands inside his pockets as he walked to his car. He had planned to go straight back to St Asaph station following the interview but something Derek Hughes had said made him change his mind. So instead he drove to Mostyn Street and the scene of the accident before heading towards the seafront. Within minutes he was pulling up outside the Butterworth's house, or what remained of it.

There was no earthly reason for him to visit especially as he wouldn't be able to enter now the site had been secured. There was also nothing to be gained. The photographs and videos said it all. But for some reason the case now snagged his attention – a complete U-turn from his initial feelings when Gaby had foisted the assignment onto his shoulders earlier.

Owen stayed behind the wheel of the car, his attention fixed on the building. Radio Two was burbling, but he didn't hear a word. The radio was background noise to his thoughts, only that.

Tony Butterworth was a man who, if Derek Hughes was to be believed, had committed suicide almost against his will. If he'd died after his wife, it would have made more sense. A person prostrate with grief, following the death of their loved one, was something Owen had come across on countless occasions. But if the daughter was telling the truth, a view confirmed by Dr Mulholland, her mother was completely dependent on her father for nearly every aspect of her daily life. By committing suicide, he'd risked having his wife mopped up by social services and most likely put into care. It would have taken a certain kind of man to allow that to happen to the person they were allegedly devoted to. His hands gripped on to the steering wheel, annoyed at

122

having found yet another loose end to tie off. But Owen Bates was nothing if not thorough. Something had made Tony Butterworth take his own life. He wouldn't be happy until he found out what.

A face peered out from one of next door's many windows, catching his attention and he suddenly realised that he'd been sitting in his parked car for far too long. If he didn't move pretty smartish, he had a good idea that he'd have a PC bearing down with a list of questions he couldn't be bothered to answer. Owen shifted into first gear and, with a brief glance at the address he'd written down in his notebook, changed his mind about heading back to St Asaph and writing up his notes before heading home. Instead he released the handbrake and made his way over the Little Orme and towards Llanwddyn, a tiny village that boasted a smattering of houses, one of which belonged to Avril and Samuel Eustace.

The drive was short, less than fifteen minutes, but through a part of Wales he had very fond memories of, the well-remembered rolling hills now lush with sheep. He paused outside The Queen's Head and checked the address again before turning right and pulling up outside a mid-terrace, stone-built cottage with periwinkle-blue paintwork and a small square of garden that was given over to lawn. The cottage was picturesque with a view over the fields opposite and his mind slipped to Kate and how much she'd love to live here instead of the two-up two-down box that was all he could afford on his salary. He pushed the thought aside and, reaching for his jacket from the back seat, steeled himself for what was bound to be a difficult interview.

Avril Eustace was exactly as Gaby described, right down to the red-rimmed eyes and drab dress sense that did nothing to enhance her death-pale skin. She looked younger than her years too, more eighteen than the twenty-three he knew her to be. She also looked trusting, far too trusting – barely glancing down at his warrant card before directing him into the small but comfortable lounge. He didn't know whether to feel relieved or disappointed that there

123

was no sign of the husband. Gaby's carefully chosen words about him had Owen thinking of his wife. Kate was very different to Avril, especially now with her swollen ankles and heaving belly, but there were still similarities. They both had blonde hair, although in Avril's case, the dark roots told their own story. They were also small-boned and, before Kate's pregnancy, probably wore the same size-eight clothes. For Avril to have chosen to marry such a flamboyant character, as Samuel Eustace was purported to be, was quite beyond his comprehension. For him to have actually bothered to propose set Owen's mind working overtime. He must have seen something in her pale, insipid beauty but he couldn't for the life of him think what.

He took a seat on the squidgy sofa and accepted a cup of tea, not that he needed it. But a couple of minutes getting a feel for the room was as important as the list of questions he'd forged on the way over. Unlike Gaby and the rest of the team, Owen's notebook remained firmly entrenched in his inside pocket, his near photographic memory one of his biggest assets to his career in law enforcement. He never forgot a name and rarely a face and could quote near verbatim any interview he'd ever conducted. But what was seen as an advantage in his working life was the polar opposite in his home one. He'd learnt the hard way the benefit of losing his keys on occasion just so she couldn't call him 'so bloody perfect' again. If he was so perfect, why hadn't he solved her sister's murder? It's not as if he hadn't been tinkering away at it in the quiet of his mind ever since joining the force.

The lounge wasn't quite square and probably a bitch to decorate but the Eustaces had made the best of the room's quirky features. A small woodburning stove was slotted into the fireplace recess and flanked by a large log basket, full to the brim. The carpet was rich cream and the two-seater sofas, on either side of the fireplace, pale yellow, which had his eyebrows lifting to his hairline. Pip would have a field day with his chocolate-covered fingers. Everything was spotlessly clean and, apart from two picture frames on the oak mantlepiece, free from clutter. He walked the two paces it took to cross the room, dipping his head to stare at the photos. The first showed Mary and Tony at some party or other, laughing up into the camera. Mary's blonde hair was cropped short and her skin etched with lines but, apart from that, Avril could have been her younger sister instead of her daughter. Tony looked pompous and well fed and the thought crossed Owen's mind as to what kind of a man he'd been. The next photo was clearly taken on Avril's wedding day. She almost passed for pretty in her virginal white gown and white rose circlet. The man by her side was tall and solid, a smug expression stamped across his face. He also looked in his mid-thirties so a good ten to fifteen years older than—

The rattle of mugs had him retaking his seat and composing his features, his hands linked loosely on his lap.

'I'm sorry to impose like this, Mrs Eustace, so soon after your loss but there are some queries that have cropped up.'

She waved a hand in reply, gently pushing a mug in his direction and indicating, with a tilt of her head, the milk jug and sugar bowl.

He cleared his throat, her silence unnerving. 'I've just come from speaking with the bus driver. He confirms the testimonies, taken from several witnesses at the scene, that your father stepped out in front of him.' He leant forward. 'The thing that's confusing me is the reason why he'd do such a thing. Did he have any financial concerns? Anyone putting pressure on him? It's obvious he took his own life but I'd like to know why.'

'I can't help you, I'm afraid.' She lifted her mug, her fingers biting into the pottery. 'At least not with the financial side of things. We didn't have that kind of relationship. Oh, as a family we were close, but not as far as money was concerned.'

'Okay. What about your husband, would he know anything?'

She placed her mug back down on one of the slate coasters that marked the table. 'Unlikely. My parents and Samuel didn't

125

really get on. You know how it is with some families. And anyway, he's away on business today. Work, you know.'

Owen nodded. 'He's a financial adviser?'

'Yes. From home mostly, unless he has to meet up with clients.'

'So you wouldn't have any idea as to wills and things?' Owen watched her carefully, unable to detect any change in her demeanour.

'There's a will with their lawyer but that's all I know.' She sat back, resting her head against the sofa. 'Being a carer is a huge commitment and that's the part I helped out with as much as I could. Mum was pretty much full-on. Oh, she had her good days but they were increasingly few and far between. We were all waiting for the inevitable.'

'Your parents – they were close?'

'Very. Sometimes I used to think too close. He was devastated when she was diagnosed. He lived one day at a time after that. In a funny sort of a way it was best that he went first. He wouldn't have been able to cope without her.'

Owen crossed his legs, his empty mug back on the table. 'And your mum. What about her? Did she say anything when he died?'

'I'm not sure she even realised.' Avril reached out to pluck a tissue from the box on the coffee table before resuming her position. 'I think that would have hurt him the most. I know the days when she didn't recognise me were heartbreaking and I wasn't the love of her life. Up until the cancer took a hold, Dad was everything.'

'That must have been difficult for you as their daughter.'

She sniffed, rubbing her nose with the tissue. 'I was used to it. Don't get me wrong. They loved me in their own way but not as much as they did each other.'

Owen was having a difficult time piecing together the various parts of the story. The devoted couple. The loving daughter. The busy son-in-law. Their interwoven lives running as smoothly as they could under the curve ball that had been thrown their way.

126

There had to be a catalyst that had made such a devoted husband fling himself under the front wheel of a bus. He frowned. He was still waiting for the court order to check their finances and he'd also like to see what was written in that will. But if he was right in thinking that the daughter would inherit, it made a mockery of someone blowing up her mother. Leave it a couple of months and she'd have inherited anyway. He glanced around the room at the tasteful furnishings, which wouldn't have come without an expensive price tag and made a mental note to check out the daughter's financial situation. If they were in debt or borrowed up to the hilt perhaps waiting even that couple of months would have been viewed too long.

The clock on the mantlepiece, making its way to half past four, was enough to prompt him to end the conversation so he could head back to St Asaph, his promise to Kate in the back of his mind.

'I know that this is difficult for you, but I'd like to ask you what you think happened to your mother?'

He'd wrapped the question in such a way as to cause the least distress but he could still see her flinching at his words. It was times like these he regretted not having the foresight of asking a female officer to accompany him – not that he wasn't up to the job. But there wasn't any comfort he could offer other than words and the only phrases he could think of all seemed a little trite.

'I don't know what to say.' She glanced up briefly before dropping her gaze to the floor, her arms wrapped tightly around her middle. 'I know I shouldn't have left her but it wasn't for long. Dad used to leave her all the time but never long enough that she'd get herself into trouble. She was sitting in front of the telly watching reruns of *EastEnders*. She could sit there for hours not moving and yet the one time . . .'

She stopped, her voice cracking, and into the silence a key turned in the front door.

Chapter 22

Gaby

Tuesday 21 July, 3.50 p.m. St Asaph

Angus Ford wasn't what anyone would term handsome. While tall and slim he missed out on that moniker by a mile. His nose was too large, his chin narrow and with a deep cleft. His eyes were a nondescript mid-blue. He had what his mother would term an interesting face. But it wasn't his looks that lifted him to the dizzy heights of female popularity. It was his personality. He'd been through two wives and was on the hunt for a third. Gaby was determined not to fall into any of his relationship categories, serious or otherwise.

At ten to four, Gaby was only fit for a shower and bed. After dismissing Marie and Malachy to Newport she'd headed to the archives department and loaded up their largest trolley with all the files that Jax hadn't already gone through. She'd started with the five boxes from the CSI team, ploughing through the list of detritus found in the Happy Valley sweep that the team had conducted – a list that included eight crisp bags and fifteen chocolate wrappers

128

not to mention five Coke cans and even a full nappy sack. Each item had been carefully collected, secured in clear plastic bags and labelled before heading to the lab for testing. A useless exercise as, apart from Leo, they'd had no suspects. However, that little fact hadn't influenced the thoroughness of the investigation. One of DI Tipping's first tasks had been to round up the usual persons of interest, which included all known paedophiles and rapists in the North Wales area. But any thoughts of an easy arrest were quickly dashed. The few that didn't have bulletproof alibis were being detained at the pleasure of Her Majesty at the time.

She'd left Jax to continue working through all the interviews, pen and notepad at hand. Apart from Leo Hazeldine's mother there was a growing list of people that they needed to re-interview and she was more than happy to let him conduct them. With all the team out of the office, she'd knuckled down and finished the last of the boxes, her plan being to knock off on time for once and start washing down the wood panelling in the lounge in preparation for painting at the weekend. Angus Ford's sharp knock on the door changed all that.

'So this is where you hide when you're not traipsing around the country on some course or other,' he said, strolling into the office and folding his frame into the only spare chair, his briefcase on the floor beside him.

'Angus, what are you doing here?' Gaby jumped to her feet with a broad smile of welcome.

'With the university all but closed I decided to see how you're getting on with the case and offer my humble services such as they are.' He lifted his briefcase and, after undoing the buckles, pulled out a bottle of red wine, placing it on the desk in front of him. 'After which I'm taking you out for dinner, no excuses accepted.'

Gaby managed to hide a grimace. While she was overwhelmed with his offer, she was less certain about the second part of the deal. Men like Angus came with a government health warning tag attached. Women like her usually took note and as a consequence

129

exercised avoidance strategies. She'd just been outplayed by the master because he knew how much she needed him to help her untangle the mess that was Angelica's murder.

Swiftly changing the subject, he said, 'I've been online to get a feel for things but I'd prefer it if you could run through exactly why you think a profiler would help?' He continued to watch her through hooded eyelids. It almost looked as if he was falling asleep but she knew he'd listen to every word and be able to recite almost verbatim what she told him.

It didn't take long for Gaby to fill him in. With only one serious suspect and a lack of forensic evidence, the case, while irritating, was annoyingly straightforward.

'So, what you're telling me is that you suspect that her murderer might have killed again and all because of a nightdress? Is it likely?' Angus said, settling back in his seat.

'No, not just because of the nightdress. There's also something Colin, our archives officer, said about the positioning of the body that rings a bell. He's going to get back to me if and when he remembers. Also if I am right, the killer must have thought that he'd gotten away with what must be viewed as the perfect crime. As time passed, the more confident he would have become. Why would he stop if he could continue to get away with it?' Gaby shook her head, her lips tightening. 'In effect, he could have been carrying on for the last twenty-five years without a shadow of doubt thrown across his path.'

'Possible but not probable. I have to say your idea of the murderer planting trophies leaves me cold. He'd have been far too clever for that.'

'Angus, you should know by now that anything's possible in this game,' she said, trying to remain calm. Taking an emotional step back from the conversation, she waited while he reached up his hand, unbuttoned the top of his shirt, removed his tie and stuffed it into the pocket of his tweed jacket. He'd travelled nearly fifty miles simply to do her a favour, something she'd best remember.

'Let's forget about the possibility of other cases for the moment and concentrate on this one. Shush a minute while I have a think,' he said, his expression lessening the impact of his words. Standing, he started pacing up and down the narrow space between the desk and the window. 'As we know, most crimes are committed by people in their teens and we also know that most murders are committed by people known to the victim. So, let's say for argument's sake that the perpetrator was a peer of Angelica's. Someone she knew. Someone that had a previous record.' He paused, swinging around to face her before continuing on his journey, backwards and forwards like a tiger in a zoo. But Gaby wasn't watching. Gaby's hand was zipping across the page of her notepad, regretting with a vengeance that she hadn't shifted the conversation into one of the interview rooms where she could have availed herself of the state-of-the-art built-in microphone.

'A previous record?' she interjected, relishing a second or two to drop her pen and try to regain a place in the conversation that was running away quicker than any bag snatcher.

'Yes, definitely. Burglary is a good one but maybe animal cruelty or petty larceny. It will be there, somewhere, waiting to be found. So you're looking for someone on the verge of middle age. Definitely a man. A clever man. A watchful man. A man that plans his crimes to the nth degree.' He paused again, retaking his seat, staring somewhere into the distance. 'He couldn't be anything but with a crime like that. He'd have sat down with a piece of paper and researched every element which means that you're also looking for someone who's finished school and who's currently in some kind of employment.' He leant back, crossing his legs. 'Tell me again about the autopsy report and what the pathologist said about her death?'

'He doesn't have any evidence as such but he thinks that she could have suffered a cardiac arrest due to fright.'

'Mmm. Interesting, that's certainly a new one on me,' he said, his eyebrows meeting. 'There's nothing I can add to that side of

131

things and there certainly wouldn't be any evidence unless you can prove that he had some kind of hold over her: some threat, not that being abducted wouldn't have been enough. Poor girl. If she'd been sexually assaulted, I'd have said that your man is probably the worst kind of predator. The kind wardens have to segregate from the rest of the prison population for fear that he'd be torn to shreds. But that's not the case here and that's what's worrying me. Why did he take her only to leave her on that hillside to die, and dressed in someone else's nightdress, to boot? If I didn't know any better, I'd think there was a ritual element to it all. The staging of the scene. The beautiful girl dressed in virginal white . . . But then what do I know?' he finished, spreading his hands.

Probably a lot more than me, Gaby thought, the scene he'd painted playing out in her mind and causing her heart to twist. But there was no room for emotion in the middle of a crime investigation, albeit a case that was a quarter of a century old. She'd like nothing better than to find Angelica's murderer and lock herself in a room with him for five minutes along with a bunch of baton-wielding members of Angelica's family. But that would be bringing her down to his level. No, she'd catch the bastard and take great pleasure in watching him receive his sentence.

She focused on her notepad, trying to think of additional questions to ask. Usually there were patterns to multiple crimes – patterns that could be linked to reveal the fuller picture. But in this instance, she couldn't think up anything other than Angus's determination that the abduction had been committed by someone who knew what they were doing. Although that in itself must be viewed as some kind of a pattern . . .

'What else can you tell me? The ritualistic side of things sounds interesting but I'm not sure how we go about exploring it. What about relationships? I remember during one of the lectures you gave that some repeating serious offenders had trouble forming relationships outside of their criminal activity?'

'That's true but it's difficult at this stage to be more specific

132

until we know if he's committed further crimes. He's probably a bit of a loner though and doesn't go out of his way to seek female company.' He hunched forward, his hands now on the top of his thighs. 'Have you thought to narrow down your search to see if any geographical patterns emerge? If I'm right and he's in regular employment that would mean that his criminal activity would have to be constrained by the needs of his job.'

'What you're saying is instead of researching trophies left with the victim I should be conducting a search of all females murdered within a—?'

'Two-hundred-mile radius at most. A place he could go to and return in the same day. Remember, he's a planner which means that he's not going to turn up somewhere and abduct the first woman that crosses his path. It probably takes him weeks or even months to select the ideal victim. All this takes time because the fewer people who are suspicious about his activities the better.'

'As you're here, are you happy to help me with this?' She stared at him, only logging in to her laptop at the slight inclination of his head. 'So, give me some parameters then. What about the counties that border North Wales for a start? It will probably give us an idea if we're onto something.'

But instead of answering her, what he said was, 'Hold on a minute. I need to think this through.' He pressed the bridge of his nose between his thumb and forefinger, obviously deep in thought.

Gaby, her wrists flexed over the keyboard, resisted the temptation to ask what was puzzling him. He'd tell her in his own time.

'Okay, what you need to do is put yourself in his shoes,' he said, dropping his hand and returning it to his pocket, his shoulders relaxing back into the chair. 'Murders like this, as we both know, almost exclusively follow a pattern. It's a bit like going to the supermarket and always buying the same brand of bread. You know what you like. It's an easy choice. It's the same with criminals. After all, why make it more difficult for themselves. They have a tried and trusted format of what works so there's no need to change it

133

unless it's to hone their skills and improve their techniques. That's where the difficulty comes in, I'm afraid.' He placed his elbows on the desk, steepling his fingers. 'Crimes like this are usually carried out by two types of criminal. The organised and the disorganised. The organised, like in this case, isn't an opportunist. He will want to eliminate as much risk as possible. That means that he'll usually choose to carry out his crime in private like the victim's house as opposed to the dark lanes and parks usually associated with the other type. In this case, Angelica was abducted from her bedroom but without any bruises to prove the abduction. It would have been much easier and safer for him to have done what he was going to in her bedroom except that—'

'He wouldn't have been able to gain entry,' she said, ending the sentence for him.

'Exactly! So instead he risks moving her, which must mean one of two things. Either she went willingly or he had help. But the latter takes time to arrange and means an increased risk.'

'In other words the nature of this case is misleading, perhaps purposefully so. He's not clumsy or slipshod and he's obviously very good at not getting caught.' She thought for a moment before squinting down at the screen and typing.

After 1995 ritual murders and rapes of girls/women Wales, Cheshire, Merseyside

She glanced up, her hand hovering over the enter key. 'Anything else we should add? The more words we use the less efficient the results.'

'Nope.'

'Do you really think that we're onto something?'

'I think that it's possible that you're onto something, not me, Gaby. I'm only in it for the ride.' He pulled out his mobile and swiped the screen. 'Chinese or Indian and, before you go all coy on me, I'm not taking no for an answer. I've booked a room in the Premier Inn in Llandudno Junction – I'll run you home first so you can drop off your car.'

134

'Indian or Chinese are both fine,' she replied, not really listening as hunger, for once, had passed her by. She knew by both his words and manner that Angus wasn't wholly onboard with her thinking about a serial killer, not that she could really blame him. Was it desperation coupled with a need to prove herself after the last two, far from flawless, murder cases that was driving her? She frowned. It was more likely the alarm at having to tell Owen that Angelica's murder hadn't been solved for the very good reason that it was unsolvable.

The programme, probably because of the late time of the day, had already pinged that it had a list ready, and without pausing she clicked on the print button for two copies. While she waited for the printer to whiz into action, she scrolled down, her eyes widening at the four thousand or so results. 'I think it's been too efficient,' she said finally, shifting from out behind her desk and to the industrial printer that stood to the left of the door. 'There has to be some way of narrowing this down without damaging the trustworthiness of the results?'

'I thought dreary paper shuffling was all part and parcel of a policeman's lot,' he teased, still staring down at his phone. 'Have you ever been to the Taj Mahal? I can ring and reserve a table.'

'Ha. I have a better idea. What about ordering a takeaway and coming around to mine? That way you can help me try and narrow this down.' He opened his mouth to speak but she interrupted. 'I know what you're going to say but I truly have no idea where to start. Someone with your insight is going to save me hours of legwork.' She handed him a sheet of paper and returned behind her desk. 'Look at this lot. I'll be amazed if we can narrow it down to half that number.'

'And I'll be surprised if we find ten that match the profile.'

'So that's a yes then?' she asked, grabbing her jacket from behind her chair and pulling out her bright scarf before wrapping it around her neck.

'As long as there's onion bhajis.'

135

Chapter 23

Marie

Tuesday 21 July, 4.30 p.m. Shrewsbury

'What are you like on history, particularly Victorian?'

Malachy slid into the chair opposite, placing a tray piled with sandwiches and cakes between them, before passing over the latte she'd asked for.

'As in Queen Victoria? Died 1901. Apart from that, not a lot. I didn't cover that era in lessons.'

'No, well, neither did I.' Marie took a sip of her coffee, allowing the smooth taste to wrap around her tongue and start spreading warmth to her insides. She only continued to speak when the mug was half drained. 'The Victorians were heavily into mourning, probably influenced by their Queen who carried on wearing widow weeds right up to her own death, forty years after Prince Albert's. But they took it one step further, often wearing jewellery that incorporated a picture or even a lock of hair belonging to their beloved.'

'That sounds all a bit barbaric.'

136

'Each to their own, Mal. I'll admit it's not something I'd ever do but, in this case, knowing about this stuff has done us a huge favour.'

'How so?' He opened up his sandwich to check the filling and removed a slice of tomato before rearranging it and taking a bite.

Marie glanced over her shoulder, but with the time heading for five the café was all but deserted, the black-haired teenage server starting to stack chairs on tables.

'Because our murderer chose to dress Angelica in a nightie that had one odd button.' She leant across the table, picking up his discarded tomato and popping it into her mouth. 'A white onyx button chosen simply because it was the same size, shape and colour as the rest but with one obvious difference. The front is made from braided hair, which means the chances are that—'

'That it might contain the DNA of the killer's granny.' He sat back and slow clapped, a beam of a smile on his lips. 'At least the boss gets to be mega pleased with one of us.'

'Actually I think she might be mega pleased with both,' she replied, pulling her phone out of her pocket and searching through the photos. 'I took the opportunity to take a couple of shots of Mrs Hazeldine's wall art.' She enlarged a picture between her fingers and slid the phone across the table. 'It's amazing what people pin on their walls. It doesn't take long for them to forget what they've got; photos and the like blur into the background, only remembered when it's time to dust and, it's a very long time since Mrs Hazeldine held a duster between her arthritic fingers.'

The phone contained a photo of Leo Hazeldine but, for once, it wasn't the man that was of interest. It was the scene behind the selfie.

Chapter 24

Owen

Tuesday 21 July, 4.30 p.m. Llanwddyn

Samuel Eustace was taller than Owen had expected. Taller. Larger. Fitter.

'Darling.' He turned to Avril, on the surface composed but his relaxed demeanour didn't deceive Owen one little bit. The man was almost incandescent with rage – he just wasn't showing it. 'Please tell me that you haven't allowed coppers into my house?'

Avril cowered back into the sofa, all trace of colour now departed from her cheeks.

Owen Bates didn't like bullies. He'd come across his fair share in his time both in and out of the force and it was the one character trait he made no allowances for despite his outwardly calm appearance. Inside, his heart had ratcheted up a notch but that was for him to know and nobody to find out. He didn't jump up and explain his presence in an attempt to extricate himself from what was turning into a sticky situation.

No. He stood to his feet, his movements slow, a smile of sorts breaking out, his hands tucked into his pockets. He wasn't as tall or as broad as Samuel Eustace and he certainly wasn't as angry. But then anger was the very last thing he needed flowing through both his mind and his body when confronted with irate members of the public.

His next action was to slide his hand out of his pocket and offer it to the man now within striking distance.

'Good afternoon, sir. I'm DS Bates.'

'I'm sure it is and you're telling me this because?' Samuel said, ignoring his outstretched arm.

Owen raised his brows. 'If you'd like to take this conversation down the station, I'm happy to oblige, *sir*,' he said, his hand back in his pocket, his fingers wrapped around his phone. He wasn't scared, far from it. All the years on the beat meant it took a lot to scare him. He could stop most things apart from a bullet and he didn't think that the smooth lines of Eustace's suit jacket held anything more interesting than a wallet or perhaps a comb – his gaze now rested on his perfectly presented hair.

'Samuel, he was just leaving.' Avril rushed to her husband's side, her hand on his arm. 'Come on, love. They do need to find out what happened.'

He shook his arm free from her grasp. 'Go on then. You know where the door is.'

Owen had two choices. To stay and ask more questions or to leave. One glance across at Avril and, unusually for him, he chose the latter option. If ever he'd met a woman in need of help it was Avril Eustace. He could almost smell the fear emanating from her pores. But there was nothing he could do. It would be unlikely that she'd agree to leave with him and if he stayed it would only escalate the situation.

'Thank you for your help, Mrs Eustace. Here's my card in case you think of anything else,' he said, placing it on the mantlepiece and walking out into the hall. But once the front door had closed behind him, he didn't walk down the path to his car. Instead he waited a moment and listened. He only moved when he was assured that all was quiet inside.

Feeling restless after the encounter, Owen decided to drop into work before journeying home. Back at the station he headed for the coffee pot, filled his favourite mug up to the brim, returned to his desk and flipped open the lid of his laptop. There, as Gaby had promised, were the two new folders detailing the Butterworth's financial circumstances and also their will.

It didn't take him long to realise that Tony and Mary Butterworth were richer than he'd previously thought. They'd been left the house by Tony's parents and had savings in excess of £100,000, which added weight to the idea of them being murdered for financial gain. He next turned to the property pages, whistling through his teeth at the sums houses along the same road had fetched during recent months. Okay, so the current state of the building would mean that it would have to be knocked down and rebuilt, but its beachside location alone meant that the plot would make a tidy sum. He pulled out his notepad, jotting down a ballpark figure of half a million – a figure that wouldn't include insurance. Tapping his pen against his teeth, his mind neatly jumped onto the issue of life insurance and whether he hadn't underestimated what they might be worth as a couple. It was unlikely the insurance companies would pay up for Tony Butterworth, purely because it looked like they wouldn't be able to prove that it wasn't suicide. But Mary was a different matter altogether.

Despite the time, he retraced his footsteps back to the coffee machine and refilled his mug. He'd promised Kate that he wouldn't be late but five or ten minutes wouldn't hurt. Back at his desk, he pushed his notebook to one side and rested his head in his arms, starting to feel the weight of the day pressing as the start of a headache loomed. What he really wanted was to speak

140

to someone about what was happening on Operation Angel but it seemed as if everyone had knocked off on time for once. He lifted his head briefly only to return it back to its previous position and close his eyes. The last thing his brain needed was a bucketload of legal jargon and no matter what goodies the will gave up it couldn't change the fact that Mary Butterworth had died within weeks of her predicted death from that brain tumour. There simply was no good enough reason that he could think of to risk expediating her death. Therefore, case closed.

The house was in darkness when he finally pulled into the drive, his headache again deciding to reassert itself along with the realisation of yet another broken promise. He didn't need to check his watch to see that he'd missed Pip's bedtime. He'd even missed the start of *News at Ten*. But this time his excuse wasn't work-related, or at least only in part. Even now he couldn't believe he'd made the rookie mistake of dropping off to sleep at his desk only to wake up hours later with a sleeve moist with spittle and a stiff neck to rival that of the pain in his head.

He pushed the door open and switched on the hall light, comforted by the warmth that greeted him. *She's probably gone to bed early* was his next thought and he pulled out his phone to double check that she hadn't messaged him. But his phone was resolutely silent as was the hall. The kitchen, the heart of any home, was a mishmash of Ikea units and yellow paint – the unique artwork supplied by Pip. But he didn't see the walls or the cabinets. He didn't notice the new addition to Pip's portfolio, his depiction of what a happy family looked like right down to Kate's protruding belly. All he saw was the set table with the good candlestick in the centre – the one that only came out on birthdays and at Christmas. Or, to be quite factual, he didn't notice the candlestick but the folded piece of paper propped up against it.

141

Chapter 25

Gaby

Tuesday 21 July, 8.40 p.m. Rhos-on-Sea

Gaby didn't know whether her lounge seemed better or worse with a petrol station map of the South West pinned to her wall. She'd laughed when Angus had arrived, takeout in one hand, a map, stickers in an assortment of colours and felt tips in the other. Two hours later and she was far from laughing.

The map would never be used for its original purpose, its surface now desecrated with thick red pen lines interspersed by coloured dots. It looked like the road to hell and, in a way, that's exactly what it was. The curry had long gone. The wine was open but barely touched. Instead, Gaby and Angus, as soon as their plates were clean, had divided the lists into two and, with Google Maps to help, started plotting what they decided to call the murder map, for want of a better term. Working together, they'd soon filled the left-hand side with an assortment of dots using a random set of colours. Red for murder, yellow for rape and blue for a combination of the two. Within the first hour they'd had

142

eight reds, two yellows and one blue. Halfway through the second the number of blues had jumped to four and the excitement in the room was palpable.

Gaby placed the fourth dot on the board and, leaning back, scanned the map, her mind in freefall. While there were no guarantees that the cases were in any way linked to each other or indeed Angelica's, which didn't follow the same pattern, it did seem like too much of a coincidence. She turned her attention back to Angus who was zipping through his list, a yellow marker pen in hand as he crossed out any cases that didn't meet the strict criteria that they'd set, a look of intense concentration deepening his wrinkles and furrowing his brow.

'I think it's time to stop,' Gaby finally said, noting the time. 'You're making me feel guilty the speed you're getting through them.'

'Actually, I think I'd like to carry on for a bit if you don't mind but a glass of wine would be welcome.' He stood and, standing tall, rolled his shoulders in a circular motion before meeting her gaze. 'I honestly think that I owe you an apology, Gaby. You're onto something, something huge. If we carry on at least you'll have something substantial to show that DCI of yours.'

'There's no need, Angus, honestly. You coming all this way and helping me like this.' She felt her eyes smart and took a couple of rapid blinks. 'You even had to supply your own food and drink,' she added, topping up his glass and sliding it across the table. 'Without your help I'd have been floundering on the edges, still investigating the leaving of trophies with the victim when I knew all along that it was a daft idea. Even the stupidest of criminals must know by now about crime scenes and the role DNA plays in modern-day policing.'

'But he did leave that nightdress?' He picked up his glass and, cradling the bowl between his hands, took a small sip.

'Yes and he's probably learnt from that mistake. It's only by luck that we didn't manage to find any DNA traces.'

'Oh, I don't think luck comes into it, Gaby, if you don't mind me saying. Remember what I said about our man being a planner? He'd have taken every precaution. Despite the lack of evidence, I think that the dressing up of the victim in that nightdress is integral to what drove him to his first kill.'

'If indeed it was his first,' she said, almost to herself.

'Yes, and that's all the more reason to battle on for a bit.' He pressed his hand down on the sofa, shooting her a look. 'I'd like to stay the night and that's in no way an invitation into your bed,' he continued in a rush. 'I'm perfectly able to read the signs when the lady isn't interested. No, if we are right and I do so hope that we aren't, then some poor woman might even now be in the process of turning into an unsavoury statistic.'

144

Chapter 26

Tuesday 21 July, 10.50 p.m. Bangor

Matilda Chivell, Tilly to her friends, is sitting alone in her one-bedroomed flat with a half-empty bottle of wine and the largest bag of Kettle crisps she can find, her attention flickering between Love Actually *on the television and her silent phone on her lap.*

She pops another crisp in her mouth, slugging it down with a mouthful of bin-end red, the effect of the wine dimming the feeling of disappointment. Callum had promised he'd text. He'd been so insistent that if there'd been a bible handy, she's convinced he'd have pulled it out like a magician and placed his hand on top. It would have been kinder for him to come up with some crappy excuse about their dead-end relationship. Kinder of him and kinder to her. She wouldn't have bothered to keep the flat at the end of term on the off-chance that they could spend some serious time together. No. She'd have boarded the train the same day that uni had broken up for the summer and, instead of being on her tod, she'd have had her mum to cosset her and her dad to wrap her in the biggest of hugs, the familiar scent of his aftershave bringing a smile to her lips and tears to her eyes. A week. A whole bloody week she'd given him to wrap up his latest project in time to pop home so that she could introduce him to her parents.

She gazes at the screen but can't even conjure up the glimmer of a smile at the sight of Hugh Grant prancing around Number 10. She hasn't seen Callum since Saturday and then only for five minutes. She hasn't heard a peep since. All her friends have been telling her to dump him and to get a life, their words ringing in her ears. He's too old, too staid. You need someone your own age, Tilly. Someone who enjoys the same things you do.

She picks up the wine bottle, filling her glass to the top. She knows they're right and, if she'd had her time again, she'd have never agreed to go on a date with him. But she didn't and now it's too late. Now she's trapped in a relationship that, when she's with him feels completely right even though she knows that it's completely wrong.

The wine helps as do the crisps. That's her diet gone to hell and back but, for once, it's not going to matter. With the clock heading for eleven, she's got a decision to make. Open the second bottle, sitting on the worktop in the kitchen, or head to bed. But she knows she won't sleep. Sleep is the last thing on her mind. To spend another night lying alone in her cold bed, the lumpy mattress digging into her flesh, is another kind of torture. She could have agreed to stay in halls for another year, but the thought of independence beckoned and renting a flat in Bangor seemed grown-up somehow. A front door of her own even if the kitchen is cupboard-sized and the whole flat reeks of an odour redolent of boiled cabbage.

She stands, wobbling a little until she regains her balance, her eyes drifting around the room with its soft cream paint and the art posters she'd Blu-Tacked to the walls, before she focuses on the door. Despite the wine she's more security conscious than most and she pauses a moment, checking that it's locked. A woman living alone can never be too cautious, she thinks, her mind now on the can of mace spray she hides under her bed. She heads to the kitchen but, instead of flicking on the kettle, she decides to start on that second bottle. Life is too short for a nineteen-year-old to stay in drinking

146

tea. Yes, she'll regret the hangover in the morning but she still has the rest of the night to get through. Her attention is back on her phone and where it's resting on the arm of her small two-seater sofa.

The television hums in the background, Love Actually *long since finished along with that second bottle of wine. Now there's a Clint Eastwood Spaghetti Western showing, not that Tilly's watching. Tilly hasn't made it to bed. Instead she's asleep on the sofa, her mouth lolling open, a small snore gurgling in the back of her throat, her mobile clutched between her hands. She has no way of knowing that Callum is fifteen miles away, wrapping up his late night at the accountancy firm, his mind on the beautiful brunette who he hasn't managed to phone. Instead he decides to drop by on his way home . . .*

147

Chapter 27

Wednesday 22 July, 8.45 a.m. St Asaph Police Station

Two more.

Two more, which made six in total and they weren't even halfway through the list.

Gaby grabbed her briefcase and laptop bag from the passenger seat before slipping out of the car and heading into the station. Angus had surpassed himself not least because of his insistence in taking the couch after they'd decided on Irish coffees to follow the Barolo. The liqueur coffees weren't in the form of a celebration. Coppers' minds didn't work like that. Proof that Angelica's murder had been an isolated incident would have been the preferred result. But Gaby was never one for ignoring what was in front of her and the evidence was clearly pointing to a very worrying set of coincidences.

She pushed open the door to the station, pausing at the loud shrieks of laughter coming from Clancy and Jax.

'What's so funny, lads?' she said, joining them at the counter.

'It's that Ian Strong, ma'am. Remember I was telling you about him?'

'What, the newest member of the team?' Gaby eyed him, her frown making a break for freedom. 'What's he been up to now?'

'They were out on a shout last night, breaking and entering, when he managed to miss the kerb outside the cathedral, impaling the bonnet of the ARV into the base of the Bible Translator's Memorial. The car's a write-off.'

'I hope he's all right?' she said, trying to hide a grin. Strong had appeared a tad cocky when she'd been introduced to him. With a bit of luck he'd learnt his lesson before any real damage was done.

'Not a scratch but that's not to say he'll still have a job after the DCI has a few words. It was one of the new cars, only 200 miles on the clock.'

Gaby allowed a brief quirk of her mouth as she tilted her head in Jax's direction, her hand clutching the wad of post Clancy had slid across the counter, her mind resolutely twisting back to the day ahead.

She had a job for Jax and the rest of the team, and she was pretty sure they weren't going to like it.

As soon as they were out of Clancy's hearing range she stopped, bending her knee up to rest her briefcase on top. She thrust her bag and the post in his direction before opening the leather straps and pulling out the map, quickly explaining what she wanted him to do. It would probably take them until lunchtime to finish going through the remainder of the list. In the meantime she had a meeting to prepare for with Sherlock – a meeting she was dreading.

She left Jax to make his way into one of the spare offices while she headed into the incident room to catch up with the team.

'Morning, Owen, Mal, Marie,' she said, nodding to each of them in turn. Marie looked better. Her hair had a bright sheen that only comes when newly washed and she appeared, if not exactly happy, then at least interested as she replied to something that Owen had just said. Malachy was sporting a plain navy suit,

149

which fitted like a glove and must have cost a fortune. He was again clean shaven, the subtle scent of his aftershave causing Gaby's nose to twitch in appreciation. Owen, however, looked the antithesis of what she'd expected. His suit bore the signs of someone who'd pulled an all-nighter while his white shirt was decidedly less white than when it had been removed from the wardrobe. Either he should think about changing his washing powder or he was wearing yesterday's shirt, she thought, her nose wrinkling a second time but for a totally different set of reasons.

She suppressed the words on her lips; obviously something was very wrong with her friend and colleague. He'd tell her in due course or he wouldn't. It was up to him but the very least she could do was to give him the opportunity.

'Malachy and Marie: I'm going to do the one thing I promised I wouldn't and use you both in a totally unprofessional manner.'

'Ma'am?'

'Don't get your hopes up, Mal,' she said, noting his look of astonishment. She removed her purse from her bag and removed a twenty. 'You're going to have a very busy morning ahead of you so go buy yourself some eats and then find Jax. He'll fill you in.'

Marie stepped forward. 'Gov, I did want a quick word about the buttons and Mal has—'

'Unless you can give me the killer's name and address it's going to have to wait.' She hesitated a moment, noting their shaking heads. 'Okay, I'll be sure to hear you out later but the job I have for you far outweighs buttons and the like.'

As soon as the door had closed behind them, she turned back to Owen, her professional mask in place, her teeth biting down on her tongue at the sight of the dark shadows bruising his skin. They'd been through a lot over the last six months. He'd even saved her life on one occasion. She viewed him as a friend more than a workmate but that didn't give her the right to interfere in his private life no matter how much she wanted to help.

'What have you got to tell me about—?'

But he interrupted her before she could finish. 'I think she's left me.' He ran his hand through his hair, causing it to stick out in clumps.

'Oh, Owen.' She didn't have to ask who. There was only ever one woman for Owen. While she might not have known him all that long, she'd never once caught him glancing at another female. She could have walked into the office fashioned like a modern-day Lady Godiva and all he'd have done was hand her his jacket. He was a one-woman man but the truth was that the one he'd chosen wouldn't be one to put up with any nonsense on a good day and, with Operation Angel back under scrutiny, no day was going to be a good one.

'She warned me that if I didn't choose between her and the force then she'd make the choice for me.'

Gaby patted his hand, at a complete loss for words. Didn't Kate realise that being a detective was part of who Owen was as a man? It defined him in a way no other job could. And what did she expect him to do? Turn into a PI or, even worse, go into security? For someone as active as Owen, who loved nothing more than the excitement of tracking down criminals, it would be a living death. Gaby swallowed a groan. She'd like nothing better than to go around and give his wife a piece of her mind but she wouldn't. Owen had a difficult choice. If he couldn't come up with some sort of a compromise, rocks and hard places would be nothing to what he was about to deal with.

Instead of saying what she wanted to, all she said was, 'Owen, you do know if there's anything I can do to help?'

'I know.' She watched as he tried to pull himself together, his hand now trying to repair the damage it had wrought to his hair. 'So, is there anything on the case?' he asked. 'I'm in need of some good news for a change.'

'I'm not sure you could class it as good.' She propped her hip on the edge of the desk, feeling her scar pull under her jacket. 'But I'll be heading into Sherlock shortly. There's a strong possibility

151

that we have a serial killer on our hands, with Angelica being the first victim. If that's the case, I want you back on the team ASAP. It's not as if you're a blood relative or anything.'

His face blanched, his beard now a stark contrast against the pasty pallor of his skin. 'Surely we'd have picked up something like that before now?'

'Not necessarily. The UK is a large place and, unless someone goes in search of tenuous links, it's unlikely they'll be found. Our killer is clever, Owen. To leave no trace takes a certain kind of intelligence we don't normally come across amongst the criminal fraternity. He just doesn't make mistakes.' She patted his arm again. 'You do realise if you hadn't pretty much forced me to reopen Angelica's murder, we wouldn't be standing here discussing this. Never forget what a good copper you are.'

Gaby paused, the sound of the door being wrenched open and flung back against its hinges making her stand to her feet, all her attention on DCI Sherlock who was closely followed by Clancy. She watched him scan the room before finally focusing on her. He looked grey, his glasses pushed back on the top of his forehead, his Adam's apple working overtime.

'I need you to head out to Bangor straight away. They've found the body of a girl,' he said, his gaze now shifting to the photograph of Angelica, pinned to the board. 'God help us.'

152

Chapter 28

Gaby

Wednesday 22 July, 9.15 a.m. A55

'While we're here, you might as well fill me in on the Butterworth case.'

Gaby returned her mobile to her bag and wriggled into a more comfortable position, the seatbelt rebelling against her movements. She'd have preferred to discuss Kate and what exactly had happened but one quick look at Owen's fixed jawline made that conversation impossible.

'Only to confirm that the husband is a complete arse.'

She glanced at him again before returning her attention back to the road ahead. 'Well, I did try and warn you. So, what did he do then?'

'Pretty much turfed me out of the house and, the biggest surprise is that I let him. I feel sorry for the wife. I wouldn't put it past him to slap her about.'

She shook her head. 'I'm not sure what she ever saw in him.'

'And that's another thing.' He slammed on the brakes, a muffled curse on his breath, narrowly avoiding a black cat that seemed

153

determined to lose all of his nine lives in one go. 'I really don't know why you wasted my time yesterday when one of the juniors could have managed with their eyes closed. Whichever way we look at it we're stuck with Tony Butterworth taking his own life for reason or reasons unknown and Mary's death being a horrid accident that should have been prevented with constant supervision but wasn't.'

'But we still had to do due diligence on the case, Owen. You know that as well as I do.'

He crashed his hands against the wheel. 'Possibly but what I'm really thinking is that having checked firstly with the fire brigade and then the gas company, there's no way now to determine exactly what happened.'

'I know you feel disappointed about being palmed off like that, Owen, but at least we now know that we can sign it off and concentrate all our efforts back to where they're needed the most,' she said, turning in her seat, her attention now on the detached block of flats up ahead and the dark-haired woman standing chatting to one of the CSI officers outside. 'That didn't take as long as I was expecting. There's a space behind that van.' She waited for him to park. 'You've been here a lot longer than me. What do you know about DS Enderlin?'

'Kay? Not a lot. A few years older than me. Born and bred in Anglesey and, by all accounts, a good copper. She's worked with the North Wales MIT a few times but before you took up post.'

'Okay, thanks for that.'

After the introductions and a brief stop at the CSI van to don the requisite hooded paper jumpsuit and overshoes, Kay Enderlin escorted them through the hall and to the back of the building, going down a couple of steps to the garden flat.

'It seems as if the perp accessed the property through the bathroom window,' she said, with the clear look of someone who'd been up half the night.

Gaby had only met her once but Kay had struck her as a career copper of reasonable intelligence. Her purpose in asking Owen's

154

opinion was in relation to Enderlin's attitude towards liaising with colleagues from other teams – she was about to find out. She led her past a CSI officer taking photographs and into the tiny bathroom, where another officer was on fingerprint duty.

Gaby took one glance at the open window and the deep marks in the frame before following her back out and into the lounge. When would people learn that there was little point in having high-end security at the front door if the rear of the property was left unsecured? It would have only taken him seconds to wrench open the window and clamber in. The fact that it was a ground-floor property made it all the more tragic.

'What's outside?' Owen asked, his frown matching Gaby's.

'A small private yard accessed by an unlocked gate at the side of the building. No CCTV cameras anywhere near and probably happened too late at night for any of the neighbours to spot anything but we'll do the interviews all the same.'

A list of questions pooled in Gaby's mind but, instead of asking them, she held back, her attention on the body arranged in the centre of the floor and the man leaning over her.

The sight of a dead body never got any easier and certainly not when the victim was as young and pretty as Tilly Chivell. The staging of her body into the foetal position must have been planned and surely not a coincidence; it echoed almost exactly the post-mortem photos she'd so recently viewed of Angelica. A shiver shot down her spine, the final bricks in the wall she'd carefully constructed slipping out of her grasp and crashing to the ground. No matter how many times she told herself to the contrary, it appeared she had a serial killer working her patch.

'Good morning, Dr Mulholland.'

'It might be morning but there's nothing good about it.' He knelt back on his heels, glaring at her briefly before returning to the body. 'As you can see, I'm busy, DI Darin, and please don't do your usual by asking a heap of questions I have no intention of answering until I've had time to examine her properly. Now,

155

if you don't mind, I have work to do here,' he said, starting to mumble into a small handheld Dictaphone.

She felt rather than saw the look exchanged between Owen and Kay Enderlin but apart from challenging Rusty on his manners there was nothing she could do. Obviously, the truce between them, for want of a better word, was over. She had no idea why. But, just like him, she also had work to do and an ill-mannered pathologist, while disappointing considering his recent behaviour, was the least of her worries. What was more disappointing was the knowledge that he never treated any other member of the team the way he treated her. But if he thought that his attitude would stop her from carrying out her job then he had another think coming. She ignored the feeling of disappointment rushing through her veins and stabbing her somewhere in the region of her breastbone. She was a big girl. She'd been disappointed before. Would she never learn that men weren't to be trusted? Her ex, Leigh Clark. Her former colleague in Swansea. Rusty Mulholland. Just another name to add to the ever-increasing list.

With her eyes darting daggers between his shoulders, she waited until he'd finished dictating, her nails digging deep crescents into her palms.

'Thank you. I won't detain you for longer than is absolutely necessary, Doctor,' she said, her voice deliberately smooth and betraying none of the mounting anger that was quickly taking hold. 'I do, however, need you to attend tomorrow's 9 a.m. catch-up meeting. If you haven't managed to complete your findings, at least bring what you can.' She watched the muscles of his back tense underneath his paper suit but she turned away before he could add anything to the conversation. After his recent outburst, more words from him were going to be far from helpful. 'Kay, I also need you to attend. I'll square it with DCI Sherlock.' She walked to the door, throwing one last glance at Tilly Chivell's body before heading out into the hall, closely followed by Owen and Kay. 'Tell me again how she was found?'

156

Chapter 29

Marie

Wednesday 22 July, 9.35 a.m. St Asaph Police Station

With no Darin or Bates on their backs, Marie, Malachy and Jax hid away in a spare office on the second floor with coffee on tap and more sweets than they could possibly eat. After a couple of minutes wrangling, the men had pressganged Marie into searching for the names they came up with while Mal managed the map and Jax continued going through the list with a yellow highlighter.

'We have to be methodical,' Marie began, logging in to the system and pulling up a new spreadsheet. 'As well as logical.'

'Come on, Marie, give us a break. You sound like someone out of *Star Trek*.'

'Mal, if I want a wise crack comment, I'll ask for it but it won't be from you.' She turned to Jax who was busily looking through the previous pages and making notes on an A4 pad. 'Tell me again what the gov said?'

He glanced up, his highlighter already starting to stain his thumb and forefinger yellow. 'Only that she's been speaking to a

157

profiler and he suggested searching through the list of *unsolveds* by geographical location in case we find more. There's six matches already and still pages to get through.'

'Okay, what are the case numbers? I can be pulling their reports at the same time.'

'It's not likely though, is it?' Mal stood from where he'd been propping up the wall beside the map, eating from a packet of marshmallows. 'So basically what you're saying is that this profiler chap thinks we have a serial killer on the loose? But it's not as if it's the 1900s. With the amount of electronic support the force has these days in addition to worldwide networks, there's no way that something like this could go under the radar.'

'You'd think that, wouldn't you, but I'm not so sure,' Marie said, her voice fading away to nothing, her attention now on the screen in front of her. 'Listen to this. Nineteen-year-old Dawn Spruce found raped and suffocated in her Manchester flat. No witnesses.' She tilted the laptop around, the image of a laughing redhead filling the screen. 'They had the boyfriend in for questioning but had to let him go after the prerequisite seventy-two hours – there was no evidence that wasn't circumstantial.'

She swivelled the screen back and continued typing, trying to ignore the sound of Malachy rustling the bag of marshmallows as she read through the next report and the one following.

'I've another potential,' Jax said. 'Twenty-three-year-old Bianca Olsson, Liverpool, case number 2970371x.' Into the silence Malachy added a dot to the board while Marie typed.

'Okay, here she is. Bianca Olsson, originally from Sweden, at Liverpool undertaking a postgrad in engineering. Found by her flatmate.' Marie's voice dropped a notch as she turned the screen to show them the photo of Bianca, her blonde hair stretching almost to her waist, her body in a tight ball as if she'd curled on her side to sleep. 'Still think we're flogging a dead horse, Devine?'

It gave her no pleasure to note the deep flush spreading across his cheeks or his uncharacteristic silence. She couldn't even think

158

to produce a smile at the way he joined Jax at the table and grabbed some of the spare sheets, another highlighter in his hand. Nothing would give her greater pleasure at that moment than to prove Gaby Darin wrong and Mal right.

Head bent, she watched him starting to score through the list, his mouth uncharacteristically grim, his cocksure voice nowhere to be heard. This was serious stuff and, for once, Malachy Devine seemed to realise it. He finally spoke, a pulse beating out on his temple the only sign of his distress.

'I think we need to think this through a little more. So far, we've come up with Angelica, young, blonde, a student, found outside – cause of death unknown. What about using the same criteria to apply to the positives and see if we can't come up with some matches?'

'Good plan,' Marie said, starting to scribble out a new list on the top of her pad. 'So, what have we got so far?'

'Well, what about age range, under 25?'

'Trust you to start with the easy, Jax. Mal, anything to add? They seem to be all students of some type. Apart from the first, we could also check out the cause of death.'

'That's the problem though, isn't it? Angelica doesn't necessarily fit into the criteria.' Mal started ticking off on his fingers. 'While all young students, she was found out of doors and, by all accounts, died from natural causes. Also there was no indication of any sexual activity.'

'Good point, Detective, and one that needs explaining. Any ideas?' she said, looking between them.

Mal ripped open a jumbo packet of M&Ms, starting to pick out the blue ones. 'You have to remember that he was probably young then, young and inexperienced. Isn't it likely that he was a peer of hers, otherwise how would he have known about her sister and the difficulties the family had with regards to her sleepwalking? That's probably why he ended up removing her from the house as he sure as hell wasn't going to be able to break in

159

through the locked window or the secure front door. He'd have needed help with that unless she went willingly.'

'Which puts Leo Hazeldine firmly in the frame?'

'Indeed yes. I've dropped off the photos by the way,' he said, turning to Jax and filling him in. 'Jason will blow up the second one to see if we can't get some kind of a fix on where Hazeldine is.' He held out the bag of sweets. 'The murderer planned everything except for the one eventuality he couldn't. Her premature death.'

Chapter 30

Gaby

Wednesday 22 July, 11 a.m. Bangor Police Station

Callum Beech would have been handsome if it wasn't for his deathly pale face in stark contrast to his unshaven cheeks. He looked like he hadn't slept in years and not the one night that Gaby knew of. He also looked to be in his early forties so a good fifteen to twenty years older than Tilly, something that had Gaby reaching for her pencil.

'My boss loaded more and more on my plate. It got to the stage I was only eating and sleeping. There was no thought that I actually had a life outside the office, that I actually needed to see Tilly now and again. I tried to keep in touch but I'm not meant to make personal calls at work.' He ran his hands down his cheeks to his jaw and left them there as if his head was suddenly too heavy for his neck. After the shock he'd had, it probably was.

Instead of interrupting, Gaby let him continue, her emotions swinging from suspicious to sympathetic and back again. She knew how easy it was for a killer to hide behind a wall of supposed grief just as she'd learnt the hard way never to trust the evidence before her. But Tilly Chivell's boyfriend was broken in all the ways possible. His unsteady hands shifted onto the side of the table as if he was worried about what would happen if he let go. He didn't struggle to meet her gaze and, if she'd had to guess, she'd have said he had no idea that he was at the very top of her list of suspects. That notion didn't seem to have crossed his mind . . . yet.

The tears had started to fall, a slow, steady stream that balanced on his chin and dripped onto the table in a kaleidoscope of grief. It always surprised her to see a man cry for no other reason than it was something she'd never observed before joining the force. But over the years she'd gotten used to all the displays of emotion imaginable and, if not exactly inured to their impact, she was now able to take their display with the suspicion they deserved. She'd heard it bandied about what an unfeeling cow she was, but it would hurt more if she believed everything she witnessed while on duty. The tragedy, of course, being that she carried the same mantle of distrust as a shield outside of the job as well as in, her thoughts swinging back to Rusty and the hurt he continued to cause with his mercurial behaviour.

She pushed the box of tissues nearer but, instead of angling her head in their direction, she plucked a couple and squeezed them into his hands, forcing herself to concentrate on the man in front of her and not the one still working on the body of Tilly Chivell, a couple of miles down the road.

'I know this is difficult, Mr Beech,' Gaby said, gesturing towards Kay and the open pad in front of her. 'Have a sip of your drink and we'll try and get this over as quickly as possible.' She replaced the tissues with the mug as if he was a child and watched as he lifted it to his mouth with all the finesse of a dog who'd just found a bowl of water on the hottest day of the year. Within seconds the mug was empty and back on the table.

'That's better. Now I feel I need to remind you that if you'd like a solicitor to sit in on our discussion, I'm very happy to wait

162

until one arrives.' She'd already asked him the very same question on entering the interview room – then the only response he'd given had been a shake of his head – but she really needed it voiced for the microphone busily recording the whole interview.

'I know I'm not guilty so fire ahead.'

'Thank you. I'd now like to take you back to last night and exactly what happened. I know it's painful,' she continued, her voice dropping a notch. 'But it's vital we get all the facts right at the very beginning.'

He heaved air into his lungs, his chest expanding under his striped shirt. 'We'd arranged to meet only I couldn't make it, something she probably wasn't too happy about especially considering she'd planned for us to visit her parents. She hadn't yet told them about me – she didn't think they'd have approved.'

'And why would that be?'

'She wouldn't say but I'm guessing it had something to do with the age difference.' He sank his head further down into his neck, staring at the table in front of him. 'I finally finished at around midnight and decided to drop by on the off-chance she was . . . she'd see me.' He glanced up briefly before returning to the fascination of the mahogany veneer tabletop.

Kay opened her mouth to interrupt but Gaby stopped her with a shake of her head. She knew that Callum Beech had only paused to gather his words and possibly his courage. It was easy for a copper to forget what it must be like to find a dead body. Finding a stranger would have been bad enough. A tramp in a doorway. A victim of a road traffic accident. A stranger in a street. But to come across the body of a loved one must be one of the worst experiences out there. When that death wasn't either expected or accidental . . . well, she couldn't possibly imagine what he must be going through. Unless, of course, it was all an act.

'The front door was open,' he said, his voice so low she had to lean forward to catch the words. 'Why would she even do that? She was so security conscious and I was always telling her to

163

make sure she had the chain in place before opening the door. I walked in and found her lying there curled up on the floor, her hair splayed around her like a halo. I thought she was asleep at first, she seemed so comfortable with her hand under her head. But she wasn't. I pulled the sheet back and—'

'Sheet?' Gaby interrupted, shooting Kay a look of surprise, which she returned with a sharp nod of her head.

'Yes, it was almost as if she was in bed but—' He jerked to his feet and rushed for the door, his hand pressed to his mouth. 'I'm going to be sick.'

'What do you think?' Gaby sat beside Kay Enderlin, waiting for Owen to join them back in the office. They'd decided to stay in Bangor until they'd fleshed out all the information on Tilly Chivell. Her life. Her background. Her death.

'It's difficult to say, ma'am,' Kay said, hiding behind a cloak of formality. 'He seems genuine enough.'

'Indeed.' Gaby turned to Owen, who'd come back and sat in the chair opposite, spreading an array of scene-of-the-crime photos out in front of them. She glanced at each of them in turn, not bothering to disguise her expression of distaste.

'We've been in touch with Beech's place of work and they can confirm that he logged out of his computer at nine past midnight, which fits in with his story of arriving at the Bangor flat a little after twelve-thirty,' said Kay. She tapped the first photo, which showed Tilly covered up to her neck in a plain white sheet. 'As you can see from this it seems as if she's just fallen asleep,' she said, her mouth compressed. 'Which is why he decided to wake her. We got a 999 call shortly after 12.35 a.m. from a distraught neighbour who was dragged out of their bed by the sound of screaming coming from downstairs.' She tapped a second photograph showing Tilly as the police had found her, the sheet nowhere to be seen.

'But there doesn't look to be a mark on her body?'

'No. We haven't got all the photos back yet but, believe me, they're there,' she now said, pointing to the blow-up of Tilly's face. 'Obviously we'll have to wait until the doc does his stuff but I'm pretty sure we'll find that she suffocated. There's a redness to the skin around her lips as if her mouth has been taped. All he'd have had to do was hold her nose. She couldn't struggle – the same redness appears on her wrists.' She gathered the photos back into a neat pile, placing them in a brown envelope. 'There's also signs of redness on the inside of the thighs but the doc will confirm or otherwise what exactly happened.'

Gaby frowned at the way Owen's attention lingered on the envelope. Had she been wrong to take him with her? She didn't need twenty-twenty vision to see how similar Tilly and Angelica were in the pretty stakes. Now she needed to work out whether looks were the sole contributing factor for his choice of victim or whether there was something else she was missing.

'Right then. For all the emotion he displayed it must also be noted that Beech is a good fit for Angelica's murder,' she said, counting off on her fingers. 'Well educated. Employed. Single. The right age and finally not living it up in Australia. I want everything you can get on him, Kay, and I want it yesterday.'

165

Chapter 31

Marie

Wednesday 22 July, 1.10 p.m. St Asaph Police Station

Marie headed back down to the incident room and the home-made cheese sandwich waiting in the bottom of her bag only to find her way barred by Malachy. After a morning spent locked away in front of her laptop, all she wanted was an hour to herself where she could think about what they'd found – ten minutes of which she'd already wasted racing up the stairs to discuss the button with Jason, the senior CSI.

'That didn't take long. What did the boffins say about the button?'

'Not a lot but then you'll never get Jason to do anything more exciting than grunt his appreciation. I left him with a miniature set of pliers and tweezers. You know what he's like. He wants to try and preserve it as evidence.'

Malachy quirked a brow. 'You'll probably find it for sale on eBay later.'

She swotted him on the arm with a laugh. 'What are you like? You know as well as I do that Jason's as honest as the day is long.'

166

'Honey, you know me. I don't trust anyone – even myself on a bad day.'

'Honey! Really! Well *honey*, it's time for lunch and, as I missed breakfast, I'm extraordinarily starving. What with you and Jax I barely got a look-in on the sweets,' she said, walking to her desk and checking her phone.

'You should have said.'

'Fat lot of good that would have done me. It's like sharing an office with children the way you dished out your favourites.' She gave an audible sigh to make her point before slinging the strap of her bag across her shoulder. 'I'll catch you later.'

'I'll join you.'

She looked up, eyeing him from under her overlong fringe. 'Why?'

'Why not? I need to eat. You need to eat and it's not as if we're excluding the youngster as Jax is meeting up with his girlfriend to go flat-hunting.'

'Isn't that a little soon? They've only been dating a few months.'

'What are you? His mother? He's still living at his parents, which, I think you'll agree, explains a lot.'

'He doesn't know he's born.' Marie grabbed her keys from off the desk and headed for the door. 'If I still had my parents I'd move back in a shot.' *Instead of living in a bedsit with less character than the inside of a shoebox in addition to being smaller*, she added silently, her thoughts never far from the mess that she'd made of everything. If she had her time again, she'd have gone to university at eighteen instead of joining the force. She also wouldn't have fallen for Ivo's softly spoken patter or have left all his birthday presents in the cupboard under the stairs for that bitch to find the first time she pulled out the ironing board!

'That bad, huh?' He collected his jacket and mobile and followed her into the corridor. 'Come on, I'll take you back to my place and, before you say no, it's only five minutes away. Far

167

more comfortable than wandering the streets and the coffee will at least be fresh.'

She came to an abrupt halt and turned, her face a picture of bewilderment. 'I really don't think that's a good idea. I appreciate that you're trying to be kind . . .'

'Obviously not hard enough. Would it help any if I said that I have a favour to ask and, while I think you're stunning and your husband the biggest fool out there to let someone like you slip through his fingers, I'm not interested in you in that way?'

Marie stared at him, trying to see what lay behind the smooth smile and laidback demeanour but it was like trying to read a potato. Giving up, she dropped her chin and studied her shoes, weighing up the options. He was younger than her by nearly ten years and a whole lot better looking. It would be easy for him to pick up someone with more to offer than she had and the truth was she was intrigued by the favour he mentioned. He didn't appear the sort to need a favour from anybody. So instead of parting at the entrance, she found herself sitting beside him in his car and turning left out of the station.

Malachy's apartment was far from impressive from the outside. She'd heard about the old disused shoe factory being renovated into up-market flats but hadn't given it a thought. But once inside the concrete-clad exterior she found herself following Malachy up a series of steps and through a large grey studded front door. Wales disappeared into the distance as she entered the New York loft-style apartment complete with steel girders, wooden beams and floating bookcase partitions competing with large chunks of pottery and books for space. It was so different from what she'd been expecting. It was so different from what she'd be returning to later that she felt her throat constrict and her eyes fill.

'Come on, let's see what's in the fridge.' Malachy led her past the living area, defined by two huge three-seater settees that barely

168

filled the large expanse of floor space and into a large steel-clad kitchen, which boasted a feature wall of red brick.

'Take a seat.' He gestured to the traditional scrubbed pine table in the centre before filling the kettle and selecting a couple of mugs from the shelf above the sink. 'Tea do or would you prefer coffee?'

'Tea is fine,' she said, pleased with the couple of minutes afforded for her to browbeat her feelings back where they belonged. She peeled off her jacket and sat down, the warm weather in conjunction with the leather car seat making her shirt stick to her back. 'So how does a DC afford a pad like this or is that a question I shouldn't ask?'

'That depends on whether you want the truth or not, now, doesn't it?' He placed a mug in front of her before returning with a plate of odds and ends from the fridge including deli ham, an array of French cheeses and a loaf of designer bread instead of the sliced white and budget cheese slices she'd been having to make do with.

'Why on earth would you think that I'd want you to lie?' she said, spreading her hands to encompass the feast in front of her. 'For instance, who has food like this in their fridge except when they're expecting visitors?' She made a point of turning her head and searching the room. 'Unless you have a stash of women sequestered somewhere,' she questioned, now examining the mezzanine ceiling and the landing above her head.

'Who indeed?' He picked up a knife, slicing off a piece of Brie. 'If you must know, it's my mother. She insists on turning up with little or no notice to stock up the larder, amongst other things.'

'Amongst other things,' she replied, her voice faint. 'What other things?'

'Do tuck in.' He cut a second triangle of cheese and placed it on her plate along with some ham, a hunk of bread and a knob of butter. 'Other things like sorting out my washing basket despite my insistence that I am twenty-six, not six.'

169

'Ah.' She buttered her bread, struggling not to laugh. 'You'd miss her if she didn't.'

'Really. I don't think so and that's where you come in.'

'Me?' She paused to swallow a mouthful of food. 'I don't understand?'

'No, well, you wouldn't. Look, Marie. You're in a bit of a pickle and so am I.'

He leant forward, maintaining eye contact for the first time since joining her at the table. Should she be worried? After all, she hadn't known him for long, only six or seven months and, up until the last few days, their relationship had been strictly that of colleagues. With everything that was going on in her life she was loath to change that. She opened her mouth to tell him only to pick up her ringing mobile instead.

'Okay, yes. I understand. Such a shame. Thanks anyway.'

She placed her phone on the table and pushed her meal aside, her appetite, despite the gnawing hunger of earlier, faded to a dull ache. She'd been so confident. Too confident. This was all she had left now. Her work. The obsessional need that had driven her to continue her job against the wishes of her husband. The obsessional need that had made her put off having a child until it was too late to do anything other than watch her marriage disintegrate around the ruins of her wish to be a mother.

She slammed the palm of her hand down so hard her drink slopped over the edge, not that she noticed. 'Damn, the button is useless. Completely bloody useless. So now we're back to square bloody one.'

'Useless. How come?'

'Because, Mal, for Jason to be able to extract any DNA he needed to have the hair root and not just the shaft. And, before you start, there's no hope of salvaging anything from the button as he had to dismantle it to check each individual strand. Presumably whoever assembled it cut off a lock instead of yanking a handful out by the root.'

170

'Makes sense though.'

'Of course it makes bloody sense but not in any way that's helpful to the investigation. If Darin's list is to be believed, we have a growing number of homicides, which could be linked. How do you think that makes me feel knowing that he was so nearly in our grasp?'

'So we'll have to look elsewhere.' He picked up his mug and walked over to the fridge to add another drop of milk before turning back to her. 'When we get back you can give me a hand tracing Leo Hazeldine and after I'll give you a hand to shift your gear back to my place.'

Marie's face lost any colour it had, her skin taking on a sickly pallor. 'You can't be serious. After what we've spent the morning doing, you're trying it on?'

'No. Just listen a minute. Please.' He held up both hands in an effort to ward off further comment. 'That didn't come out the way I intended. The fact is that you're living in a dive by the sounds of things and, until you're paid, haven't got two pins to rub together while I've got all this. But believe me I'm no charity. Make no mistake. I do have that favour I'd like to ask.'

'That's what's worrying me and why my answer is an inexorable no.'

'You haven't heard me out yet.'

Marie stood, grabbing her jacket and bag, a flush of colour scoring both cheeks. She couldn't believe what she was hearing and from someone she'd been starting to think of as a friend too. After what Ivo had done that was a major achievement in itself and yet here he was spoiling it and all for what – a quick fumble between the sheets. He could go to hell. She'd even pay for the petrol.

'I've heard far too much all ready. You really don't want to know what I'm thinking of you right now but despicable comes to mind. Now are you going to drive me back or make me walk?'

He picked up his keys, swivelling them through his fingers. 'I

171

can't blame you for jumping to the obvious but you're way off base, Marie. I'm not offering to share my bed only my home for as long as it takes for you to get back on your feet and in return you'll get a bedroom with a lock and key and I'll get someone prepared to act like my girlfriend but only around my parents. There, that wasn't so bad, was it?'

She flung back her head and laughed. 'You take the biscuit. What makes you think I was born yesterday? You must have girlfriends knocking on your door as it is.'

'But none I choose to share my life with at present. I'm not going to beg, Marie, but it's the only thing I can think of to get her off my back without falling out with her and, contrary to what you might think, I happen to love my mother. I just need her to let me lead my own life. Take it or leave it – I won't ask again.'

172

Chapter 32

Gaby

Wednesday 22 July, 2 p.m. A55

The mood in the car back to St Asaph's was miserable at best. It was also silent with Gaby not knowing what to say to the man sitting in the passenger seat by her side, presumably lost in a world populated with blonde-haired angels of his own making. She had priorities, which were usually headed up by the cases she was working on. But she also had responsibilities and, currently Owen topped both lists. She only spared a couple of seconds' thought for Rusty and his mercurial temperament – wasted seconds that did little to add to her mood. He wasn't going to change and stupid her for ever thinking that he might. She pushed him into the corner of her mind, slamming the door shut and slotting the deadbolt in place. There would need to be a large incentive like wine for her to drag him out again.

'Owen, we're going to take a little detour,' she said when the silence had started getting to her. 'I have a message to run and we might as well do it on the way past.'

173

It didn't take him long to realise what she was up to, the silence erupting in an explosion of words.

'With all due respect, DI Darin, what the hell do you think you're playing at?' he said, eyeing the end-of-terrace house on the outskirts of Llandudno with a belligerence that was out of keeping with his usual passive demeanour.

'I'm doing what you should have done before showing yourself back in the office this morning, Owen.'

'There's work to be done.'

'Agreed. Work that will get done with or without you. However, there's a woman in that house. A woman and a child that deserve more than you're currently giving them.' She pulled into the drive and switched off the engine, twisting in her seat to look at him. 'You're perfectly in your rights to call me an interfering cow but do it later,' she continued, tilting her head to where Pip's face was pressed up against the window of his granny's front room. 'Now there's some bridge building with your name on it. I don't want to see you back in the office until tomorrow morning's briefing, there's time enough to finish off the Butterworth paperwork then. That's not a request, Detective,' Gaby said, making a mental note about the bottle of wine she owed Clancy for looking up Kate's parents' address on the system earlier.

Gaby had missed lunch but, after the morning she'd had, it was more than she could stomach. Instead she grabbed a coffee and plonked herself down behind her desk, resting her head in her hands. There were things she needed to do. So many loose ends that needed chasing and, of course, she still had to inform Sherlock of her suspicion that there were now more murders than the two he currently knew about. Lifting her head, she reached for her phone and quickly made an appointment to see him at four-thirty, in the hope that by then she'd know what she was going to say. Afterwards, instead of returning the receiver to its cradle, she checked her diary and dialled Angus's number. Gaby was still feeling guilty about the way she'd used him and hoped that there was a way she could make it up to him without prejudicing either her principles or the investigation. She was about to find out.

He answered on only the second ring, which confirmed her view that he was waiting for such a call.

'I've had the most amazing morning,' was the first thing he said after the usual pleasantries were dealt with.

'It's lucky for some!'

'Ha, Yes. I didn't think that, after yesterday, today would be so enjoyable but a trip up to the Great Orme copper mine did the trick.'

'Look, Angus. Are you hanging around for a couple of days?' she said, with a swift change of subject. 'I'd like to buy you dinner as a thank you.'

'Heading back early tomorrow, my dear, but dinner would be welcome before I return to the Premier Inn. No offence but I'm not sure I can cope with another night on that couch.'

She ended the call, a smile lingering. An evening away from the case was exactly what she needed to concentrate her mind and organise her thoughts.

175

Chapter 33

Marie

Wednesday 22 July, 2 p.m. St Asaph Police Station

Marie and Malachy had formed a truce, if ignoring the situation they were in could be called that.

They arrived back to the incident room only to find that Jax still hadn't returned from lunch so, by tactical agreement, Malachy joined her at her desk, placing an A4 photo between them.

'Right then. Here are the pictures you took of Hazeldine when we visited his mum,' he said, lifting his head and flashing his teeth. 'I asked Jason to enlarge them earlier but, with one thing and another, I haven't had the chance to check them out.' He nudged it towards her with the tip of his fingernail before adding a second beside it.

Marie picked up the first: a headshot of Leo Hazeldine. She'd seen the pictures on file of him as a teenager but they in no way matched the image of the man staring back at her, his cautious smile at war with the thinness of his cheeks, his skin the colour of the ash she used to scrape from the grate. He appeared ill, she thought, ill in addition to being ill-at-ease despite the attempt at the smile tugging at his mouth. She laid it back down and picked up the second. This one wasn't quite so clear and she had to squint to see the detail. Instead of a headshot it was a photo of a group sitting around a table. There were six people in all and she could easily spot Leo with his arm around the shoulder of a woman, her blonde hair scooped up into a careless bundle. By the looks of the men's suits and ladies' party frocks it was some kind of a formal do – the glasses full of ruby-red wine, the dinner plates layered with the makings of a traditional roast right down to the Yorkshire pudding positioned next to the roast potatoes. She scrolled over the photo, trying to find anything that would tell her where the meal had taken place but there was nothing.

Without moving her head, she said, 'Fetch my magnifying glass from the top drawer, would you please?'

But after a moment spent peering through the lens she sat back and rubbed her eyes, shoving the glass in his direction, 'Here, your turn.'

'What am I supposed to be looking for?'

She glanced across but instead of the snappy comment on her lips all she said was, 'Anything out of the ordinary that will pin either a place or a person in that group.'

'What, like a needle in a bloody haystack—' He stopped abruptly, placing the magnifying glass down on the table with a deep chuckle. 'Well, I never knew that this detecting lark was so easy.'

'You're having me on. There's nothing—'

'Maybe not for you but then again you're not a bloke,' he said, flashing his teeth a second time.

'A bloke? What? Surely that's sexist?'

'Sexist it may be, but it's also opened up the largest can of worms imaginable. Well, who'd have thought it?' He sat back in his chair, a heavy frown now worrying his forehead, his attention still on the picture between them.

177

'Go on then or are you going to keep it to yourself?' she said, grabbing the magnifying glass again and holding it over the picture.

'There. Who does that remind you of?'

She followed his finger, which was pointing at a woman in the foreground whose facial features were all but blotted out by a head of mousy-blonde-coloured hair, her slim hand reaching for her wine glass. A woman who shouldn't have been there.

'I don't understand.'

Malachy and Marie had pounced on Gaby as soon as she'd strolled into the incident room, shattering any plans she might have made for an afternoon continuing to investigate the distribution of murder cases in and around North Wales.

'Neither do we, ma'am,' Marie replied. 'To be honest, I don't think I would have spotted it without Mal pointing it out.' She placed another photo beside the first, this time a blow-up of the woman's face. 'If you look hard enough there's something in the angle of the jaw and the bone structure, not of course forgetting the nondescript hair.'

'Even so, well done to both of you. Very well done indeed. Now all we need to do is find out what Avril Eustace is doing in a photograph hanging in Hazeldine's mother's bedroom and if she has any idea as to his current whereabouts. There's obviously an age disparity with Avril being in her early twenties to Leo's mid-forties. Any ideas?'

'Not really, unless it's something to do with—'

'The Penrhyn Yacht Club.'

They all turned at the sound of Jax's voice as he hurried into the room, dumping his laptop bag on the top of his desk and scattering a fine shower of raindrops in his wake. 'God, I've heard of April showers but in July? The weather's bloody awful out there,' he said, mopping his neck with the end of his scarf. 'It was blazing sunshine earlier. Now look at it! Sorry I'm late by the way. I'll make it up later.'

178

Gaby waved a hand in dismissal. 'Don't worry about it. I'm sure we owe you more time than you owe us. So, what was that you were saying about the Penrhyn Yacht Club? That's where Angelica and Leo used to work, isn't it?'

'Yes. I was viewing a flat near there during my lunch break so I decided to pop in and see if I could make a start on those interviews. The steward couldn't have been more helpful even though he was too young to be of any use.'

Gaby murmured a word of encouragement instead of the sharp retort that she kept back in deference to his stutter.

'He got on the phone to the chief bar steward who's been there for thirty years or more. A Vanessa Mahy,' he said, his diction slow and deliberate. 'She remembered them all, probably because of Angelica's murder – it does have a tendency to focus the mind.' He dropped into his chair and lifted his head, his hair sticking flat against his scalp. 'The upshot is that during the summer months they have to employ students to help with the influx of visiting yachtsmen. Vanessa checked her records and at the time of the murder that list included Angelica and Leo Hazeldine. But somewhat surprisingly it also included Tony and Mary Butterworth, or Mary Stone as she was then.'

179

Chapter 34

Gaby

Wednesday 22 July, 3 p.m. Llanwddyn

Gaby decided to take Malachy with her when she went to visit Avril Eustace, her decision based solely on his superior height and breadth. She left Jax and Marie to continue the search for Leo from the comfort of their desks while she braved the suddenly inclement weather with Mal by her side, simply because men like Samuel Eustace ate the Jaxs and Maries of this world for breakfast, using any bones left over to pick their teeth clean. Malachy Devine was a completely different animal. While certainly not as imposing as Eustace there was something about him that spelt danger. But, funnily enough, that something wasn't only down to his physical attributes. There was a look about his person that made Gaby very glad that he'd decided on her side of the fence in which to operate.

Arriving at the property, she had hoped that they'd be lucky enough to find Avril home alone. After all it was only Wednesday and a couple of hours from the usual 5 p.m. finish. But one glance at the two cars parked outside the house had her frowning across at Malachy.

'I'll do the talking, Mal. If you think we're in danger get us out of there any way you see fit, bearing in mind I can't afford any rough and tumble with the state of my insides following the last time. Right, let's do this.' She opened the door, her black mac shrugged around her shoulders. 'I think he's all bluff but I don't want to be proved wrong.'

The door opened on the third ring of the bell but not a minute too soon as the porch offered little protection from the driving rain, which had turned the front garden into a mud bath. She stared out through the mist at the field opposite and the smattering of sheep huddled together into one conglomerate mass of white before turning and planting a smile on her face for the woman pulling open the door.

'Afternoon Mrs Eustace. Please excuse the intrusion but we do have one or two questions about . . .' She paused, noting Avril's frantic look and sharp shake of her head.

'He's out back in his office – happen he won't have heard the bell, if we're lucky. What is it you want?'

They were barely in the hall. Most people would have hastily slammed the door against the onslaught of bad weather before directing them into the comfort of the lounge but not the woman in front of them. But then Avril Eustace wasn't like normal women. It took only a second for Gaby to note the bleakness around her eyes that matched the pasty tone of her skin and drab, ill-chosen, mismatched clothing. Avril was clearly at the end of whichever tether bound her to such a man as Samuel Eustace. The most distressing thing, of course, was that unless a crime had been committed, and Gaby had no proof of that, there wasn't one blasted thing she could do about it. She was suddenly reminded of the phrase her parents often used about it being impossible to know what went on between a couple once the front door shut behind them. As a woman, Gaby had no interest in gossipmongers.

181

She'd seen too much damage caused by loose tongues for that. But as a copper she couldn't afford to overlook what was staring at her from all the four corners of her mind. Avril Eustace was a victim – but until the woman admitted it to herself there wasn't a single solitary thing that they could do about it.

'This won't take long but it would be more convenient to speak to you in the lounge, don't you think?' Gaby said, moving forward so that Malachy was able to shut the door with a gentle click.

She chose the sofa nearest the fireplace, placing her bag by her feet while she waited for Avril to settle on the couch opposite. Gaby suppressed a grin at the sight of Malachy propping himself up beside the door with his arms folded across his chest instead of joining them. As her self-proclaimed guardian he obviously took concerns about her safety seriously.

'As I said, Mrs Eustace, this won't take long. We just need to ask you whether you know the whereabouts of a Leo Hazeldine?'

'Leo who?'

Despite watching her closely, Gaby couldn't discern any noticeable changes in her demeanour. She could have just asked her what she was having for her tea for all the difference it made.

Nonverbal communication was a science that coppers excelled in but for Gaby it was a bit of an obsession. After her initial training on the subject she went on to further her relationship with the subject by buying select texts, which buttressed her books on criminal profiling. It wasn't good enough that she had an overview of the subject. Assessing body language was something she did automatically without even thinking about it – she was positive that Avril had no idea of who Leo was.

'Leo Hazeldine is a former colleague of your parents who we're trying to locate as a matter of urgency with regards to another enquiry.' She lifted a brown envelope from her bag and withdrew the same photograph that she'd been presented with earlier by Marie Morgan. 'As you can see it appears that you have met even if you didn't know who he was.'

182

Avril stared at the picture briefly, her expression partially obscured by her hair falling forward to cover her cheeks. But there was no evidence of any emotion when she lifted her head and handed it back.

'At the end of last year, the bank held a party for my father when he decided to take early retirement.' She laughed. 'Well, not really retirement as he planned to work from home – it meant that he could look after Mum and do a bit of bookkeeping on the side. Anyway, while I agree that it's me in the picture, I have no recollection as to who I was sitting with.' She lifted her hands to her throat, rearranging the pretty blue and white chiffon scarf at her neck. 'Sorry I can't be of more help.'

'What about your husband?'

'Samuel? But he wasn't there.' Gaby watched the muscles around her jaw clench as if she was fighting some inner demon. 'If you must know, my mother, to put it mildly, wasn't fond of my choice of husband. My parents pretty much told me that if I married him, they'd have nothing to do with me,' she said, twisting her fingers together. 'It was only in recent months when my dad realised how desperate things were that he allowed me to visit. By that stage I could have been one of my mother's carers for all she recognised me.'

And you'd have done best to follow your mother's advice, Gaby thought, but all she said was, 'Okay that's fine. Thank you for your time.' She placed the photo back in the envelope before standing and making her way to the door only to pause and turn. 'Oh, one last thing. Where was the retirement do held?'

Chapter 35

Gaby

Thursday 23 July, 8.55 a.m. St Asaph Police Station

Thursday morning wasn't usually that busy at the station. Certainly not as busy as Mondays when they caught up with the fallout from the weekend. But this Thursday was different. This Thursday they had a host of crimes to solve – crimes that suddenly, crazily, unbelievably all seemed to be linked. The incident room, which on an average working day had six people at most, was now standing room only with additional chairs borrowed from the rooms leading off the first-floor corridor. The other thing that was odd was the silence. On a normal day the chatter and chink of china had to be controlled by an iron fist thumping on the table in the same way a teacher might use to get his pupils to behave. Now the silence was only broken by a soft greeting, a shuffle of chair legs against wood laminate flooring, a muted cough.

Gaby was early but there was nothing unusual in that. Some of the team thought her a control freak while others thought her

184

born with a warrant card in her mouth. The more benevolent of her colleagues, like Owen and Clancy, rationalised that the only thing missing from her life was the love of a good man. Little did they know that Gaby agreed in principle but up to now the availability of a suitable candidate was scarcer than snow on a sunny day. She kept her gaze to the front thus avoiding clashing with Rusty who she'd decided, late last night while lying in bed unable to sleep, she was going to avoid at all costs. The same didn't apply to Angus who knew the score and had quickly learnt to treat her accordingly. In return for the smile he offered when entering the room she gestured to the seat she'd been saving. It had been intended for Owen but Angus wasn't to know that.

'Wasn't sure if I'd make it,' he said, lifting his cuff back with the tip of his finger and glancing at his watch. 'The traffic between Llandudno Junction and St Asaph was bumper to bumper.'

'Probably this lot rushing to nab a seat,' she whispered back, her attention drawn to DCI Sherlock and, surprise surprise, Chief Superintendent Winters, a man who rarely left the comfort of his office. But for all his lack of visibility on the floor, Murdoch Winters was a man who kept a close interest in all the goings-on in his area. Gaby had learnt to never underestimate either his work ethic or intelligence. He was here to support the team, only that.

'Right then, settle down people.' DCI Sherlock stood up front, gesturing to the couple of latecomers to reduce the noise. 'Morning. Firstly thank you to everyone who's made the effort to come to the meeting. There're a few people here that some of you may not know.' He went on to introduce the team from Bangor. 'We also have Dr Angus Ford, criminal profiler over from Liverpool University. Needless to say everything we discuss today is strictly confidential. If the media get to hear about our concerns, there could be widespread panic on the streets.' He paused to glance across at Murdoch Winters who was now standing by the window with his hands in his pockets. 'I also have the personal guarantee from Chief Superintendent Winters

185

that all the resources needed to help catch the perpetrator will be made available. Now, down to business – as you already know, the body of a young woman was discovered in the early hours of yesterday morning. Tilly Chivell, nineteen years of age and studying English Lit at the university. We've informed her parents and they've identified the body.' He lifted his head from the sheet of paper he was holding, directing his attention to the back of the room. 'Dr Mulholland, what can you tell us?'

Gaby refrained from turning her head, instead she pulled the cap off her pen and started writing on the A4 pad on her lap, her ears channelled to pick up the soft burr of his voice.

'I was bleeped at 6 a.m. to view the body, arriving on the scene at a quarter to seven for a preliminary examination before she was transported to St Asaph and I subsequently performed the autopsy yesterday afternoon. I'm still waiting for the lab results but in brief Miss Chivell's toxicology report came back with a blood alcohol level of 280 milligrams of alcohol per 100 millilitres of blood, which indicates that she would have been heavily under the influence. This is underpinned by the two empty bottles of wine that the CSIs found, one on the floor by the sofa and the other on the kitchen worktop. There is also evidence that she was restrained. By the marks on both of her wrists and across her mouth I would suggest that some sort of tape was used although there was nothing found on the scene to indicate what sort. I'll know more when I get the results back from the skin scrapings, which should tell us a little about any adhesive residue left.' Gaby heard a rustle of paper and a brief cough before he continued to speak. 'There is some evidence that a struggle ensued: the faint scattering of bruising to her upper torso and her inner thighs – this despite the lack of evidence that her ankles were taped. There was also redness to the nasal region indicating that at some point he restrained her by holding her nose closed. This leads me to conclude that the cause of death was suffocation. I also don't have the results

186

from the rape kit as yet but the indication is that sexual activity had recently taken place.'

If Gaby hadn't noticed the silence on entering the room, she certainly noticed it now. It was the type of quiet that could be sliced with a knife and served along with the mugs of coffee scattered across nearly every surface. No one, after such a report, wanted to be the first to speak but that didn't stop her from standing and joining Sherlock at the front, her hands dug deep inside her trouser pockets, mirroring the body language of the Chief Inspector. It was clear that she'd annoyed Rusty. She had no idea how or why. But that was in no way going to interrupt how she conducted herself in his presence.

'Thank you, Doctor. So, what you're saying then is that she was intoxicated before being restrained, raped and then suffocated?'

'No, that's not what I said, Detective. It's my job to extract the evidence from the victim. It's not my job to then fit it into a tidy package of explanation. That's your job.'

Gaby's raised brow was the only indication that Rusty Mulholland was being an arse. In truth she was seething with rage but there was very little she could do about it in front of the DCI and Super. Instead she promised herself that the very next time she saw him, she'd tell him exactly what she thought of him, no matter what the circumstances.

'You didn't tell us about an approximate time of death?'

'No. I didn't.' She watched him clench his jaw and hoped that no one else was noticing his behaviour towards her which, in a room full of detectives, was highly unlikely. 'When I arrived on the scene rigor mortis had started but was in no way complete,' he continued. 'Hypostasis which, as you'll know leads to skin blanching and therefore is a useful tool in determining whether she was moved following death, was present on the body where skin met pressure. So the side of her head, one shoulder, her left hip and elbow and the palm of her right hand. Taking all this into account, alongside her rectal temperature at the scene and liver

187

temperature back at the hospital, I can hazard an informed guess at the time of death being between 10 p.m. and midnight. He might have shifted her from the couch to the floor but no further.' He pushed his chair back and, grabbing his notes, started placing them in his briefcase. 'If that's all? I have a busy day ahead of—'

'Actually I would prefer if you could stay a little while longer, Doctor. We have a lot to get through in a very short period of time and your input would be invaluable.' She made a point of watching as he sat back down and folded his arms across his chest, before she turned to the rest of the room.

'Thank you, I know all your time is precious.' She walked over to the whiteboard, pointing to the picture of Angelica. 'Something has come to the attention of our team here at St Asaph, which I would like to suggest links the 1995 murder of Angelica Brock to not only the recent murder of Tilly Chivell, but also potentially at least nine other victims that we know of.' She lifted her hand to stem the tide of questions being thrown at her. 'Yes that's right. There's a strong possibility that we have a serial killer on the loose. But before I go any further, I'd like to introduce you to Dr Ford who, as you've already heard, heads up the criminal profiling unit over in Liverpool.' She settled on the edge of the table and, with a sweep of her hand, said, 'Over to you, Doctor.'

'Thank you, Detective.' He stood and faced the room, his attention hovering on Dr Mulholland briefly before focusing on some point in the distance.

'Right then. I first became acquainted with Detective Darin's little problem three days ago when she contacted me for advice relating to a cold case her team have been looking into. The murder of eighteen-year-old Angelica Brock.' He nodded towards the whiteboard. 'As with most things my involvement snowballed into a completely different direction following our initial discussion. My understanding is that if it hadn't been for the nightdress, which didn't belong to the victim, the police would have come up with a completely different opinion as to the circumstances

188

surrounding her death. But that's irrelevant. There was a night-dress and, as the saying goes, we are where we are. The question of criminals leaving trophies on victims as opposed to removing them was an interesting construct but one I felt, in this instance, wasn't pertinent. However, the murder intrigued me not least because, with no cause of death, no crime could be proven outside of the initial abduction. But as we all know, rapists and murderers change over time, which got me thinking. What if Angelica's murder had been the first, a murder he botched but had learnt from the experience? So while Gaby and her team went fishing on the database for similar emerging patterns, I decided to put together a preliminary profile.' He retook his seat. 'I think you should handle the next bit, Detective.'

Gaby started, picking up his thread of conversation after only a brief pause. 'At this juncture there's not a huge amount to say other than Jax, Malachy and Marie undertook a search only to uncover a worrying trend in young female students being raped and murdered within a 200-mile radius of the Great Orme, the location of the first murder.'

'But that's ridiculous. Surely something like this should have been spotted years ago. It's not as if we don't all know about trends within crime. It's something we sprinkle on our cornflakes for breakfast,' Colin Wynne said, peering over the top of his spectacles, two bright red patches appearing on his cheeks.

'Yes, Colin, and in most cases, I'd agree that something like this couldn't be missed but our man is clever and each one of the cases that we've examined so far has one common theme. A complete lack of physical evidence apart from his choice of victim and the interesting fact that they all seemed to have been arranged in a foetal position, post-mortem, as if they'd just curled up to sleep,' she said, softening her words. 'You might remember you told me yourself you thought you'd seen that exact pattern before.'

'So, who are we looking for, Doctor?' Rusty interrupted, totally ignoring her.

189

'Ah yes.' Angus withdrew a sheet of paper from his pocket and carefully unfolded it. 'Someone who was living in and around Llandudno in 1995. Age wise, at the time of the first attack I suggest that he'd have been somewhere in his late teens and probably known to the victim, which translates to early to mid-forties now. He also would have had some previous contact with the police but only in relation to petty crime. With regards to his character, he'll be someone with few friends. Probably unmarried – difficulty forming relations with women is key here.' He glanced up, managing a brief upward tilt of his mouth. 'We also know that he's highly intelligent and organised. Remember he managed to abduct Angelica from her first-floor bedroom when the house was securer than Fort Knox. While that might be something he could have managed alone, especially if he was known to the victim, it's likely he would have needed help to get her up the Great Orme. Also the targeting of students could very well mean that he's somebody that's attended university – it follows that he's currently in some kind of skilled employment.'

'So, reading between the lines, I take it that you'd like me to look over all the other cases in question from a medical point of view, Detective?' Rusty rose to his feet and waited, one hand on his briefcase. 'Because if that's the case I'd like to get started unless there's something else I need to know?'

Gaby simply shook her head, unable to equate the man who'd sat in her lounge drinking her tea only a few days ago with the arrogant tosser now turning on his heel and heading out of the door, allowing it to bang sharply behind him.

CS Winters removed his hands from his pockets and stepped forward. 'Thank you. Does anybody have anything that they'd like to add?' He scanned the room, his gaze landing on each of the coppers in turn before focusing again on Angus. 'Good good. As DI Darin is the senior officer, I would like her to continue heading up the investigation but liaising closely with DS Enderlin with regard to the Bangor side of things. We'll iron out the final

190

details later. Thank you once again for your time.' He shifted his head in Gaby's direction. 'I'd like to meet with you in DCI Sherlock's office. ASAP.'

Gaby nodded, trying to ignore the dart of fear tracing up her spine. She'd done nothing wrong, had she? But instead of dwelling on something she couldn't change, she turned to Owen, who, she was pleased to note, was looking almost back to his old self.

'Bates, round up the troops. We'll meet back here at ten to divvy out the work.'

Chapter 36

Gaby

Thursday 23 July, 9.20 a.m. St Asaph

'Hold up, Gaby. What's this with you and the eminent Dr Mulholland then?'

Gaby glanced over her shoulder at Angus, who'd followed her out of the room and into the corridor. 'What? Really? I don't have time for this now. You heard what Winters said. Angus, you know how grateful I am for all the work you've put in but I can't afford to be late for this meeting.'

'You can't afford to miss what I'm about to say either. I'm heading back to Liverpool shortly and this will be the only opportunity we have to talk.'

Gaby came to an abrupt halt and turned, staring at him for a moment while she tried to think up the reason for his urgent need to speak to her. She couldn't. Suppressing a sigh, she reached for the handle of one of the empty offices the corridor housed.

'Come in here then but it can only be for a minute.'

But once the door closed behind their backs, he went to lean against the wall, his hands jingling what sounded like a pocketful of change. She knew he wasn't a man of many words but some at this juncture would be helpful. She resisted the urge to check the time on her watch.

'You do know that I got a degree in psychology before going on to specialise?'

'No, I didn't. But how is that relevant to the case?'

'It isn't. But it is relevant to your relationship with Dr Mulholland.'

Her jaw dropped open. 'Now you just hold on—'

'No. You gave me a full minute and I intend to use it.' He shifted from the wall and strolled across the room to the window, his back to her. 'The thing is I like you, Gaby, and I don't want to see you make a mess of your life.'

'But I'm not.'

'Really? You're happy to go home every night to your ready meal and single glass of wine, sitting in front of whatever inane programme that takes your fancy?' he said, finally turning back to her. 'Work is all very well but it won't keep you warm at night. It won't fill your dreams and it certainly won't be around when retirement age hits. So you can listen to me or get a cat to keep you warm. Your choice.'

Gaby eyed him warily, not quite able to believe the tone of the conversation. Apart from Amy and Owen's teasing, she was pretty confident no one had noticed the rather skewed relationship she had with the doctor. The one thing she did know, however, was that saying nothing would make her late for her meeting.

'Go on then, Angus, speak your mind but I won't promise to listen.' She tucked her hands behind her back and waited.

'Dr Mulholland couldn't keep his eyes off you, Gaby, but only when you weren't looking in his direction, which suggests to me that he's well and truly smitten. And, I might add, I don't need to be a psychologist to notice that you behaved in exactly the same

193

way. Obviously something's gone wrong with your relationship, something that you need to sort.'

'We don't have a relationship, Angus. We're colleagues and most days he can barely be civil.'

'And on the days when he is civil?'

She blushed even though blushing wasn't something she made a habit of.

'Exactly my point, Gaby. Your minute's free consultation is up. I'll continue working on your little puzzle when I get back to Liverpool.' He pulled open the door only to pause, his hand on the frame. 'Has he been round to your house?'

'What?' She lifted her head from where she'd been in the process of checking her phone. 'Yes, but only a couple of times and that was business.'

'Recently?'

She glared at him but answered all the same. 'At the weekend. Angus, I really do need to go,' she said, freeing the door from his hand.

'So if he'd driven past your house the last two evenings for instance, he'd have noticed my car in the driveway? Something to think about. Enjoy your meeting. I'll be in touch.'

Gaby forgot about the tight schedule she was on. Instead of rushing up the stairs like she'd intended, she walked at a snail's pace, her mind for once diverted from the investigation. It was only the sight of Sherlock's office up ahead that made her straighten her jacket and fix her mind on the matter at hand and not the muddle that was suddenly her existence. All she'd ever wanted was the satisfaction from a job well done and a contented home life. She'd never for one moment thought that she'd be in the middle of a soap opera storyline. If it wasn't so tragic and confusing, she'd find it funny. She was far from laughing.

The anticipated reprimand for being late never materialised. Instead both men stood and smiled when she entered the room, the fleeting nature of the latter probably due to the current

194

situation rather than a comment on her poor timekeeping.

'There's no need to look so worried, Detective.' DCI Sherlock nodded for her to take a seat before retaking his own. 'The reasons we've dragged you away from the investigation are twofold. Firstly to add our support and thanks for the effort that you and your team are giving to this enquiry.' He sat back in his chair, folding his hands across his lap, obviously waiting for Murdoch Winters to take the conversation forward.

'Yes indeed. Sterling effort, Darin, and right on the back of your last escapade,' he said, smoothing his hand over his trousers to remove an invisible thread. 'But the main reason you're here is to inform you of Stewart Tipping's decision to take early retirement. Obviously we'd like you to continue in the role of acting DI until a suitable replacement can be found but also we heartily recommend that you think seriously about applying for the post when it's circulated.'

195

Chapter 37

Gaby

Thursday 23 July, 9.50 a.m. St Asaph

Gaby sank behind her desk in the incident room, resisting the urge to slip her feet out of her shoes and wriggle her toes. There'd be time enough for such luxuries at the end of her shift and not the beginning. There wouldn't be a moment for anything but work over the next few days. So much work that she barely knew where to start. She turned to a new page of her pad and started writing a rapid list. As the prime suspect in Angelica's murder, finding Leo Hazeldine was the main priority. She hadn't quite puzzled out how she could tie him in with the rest of the cases but eliminating him from the enquiry, or alternatively, proving his guilt was key. She also had to think about informing the other police forces around the country about the possibility of their cases being linked to a much larger enquiry – something she was dreading. It was all very well Sherlock and Winters recommending her for the post but, from what she'd seen already, the role of DI was far from a sinecure. Yes, the extra hours and responsibility would be counteracted by an increase in salary but she wouldn't have the time to spend it. Her mind jumped the short distance to her cottage in Rhos-on-Sea and the, as yet, unopened tins of emulsion. At this rate she'd still be staring at it at Christmas; not this one – the one after.

Instead of writing, she started drawing random squiggles on the side of her jotter, allowing her mind to drift over what they knew to date. They had to find Leo. That was central to everything. She'd also like to know the depth of his relationship with the Butterworths and whether Avril Eustace had been telling the truth about not knowing him. The Eustaces worried her, not least Avril's comment about her parents disliking her husband but, while a niggle, it wasn't vital to the investigation. She could think of a hundred and one reasons for them to dislike their son-in-law but not one of them that would link him to the case simply because of his age. No. Leo Hazeldine or even Callum Beech were more in the frame than Eustace. It was just another loose end that she'd like cauterized.

The squiggles had stopped. Now Gaby was leaning over her pad thinking about coincidences and the strands that joined the deaths of Mary and Tony Butterworth to Angelica's murder and how Leo or Callum could possibly be implicated. Oh yes. Contrary to yesterday's take on the situation, Mary and Tony Butterworths' deaths were now back on the agenda. Another interview with Callum Beech was also a priority, she thought, remembering Angus's comment about criminals developing over time. He was exactly the right age for a start and in the right place instead of Australia. He was also an accountant so obviously intelligent.

'Hard at it, I see.'

Gaby raised her head, smiling at the vision of Owen bearing down with a couple of mugs. 'How did you know that's exactly what I needed?' She dropped her pen on the pad, pushing the cap into place and shifting it to one side to make room for the drinks. While she'd like to ask him how he was, the incident room

197

was too busy for any kind of personal conversation unless they wanted it spread around the office – as a portal for gossip sharing it was invaluable. Instead she asked him to pull up a chair and, lowering her voice said, 'How's Kate holding up? Not long now.'

'Only two weeks or so. This morning she looked like she was ready to pop.' He took a sip of his drink, his eyes meeting hers over the rim. 'We had a long chat about things . . .' He paused, his frown deepening. 'But at least we're back on the same page. I never realised how difficult it is to talk to someone with a toddler around unless it's about kid-related stuff. We never talk, not really, not about the important things. We took a drive along the coast while her mother minded Pip and sorted out a few things, some of which will affect my future.' He placed his mug down and started fiddling with the end of his tie. 'I do need to see you in private for that but for now I'd like to ask to take my lunch breaks out of the office? I know it'll be a stretch with the increased workload but I can't end up in the same position as yesterday. It's not fair on either of us.'

Gaby would have liked to have questioned him further on why he needed to speak to her alone but now wasn't the time or the place especially as she could hazard a guess as to what he was going to tell her. Instead all she said was, 'I wouldn't have it any other way. Anything that I can do, Owen. We both know the pressure's on but if we can't look after our own, it's a poor job.' She picked up her mug and, standing, patted him on the shoulder before gathering up her notepad, pen and mobile. 'Come on. Let's have that catch-up with the rest of the team – we've got more work to get through than I ever imagined. So much for this time last week thinking we had the luxury to scrutinise a cold case, huh! That's what chancing fate gets us. A prolific serial killer and no bloody clues to play with.' She made her way to the front of the room, noting the rapidly filling chairs with a nod of approval even as she stuffed Owen's personal problems into the corner of her mind alongside the up and coming conversation she owed

Rusty Mulholland. If Owen could pluck up the courage to sort out whatever issues he had with Kate, then she had no excuse not to iron out her current difficulties with the irascible Irishman.

'Morning for a second time. I'd like to reiterate a warm welcome to Kay and—?' She switched her gaze from Kay Enderlin to the pretty blonde with rounded cheeks and a nose that unfortunately took over her face to the exclusion of any of her other attributes.

'DC Florence Harlow, ma'am.'

'Welcome Florence. We're a small team but hopefully a friendly one. Any problems, my office door is always open.'

'Although she's rarely in it.'

She raised her eyebrows at Owen. 'Trust you to ruin my usual spiel, Bates. I'm never in it because I'm too busy keeping tabs on you,' she said, her expression belying the seriousness of her tone. 'Right then, back to business. As you can see from the extra whiteboard, any more victims and we'll need a larger incident room. We now have the murder of Tilly Chivell in addition to that of Angelica to investigate. There's also the little issue of Mary and Tony Butterworths' untimely deaths which, considering the link with both Angelica and Leo Hazeldine, must now be viewed with suspicion. So, I think you'll agree that it makes sense for Kay and Florence to continue looking into the Bangor side of things but to base themselves here for at least some part of the week – we'll play it by ear.' She paused. 'Kay, what have you got for me on Callum Beech?'

'Callum Lewis Beech, age forty-two. Born in Abergele. Went to Southampton University to study maths and subsequently was taken on by an accountancy firm. He's been working in his current job for six years. He's known to us but only for the odd parking ticket and a couple of speeding fines. Unmarried and up until recently lived with his mother, which tallies with the start of his relationship with Tilly.'

'So a mummy's boy but now he's off the leash. Anything else?'

199

'Not yet, but I'm still searching.'

'Okay. I want his work visited to check on his alibi. Also see if you can chase down Tilly's friends to see what they have to say about their relationship.' She lifted her hand, her thumb and forefinger only a millimetre apart. 'I'm this near to hauling him in. The only thing stopping me is a distinct lack of anything that's not circumstantial. What we really need is a juicy bit of DNA or CCTV evidence. Even his car somewhere it shouldn't be on the ANPR system would be good.'

She tucked her hands deep into her pockets and stared at the floor, running the case over in her mind before returning to the very start and Angelica's murder. All they needed was one mistake, one break and they could lock him up and deep six the key. But their man was smart. He didn't make mistakes expect perhaps during his first murder . . .

'So, going back to Operation Angel, what about the pebbles and footprints I asked you to look into, Jax? Any luck?'

'Not good news, I'm afraid. The trainers, one set of footprints, were a popular brand of Nike that sold in their hundreds of thousands. There were pebbles too but no DNA. Jason thinks gloves must have been worn.'

'And why would I think anything less from our killer! Anything else?'

'A ladder was definitely used but again nothing of any use was found either then or now.'

'Thank you.'

She took a step back, resting her hip against the table, deeply disappointed but far from surprised. 'Right, everyone, for now these four deaths are our focus: Angelica Brock, Tilly Chivell and Tony and Mary Butterworth. Yes, it's possible that there are at least nine others that need to join them but there's a lot of work to do before that happens,' she added, turning towards Malachy and Marie.

If she didn't know any better, she'd say that they'd fallen out. There was just something in the way that they'd walked into

200

the room. It was almost as if Marie couldn't bear to be in his company. Malachy wouldn't be the easiest of people to get along with, Gaby had had her own difficulties with him in the past. But if there was a problem, they'd have to either live with it or sort it out. She sure as hell didn't have the time to spoon-feed them on this gig. So, instead of asking Malachy to follow up on the Avril Eustace interview and also continue the search for Leo, as she'd planned, she decided to mix things up a bit.

'Malachy, I'd like you to work with Marie, concentrating all your efforts on continuing to hunt for possible victims that fit the profile you produced.' She angled her head to look at Florence, who was busily writing down everything in a jotter. 'Young female students living in digs,' she said, directing her attention back to her two detectives who appeared to be less than impressed with their new task. 'Go and find a spare office, somewhere out of the way. I want to keep what we're doing as quiet as possible for now.' She slid her gaze back to Malachy. 'I also need you to liaise with Dr Mulholland, Mal. Send him what we've got on the potential cases to date and please ensure you encrypt them,' she said, her voice sharp. 'We have enough to do without breaching any GDPR regs. I do have some good news though. I've spoken to CS Winters and DCI Sherlock and they've agreed to find me some more staff from somewhere. But until then you're both on your own unless Kay and Florence find that they have some free time to assist. I'll also need you to give me a list of the lead officers and their contact details for each of the cases listed.' She twisted her mouth. 'That will be my next job.' Turning to Jax, she said, 'I'm sure you could do with a break from all the research you've been lumbered with. So, instead I'd like you to concentrate on locating Leo and, luckily for you, I have a lead.' She opened her notebook and rifled through the pages. 'Ah, here it is. Avril Eustace states that one of the photographs depicting Leo was taken when he attended Tony Butterworth's retirement do at Paintings Hotel, Betws-y-Coed. It's a pot shot but they might have something on

201

record to help us. I'm not sure how he could have been involved with any of the other murders being as he was living abroad at the time, but I want him in for questioning, pronto.' She pocketed her notebook, a clear sign that the meeting was over.

The clock on the wall above the door was a surprise being as it was a full hour earlier than she'd thought. There was a lot she could do with that spare hour but one thing took precedence. 'Owen, if you can make sure that Kay and Florence have everything they need. I'll be in my office. I have a job for us but there's something I need to do first.'

Chapter 38

Gaby

Thursday 23 July, 10.30 a.m. Gaby's Office

Gaby let the phone ring through until the answer-machine picked up. She didn't know what she felt about not being able to speak to either Sheila or Stewart Tipping. The coward in her was relieved but it was only prolonging what could only be viewed as one of the most difficult of conversations. She finally left a garbled message before returning the phone to its receiver, her fingers still gripping on to the handset. The problem was that she liked Stewart as both a detective and a person. He was good at his job despite never managing to catch Angelica's killer, something that couldn't in any way be viewed as his fault. The man they were chasing, with all the resources and skills they had available, had only managed to evade capture because of one little issue. Luck. He must have been seen. There's no way that someone could be that careful. There was also no way that he couldn't have left a clue. Just one. That's all she was after. She'd go through all of the files until she found it and if they grubbed around for long enough, they'd get him. The only hope was that another woman wouldn't have to die in the process.

The knock on her door pulled her out of her reverie. It could only be Owen.

He entered, closing the door behind him and slouching down in the only chair, situated at a right angle beside her desk.

'I'm surprised you were able to find your office. When was it you were last here? It must be a couple of weeks.'

Gaby scowled. 'I'll have you know I was in here at the weekend working.'

'God, Gaby. You really do need to get a life,' he said, lowering his brows so that they joined into a beetling frown.

'Yes, well. I might think of it but only after we've caught the bastard.' She settled back in her black swivel chair, slipping off her shoes under the privacy of her desk. 'I'll also have you know I bought some tins of paint all of two days ago.'

'Wonders will never cease. What colour is it?'

She stilled, trying to think back to her five minutes in the store when she'd pretty much picked up one of the first tins she'd spotted. 'Yellowish.'

'Could be interesting. Kate bought some to brighten up the kitchen. It took three attempts to get it to stop resembling the inside of a daffodil! I would have suggested a nice tasteful cream to start off with if you'd asked.'

Gaby examined him for any sign of laughter but for once there wasn't a trace. He'd had a tough couple of days but, along with the sharp repartee, he could usually be relied upon for more than the bland look he was aiming in her direction. She watched him withdraw a plain white envelope from his breast pocket and place it on the desk between them like an unexploded bomb, her heart dipping under her grey Zara jacket. It didn't take a *Mastermind* contestant to know what he was doing or even why he was doing it, but it was a shock all the same. They were a team. No. They were family. You didn't need to share the same genetic profile

204

or have the same blood running through your veins to be a member of the same clan. It ran deeper than that, especially in the force. They worked together, often late into the night, sharing the emotional rollercoaster of horrors that the job entailed. She'd take a bullet for him if she had to. He'd already set the precedent on life saving. He and Amy were the closest things within shouting distance that meant something and it broke her in all the ways possible that he was even thinking of leaving.

She finally spoke, her voice for once lacking its usual strength. 'I don't even want to know what that is, Owen. You can just stuff it back where it came from.'

'No, Gabs. I can't. I promised Kate and I'm not prepared to break that promise, I've broken nearly all the rest.' He stretched out his arm, pushing the envelope further towards her with the tip of his index finger.

'But what about the case and finding Angelica's murderer?' Gaby said, her gaze fixed on the envelope and therefore missing his fleeting expression.

'What about it? You're a good copper, Gaby. Loath that I am to admit it but you're a much better one than me. If you can't solve it, it's unsolvable. You have me for another month. No longer.'

'Well, in that case, I'd better make use of you, hadn't I?' She placed the envelope in the top drawer of her desk and picked up her bag. 'We're going to run over what the CSIs found at the Butterworths'. It's bugging me that the minute Avril popped out, Mary decided to turn her hand to baking. There's something about it that doesn't gel.' She picked up her keys and handed them to him. 'After, we'll visit the house, that is if the fire officer says it's safe. You can drive. I need to think.'

If he was expecting her to plead, he was in for a shock. Pleading wasn't her style. But in Owen's case she knew she wouldn't get anywhere. He was probably the most stubborn man she'd ever met. No, the best way to handle the situation was to ignore it. Perhaps then he'd realise that he wasn't quite as indispensable as

205

he'd first thought. She walked to the door with her head held high, the feel of his eyes burning a path into her back causing her mouth to curl. There'd be time enough to think about his resignation later. With her hand on the side of the door, she considered the folly of opening a bottle of Barolo as soon as she got home but immediately shelved the idea – common sense finally catching onto where her emotions were leading her. The way her day was going she'd be tempted to finish the bottle.

Chapter 39

Owen

Thursday 23 July, 1.15 p.m. Owen's House

'I've handed in my notice,' Owen said, walking into the kitchen and sitting beside Pip, unable to quite meet Kate's eye.

He watched her push her mug away before easing to her feet and making her way to his side of the table, despite the difficulty it caused her to move.

'I know how hard that must have been,' she said, wrapping her arms around him and pressing a deep kiss against his lips. 'But it will be the best thing in the long run. You'll see. We'll spend much more time together as a family.'

Owen knew all that just as he knew he was letting both Kate and Pip down every time he thought of work when he was with them. But he couldn't help himself. Solving crimes was like a drug and he didn't know, now the decision had been made, how he was going to cope without his daily fix. He reached up and pulled her into his arms, their combined weight causing the chair to creak in an alarming fashion. Nestling his head in the crook of her neck

207

he breathed in her signature scent of soap, shampoo and a hint of lilies, his arms a protective cradle around her stomach. This was home and where he needed to be. As to the rest, he'd have to find a way to manage. Gaby was right in saying that she couldn't see him as a security guard but the reality was, he wasn't qualified for anything else and at least he'd be able to sign off on time and help the way dads were meant to. The way his father had.

He pushed aside any thoughts of Angelica. His life was a tangle of his own making but the original knot had been tied when he'd first learnt of her death. Kate had come onto his radar when Owen was a twelve-year-old lad obsessed with football. He'd known of Angelica, the head girl, and like every pubescent boy up to A level had drooled a little at the image of her long legs and white-blonde hair. But Kate had been just another of the annoying chattering girls in his year until the day he'd found her crying into her locker. It had taken another three years before he'd picked up the courage he'd been nurturing, to ask her out. They'd been together ever since.

The sound of Pip banging his spoon on the table pulled him back into the present and, with a gentleness born out of the love and respect he had for his wife, he eased her onto her feet and helped her settle into her chair, arranging a cushion behind her.

'You stay there and I'll make us a sandwich. Corned beef and pickled onion all right?' he said, unscrewing the jumbo jar she seemed to always be running out of. There must be worse things than having a pregnant wife obsessed with pickled onions but currently he couldn't think of a single one.

'Any news about the case?'

Owen paused in the act of trying to jab the last elusive onion, currently evading capture at the bottom of the jar. While there wasn't much he didn't share with her, current investigations were usually out of bounds. But there was nothing usual about being involved with a case that centred around his wife's sister's murder.

'Gaby's brought a forensic psychologist in from Liverpool so I

208

should think the investigation will start gathering pace. The super is determined to invest all the resources needed. But . . .' He placed her plate in front of her, his hand settling on her shoulder. 'You don't need me to tell you that there are no guarantees that they'll be any more successful. I'll make sure I use all the influence I can while I'm still at the station but after that . . .'

She reached up, grabbing his hand. 'I know you will and I feel a right bitch dragging you away from the case and the job you love.'

Owen dropped a kiss on the top of her head and, glancing at the clock above the cooker, picked up his sandwich. It wasn't her fault that he'd decided on a job in law enforcement or that he'd become obsessed with finding Angelica's murder, a little fact that he'd managed to withhold from her all these years. The one single truth was that he had no intention of stopping his search. It would be easier to chop off his arm than admit to failure. No. He planned to continue working on it in any spare time he could afford. But he wouldn't tell Kate. That was a secret that could never be shared.

209

Chapter 40

Jax

Thursday 23 July, 2 p.m. St Asaph Police Station

Jax eased his long frame into his chair, trying to avoid looking at either Malachy or Marie. There was something up between them. He didn't think it was sex but he wouldn't put it past Mal to try it on now that Marie had split up with her husband. She was certainly attractive enough to invite more than a passing glance. In a way he hoped it was exactly that. Marie was one of the sweetest of ladies but with a core of steel, which had strengthened over recent weeks. It wouldn't do Mal any harm to occasionally come up against a flat refusal – it would probably do him a whole lot of good.

But that wasn't his problem; his mind flitted instead to Georgie and the one-bedroomed flat that they'd decided to rent. Subject to references and being able to cobble together the deposit, it was all theirs. With a bit of luck he'd finish work on time and take her out for a celebratory drink.

Instead of phoning Paintings, he decided to give the car a run being as the hotel was situated in one of his favourite parts of the world. Betws-y-coed. There was something niggling at the back of his mind. Something relevant to the case that he couldn't quite remember. Maybe a few hours away from the office might be the thing to ferret it out from where it was hiding. He grabbed his fleece from the coatrack behind the door, coiling his stripy scarf around his neck before pulling out his beanie and dragging it over his blonde head. The weather had continued to deteriorate and, instead of the balmy weather he'd been hoping for, there was a distinct chill in the air not to mention the threat of more rain.

The trip to Betws-y-Coed, the scenic route, did much to clear his head but little to reveal that niggle. He found a parking space opposite the train station in between the coaches that had pulled up to take in the sites around Swallow Falls. His parents used to bring him here when he was little and he'd loved it ever since. There was something unique about the place. It was almost as if someone had plonked the village down in the middle of the Conwy Valley, herding it into place by a flourish of trees. Apart from the cars and coaches all it would take was a few horse-drawn carriages and he could almost think he'd lost a century or two.

He took a shortcut across the village green, heading for Paintings, the large boutique hotel slotted in between Anna Davies' string of shops and The Royal Oak, flapping his arms in an effort to keep warm, the air from his lungs preceding him in a white frosty mist. For someone brought up on a council estate in Llandudno, the granite-fronted building was all a little too overpowering.

Foot on the top step, he paused a minute, tucking his beanie back into his pocket and smoothing his hair, his other hand on the door. Before his last block of speech therapy, he'd have been a trembling mass of blood and bones by now. Nothing could have persuaded him to approach the desk, manned by the perfectly styled receptionist. It was only thanks to the latest in a long line of therapists that he'd finally managed to mostly regain control

211

over his speech but it was his girlfriend who'd given him the confidence not to care a jot if he stumbled over his words – the sharp corners of his warrant card did the rest.

He thrust his shoulders back and strode over to the desk as if he owned the place. 'Morning. I'm D-D-DC Williams, from St Asaph station. I'm like to speak to the manager if I may?' he said, his chin raised, his warrant card laid open on the mahogany surface.

Within seconds he was being invited around the other side of the counter, his badge securely back in his pocket, while the receptionist made a hasty call. He struggled not to show the smile that was trying to break free. Despite her looks and snooty attitude, he was the one in charge of the situation. The presence of a copper in their hotel wouldn't be the kind of publicity they wanted, and he wasn't surprised at the speed with which he was propelled into the manager's office. By the expression of distaste on the man's face, if he had his way, he'd be propelling him in a completely different direction.

Jax's smile broadened, his hand extended in the firmest of handshakes much to the angst of the short balding man in possession of the loudest pinstripe suit he'd seen outside of a gangster movie. Policing was all about image and the image that Jax was determined to show was that of self-assurance mainly because he was at a huge disadvantage. But that was something, for the present, he was prepared to keep to himself – the little fact that he didn't have a search warrant. The hotel was within their rights to protect their clients' records just as he was determined to stop them.

It didn't take long to direct the conversation into the corner he wanted but not before he'd discussed the problems of underage drinkers in North Wales and the initiative to have uniformed officers visit *all* premises to check ID.

'But this is a respectable establishment,' Mr Surridge blustered. 'Even if they managed to get past reception, it's unlikely they'd be able to afford the prices.'

212

'That steep? I'll have to remember that when I bring my girl-friend over.' He'd been half thinking of booking dinner as a special treat, now he canned the idea as being too far out of his league. 'Right then, down to the reason I'm here.'

He produced the picture of Leo Hazeldine and laid it on the desk between them. 'This was taken seven months ago here in your hotel. Now, while I know that there's very little chance of anyone recognising him after this length of time, I do need to see all your records for a retirement party held on the 5th December last year.'

The cappuccino that materialised within minutes was finished off with a cocoa powder dragon and, instead of the tiny circle of shortbread he'd been expecting he had a plateful. The manager had set him up behind his secretary's desk and left him to it with strict instructions to ask for help if he needed it.

The records were printed off in spreadsheet form. The first was the original booking for eighty-odd guests and the name and contact details for the bank Tony Butterworth had worked for. The second was a run-off of all the payments taken from the party on the night. It was simple maths to discover that most of them had paid by card and a quick process of elimination to realise that Leo's name didn't appear on the second sheet. So either he was one of the two couples that had paid by cash or he was using a different name.

Jax stood and walked over to the window and the view of green leafy trees swaying in the breeze that was continuing to build. If he had the time, he'd grab a sandwich and a coffee from the convenience store and take a stroll over the Pont-y-Pair Bridge and the picnic benches below. It was a shame that Georgie was working a split shift at the hospital or he'd have been tempted to break all the rules and bring her with him. It was also a shame about the prices. Trust him to choose one of the most expensive hotels around for his romantic gesture. He turned away from the window, his thoughts now on the problem of how to stretch his

213

money, something that was never far from his mind these days. The disparity between what he had and how much he needed to live on was a quagmire fuelled by the bills that appeared through the letter box at an alarming rate. The way it was going, he'd be lucky to afford a bunch of roses for his romantic gesture let alone a meal; the vision of a starlit walk by the riverside disappeared into the mist. After all, there'd be no point in coming all this way for a meal if one of them had to drive home. Better to book for the night . . .

He smiled again. Not his usual lopsided grin with a band of wariness in its depths but a broad beam that quickly turned into a laugh. Lifting his hand, he fisted it into the other and performed a brief little two step across the room to the internal telephone. If the niggle, which was now storming through his mind, was right, he'd be the toast of the station.

Chapter 41

Leo

Thursday 23 July, 2 p.m. Montford Bridge, Wrexham

Leo Hazeldine was a wreck of a man. It was there in the downward stoop of his shoulders, which was only matched by the downward turn of his mouth. Propping up the bar of the Montford Bridge Inn, situated on the outskirts of Wrexham, people could be forgiven in thinking that he looked almost twice his forty-four years – he certainly felt it. The last few months had been particularly trying.

Jessie had been the love of his life. They'd met in Australia, a place he'd called home for nearly twenty-five years. The place he'd run away to, seeking sanctuary after the episode that he couldn't bear to think about. Australia had been both his home and his salvation. He'd met Jess within days of landing at Sydney airport and they'd been together ever since. When he closed his eyes, he could almost imagine that time had shifted back to his wedding, the happiest day of his life. The sun had shone down on them both and it had continued to shine right up until the very end.

He'd never regretted even one second of the time that they'd spent together. They'd felt blessed and cursed in equal measures. To know that their time was only finite meant they were able to achieve far more in those last couple of years than most people achieved in a lifetime. But just as he couldn't dwell on what had happened to Angelica, he couldn't allow himself to stray to the darkest days of all. Even the thought of that dimly lit hospital room was enough to break his resolve and return him to his latest mistress.

Leo knew that there was no future to be found in the bottom of a whiskey bottle. Part of him, the cowardly part, wanted to crawl inside and let the amber coloured liquid seduce him with its warm glow. But so far, he'd managed to resist the temptation by limiting his intake to a couple a day. He'd returned to Britain to start a new life away from the memories of the old and turning to booze would put all that in jeopardy. He still had his mother here and quite a few pounds in the bank after selling up abroad. It also helped that there was nothing left for him in Australia that he didn't have inside both his head and his heart. The future as far as he was concerned was dead.

The second glass was almost empty, the remains of ice now only a sliver of memory, the bitter-sweet taste an ugly siren slipping under the railing he'd erected in his mind. He really should leave. There were the makings of a meal in the fridge and an afternoon sitting in front of the telly to look forward to. But the bar was warm and inviting. Mick, the landlord, was his only friend in the small village he'd chosen to call home simply because of its location near to his mother. So one more drink quickly slipped into two and, before he knew it, he'd stopped counting. He forgot yesterday. He forgot today. There was no tomorrow.

It was Mick who helped him off his bar stool and Mick who ensured that he was wearing his jacket for the short walk home. Leo stumbled along, his hands tucked into his pockets, his fingers clutching on to his keys. If he had any thought, it was a simple

216

one. Curling up in front of the gas fire for a mid-afternoon snooze. He didn't see the shadow chasing his steps along the quiet lane where he'd rented a one-bedroomed apartment just as he didn't notice anything untoward as he fumbled for the lock.

If he could have guessed what was about to happen, apart from the sharp pain in the centre of his back, he probably wouldn't have changed a thing.

Chapter 42

Gaby

Thursday 23 July, 4 p.m. Incident Room

'What a complete waste of time.'

Gaby stormed into the empty incident room and dumped her coat on the floor beside the desk, her nose wrinkling at the distinct smell of smoke before placing a battered shoebox down on top. She had no idea of what she'd been hoping to achieve walking through what was left of the property along Colwyn Road but all she'd managed to do was earn herself a trip to the dry cleaners. The problem was she also had no idea what she'd been looking for. Suspecting a link between the Butterworths' deaths and that of Angelica was very different to proving it. At the very least, there needed to be a motive.

Trawling through Mary Butterworth's drawers proved more an exercise in self-loathing than of any real use. There was nothing left of the essence of the woman that now lay in the morgue, her body still waiting to be released by the coroner. The rooms that were left undamaged held nothing personal, nothing for them to

218

get their hooks into as to a reason for her death. All she'd come away with was a shoebox of letters, carefully hidden under a pile of blankets in the bottom of the airing cupboard. The fact that they were hidden was what had tempted her to bring them, but did she really want to read a pile of faded to yellow love letters when both parties were dead? After a wasted morning she'd dropped Owen off at his car so that he could go and fetch Pip from his mother-in-law's. Now she was out of ideas.

'What's a complete waste of time, ma'am?' Jax said, walking into the office and starting to unravel his scarf.

'Nothing.' She lifted her head from where she'd been idly flicking through her notebook in desperation. 'You seem very pleased with yourself. You must have a date this evening?' she said, not really expecting a reply as she watched his expression change into an easy smile.

'You're not going to believe this, but I think I've got Hazeldine,' he replied, ignoring her comment.

'You're kidding me!'

'Nope and I've even got his address. Come on. I can explain on the way. If the traffic's with us we shouldn't be too late back . . .' He paused, his nose twitching. 'What's that smell?'

'Don't ask, Jax.' She opened her bag withdrew a bottle of perfume and sprayed her wrists. 'After a whiff of Coco Chanel you won't even notice. Now before you drag me off to God only knows where, pause for breath a sec and tell me what this is all about? After the morning I've had, I want five minutes sitting in one place and behind my desk is as good as any. So, sit and tell me exactly what's going on.'

He folded his frame into the nearest chair. 'Remember when DS Bates told us that Kate's mum never suspected Leo Hazeldine because she always thought he was gay? That got me thinking about how a man could simply disappear like that unless they changed their name? It's okay for a woman. It's the norm mostly for them to take on their husband's when they get married. It

219

didn't even register that it might be the same for Leo. We knew he was in Australia where, by the way, it only became legal to marry within a same sex relationship in 2017 – the same year he disappeared. Once it hit me, I found him in a couple of clicks. Leo Hazeldine became Leo Martinez on the 14th October 2017. But not only that, he stayed the night at Paintings in December, paying by credit card.'

'Jax Williams, if you weren't going steady, I'd kiss you. Purely in a platonic way, you understand. So there's no need to slap a sexual harassment notice on my head for inappropriate behaviour,' she elaborated, giving him a wide-eyed look. 'What else did you find?'

'Not a huge amount more. His partner, Jessie Martinez, died a few months ago, around the time Leo's mother moved into care so he sold up everything and returned to live in the UK. He's currently renting a flat outside Wrexham.'

Gaby picked up her phone, checked through the list of stations in the North Wales network and quickly tapped in a number. With the receiver cradled under her chin she said, 'Let's check he is where you think he is. No point in wasting a good hour's round trip if he's gone walkabout.'

220

Chapter 43

Gaby

Thursday 23 July, 4.40 p.m. St Asaph Station

'Owen, am I pleased to see you! There's been a development, which is confusing the hell out of Jax and me.'

'Ma'am?'

'Before I tell you, how's Kate doing? It's best to keep our priorities in the right order,' she said, tilting her head in Jax's direction and where he was working on his laptop. 'He's meeting Georgie after her shift finishes and I for one am going to ensure that he isn't one second late. So, how is she?' she repeated, leaning back in her chair.

'Doing well, considering. They're keeping a close eye on her now she's nearly on her due date, especially after the difficulties she had with Pip.'

'Well, you do what you have to with regards to work. I mean that, Owen. I'm not sure how many favours I owe you in return for saving my life but, as far as I'm concerned, the debt is far from paid.' She pushed her chair back and, twisting on her heels, headed for the window.

221

The rain was pelting down; apart from a brief respite around lunchtime, it hadn't stopped all day. But there was nothing she could do about that. She'd make sure both Owen and Jax left on time for once even if she had to escort them to the door. All she could think about was the way the case was running away from her. It was almost as if it was taking on a life of its own. If she wasn't careful, Sherlock and Winters would remove it out from under her and call in the big boys from Scotland Yard – a part of her was surprised that they hadn't already mentioned the possibility.

She continued to stare out at the view, trying to draw inspiration from the less than inspiring car park below. 'Jax has managed to find Hazeldine but it was sadly all a little too late because some bastard got there first.'

'What?'

She turned, the lines around her eyes and mouth etched deep in the harsh overhead lighting, an echo of the old woman she'd become held between their folds. 'To cut to the chase, he was found on the doorstep of his flat earlier on today with a single stab wound in the centre of his back. It looks like a lucky aim as the blade severed the aorta. Even if there'd been anyone around, there was nothing that anyone could have done.'

'What?' Owen repeated, his face now adopting the same lines as his boss. 'I don't understand? What would there be to gain?'

'Join the club, Owen. Any more bodies and we'll be able to ask for a discount at the undertaker's,' she joked, but without a glimmer of humour on her lips. 'There's something here that we're not seeing and I'm blowed if I can work it out.' She pulled her shoulders back in an act of defiance. 'But because I'm not seeing it doesn't mean that someone else can't.' Her laugh was hollow. 'Jax, you're the youngest, go and dig out the rest of them from where they're hiding. We'll have an emergency powwow to see if we can't bash out some ideas and, in the meantime, Owen, you can chase up Rusty.'

222

'No.'

She waited for the door to whisper closed behind Jax's back before replying. 'No? Forgive me. I think I heard wrong. Did you refuse to contact Dr Mulholland?'

'Gaby, I really don't want to have to say this to you, especially with how supportive you've been. But you can't have everything your own way just as you can't run everyone else's lives for them without expecting a dose of your own medicine in return.' She opened her mouth to speak only to close it when his palm flicked up to stop her. 'No, you have to let me have my say for once. You were very quick to act intermediary between me and Kate—'

'But that was different.'

'God damn it, woman. For once in your life shut up,' he said, his voice unusually sharp, his skin flooding with colour. 'Jax will be back in a minute and I'm one hundred per cent sure that you won't want him to hear what I have to say. The whole station is starting to cotton on that there's something going on between you and Rusty and, I don't care if you do mind me telling you that it's partly your own fault. I don't give two pins if you get it on with him or not but I don't want to hear you ridiculed in the canteen for not being able to stand up to him. Yes, he's an arrogant so-and-so but like most men he's also wary of women, especially women like you who do tend to eat babies for break-fast.' He reached for the phone and lifted the receiver, stretching it out to her. 'It's about time you started doing all of us a favour by carrying out your own dirty work.'

Gaby lowered her lids over her eyes, not prepared to let Owen see that his words had hit the target dead centre. If Rusty had been damaged then so had she and yet she was the one being shouted at. She was the one being asked to paper over the cracks of their fractured relationship and all this in the middle of trying to coordinate one of the largest murder enquiries ever to hit the UK.

Without a word she punched in his number, her hand clenched so tightly around the receiver as to almost cut off the circulation

223

to her wrist. His terse 'Mulholland', did nothing to alleviate the tension in either her arm or the room in general. She didn't see Jax return to the room and throw Owen a wink or, if she did, she didn't respond.

'Afternoon, Doctor—'

'I'm just finishing up here, Detective,' he interrupted. 'I'll have Tilly Chivell's report on your desk first thing in the morning.'

She withheld a groan, her attention fixed on her desk and not on the shuffling going on behind her as her team pretended not to be listening to every word. Resisting the strong urge to reply in kind all she said was, 'Thank you. If there's anything you can share now, I'd be grateful. I'm about to put you on loudspeaker for the rest of the team.'

She could almost hear his anger pulse down the telegraph wire as she pressed the speaker button, but she was determined not to let it bother her.

'No, it happened exactly as I thought. Suffocated to death by the perpetrator taping her mouth to cut off her airway and then pinching her nostrils. There is one thing, however, that might be of use. I've only had a chance to flick through the files you sent me but in each instance, he took the time to wash the body post-mortem. However, with Miss Chivell that's not the case.'

'So, there's a possibility that he was disturbed,' she said, almost to herself. 'And if he cut corners the once, he might have again?'

'Exactly. It's worth mentioning to the CSI team to be extra vigilant about how he exited the property. There's even a chance he might still have been in the flat when the boyfriend arrived. I take it you've ruled him out of your enquiries?'

'Not as yet but my team are on the case. Thank you again, Rusty. We really do appreciate the effort you're putting in on this. I take it you'll be performing the autopsy on that stabbing over in Wrexham?'

'Scheduled in for nine o'clock tomorrow.'

'Okay. The results at your earliest convenience please.' She went

224

to disconnect only to stop at the sound of his voice, her finger hovering over the hook switch.

'It looks like you'll be putting in an all-nighter?'

'Well, it's certainly going to be a late one. If you have anything more, I'd appreciate you giving me the heads up earlier rather than later. Thank you again.' She disconnected but instead of replacing the handset she quickly punched in Jason's number and asked him to concentrate their efforts on the bathroom and the area outside of Tilly's flat. Lack of time made criminals sloppy. All they needed was one mistake and they'd have him locked up where he belonged.

Ending the call, she made her way to the whiteboard and stared at Angelica's photo. They'd now gone through all the case notes and there wasn't even one query that Tipping had failed to follow. Part of her was happy about that. But there had to be something they were missing. Why had she been chosen for a start? Was her distinctive, pale blonde hair relevant? It was so pale that it could almost be mistaken for white. She picked up a red marker and added a huge question mark beside hair colour before replacing the cap and facing the room.

'Right then,' she said, checking her watch. 'I know it's home time but, before you head off, I want an update. Where are we with the search for possible additional matches?'

Gaby watched Marie glance uncertainly at Malachy. She was more convinced than ever that there was something up between them. But whatever it was they'd better not let it interfere with their work or she'd ship them off the team. There were plenty of other officers eager to take their place.

'We have fifteen women now that fit the bill, ma'am,' Marie said, spreading a small pile of photos out on the table at the front. 'As you can see, they're all of a type. All with long hair, albeit with no pattern with regards to colour. There is one thing though . . .'

'Yes?'

'Well, Kay came up with a good point before she headed back

225

to Bangor. Due to time constraints we made a judgement call to concentrate our efforts on crimes that included both rape and murder but what if he didn't kill them all? Because, if that's the case, then we could be looking at a whole bunch more and—'

'And there might even be some witnesses.' Gaby picked up a black marker and started to write. 'Okay, we did some preliminary work on this so at least we have a starting point. Sadly that does mean that we're going to have to widen the database search and we simply don't have the manpower. If there are any live victims they'll all have to have their statements checked and most likely be re-interviewed.' She recapped the pen again but, instead of setting it back down on the table, she twirled it through her fingers. 'The other bit of news, of course, is that Leo Hazeldine has turned up with a four-inch kitchen knife sticking out of his back so it's more likely than ever that he's linked in some way to Tony and Mary Butterworth's deaths.' She uncapped the marker again and scrawled Leo's name underneath that of Mary and Tony's, hesitating a second before adding Angelica's name, but in a different colour pen. 'So, what's the connection apart from all four of them working in the sailing club?' She turned back to the room, well aware that she wasn't about to get any kind of response from their empty faces just as she was aware of how tired they all looked. It had been one hell of a week already and she wasn't going home any time soon. 'Okay, tootle off then. See you back here bright and early tomorrow.'

226

Chapter 44

Malachy

Thursday 23 July, 5.30 p.m. St Asaph Police Station

Malachy threw his jacket into the back of his car, settled in the front seat and switched on the ignition. He had plans for his evening not that they were exciting or anything but a lager and the latest Valerie Keogh thriller were about as much excitement as he could muster after the day he'd had. He still had the problem of his mother to sort out and the small question of who to invite to his sister's wedding, but he'd tackle that over the weekend. The one thing he didn't need was hassle, he thought, his attention drawn to Marie and what looked like her husband trying to make her get into his car.

For all his brazen, upfront manner and career choice, Malachy shied away from awkward situations. He'd joked with Marie about his rash of girlfriends but that couldn't be further from the truth. He was a loner by nature, enjoying nothing more than a good book instead of the late nights and bedroom exploits his colleagues expected from him. While

227

he was happy enough to fuel their imagination with a few stories, that was as far as it went. There were very few people he actually liked – only a handful – but funnily enough Marie Morgan fell within the high-walled boundaries of that elite group. But watching the scene ahead unfold, he was in two minds whether to intercede in her problems in light of the way she'd been brushing him off all day. Marie Morgan was in trouble and not of her own making, but it didn't necessarily follow that it should be up to him to rescue her. However, that errant thought didn't prevent him from switching off his engine and climbing out of the car, the picture of an ice-cold glass of lager drifting out of reach.

'Darling, there you are.' He strolled up to her, a broad smile carved on his lips. 'Come on, I've booked the restaurant for seven. By the time we've showered and changed we'll be hard pushed to make it.'

'There's no point in continuing the act,' Ivo said, flexing his shoulders. 'I know that my wife is renting a bedsit and has been for the last few weeks. Now run away and play with women your own age. This is a private conversation.'

Malachy glanced between them, his lager disappearing from his mind with a sudden snap. For all her belligerent behaviour of earlier the Marie Morgan standing in front of him wouldn't currently have the wherewithal to boil a kettle let alone stand up to the man she'd married. He could, of course, walk away but his mother, for all her faults, had tried to bring him up to always do the right thing whether he wanted to or not.

'Darling, it looks like you have a choice here. Him or me?' He folded his arms across his chest, now staring at Ivo. 'I'm not leaving until the lady tells me to. Marie?'

He watched her close her eyes, part of him feeling some degree of sympathy at the sight. She looked as if she'd swallowed a wasp, perhaps even a whole nest, the way her mouth was pursed. But he couldn't do anything to lessen the impact of the situation – a

228

situation that had begun the day she'd decided to get hitched to the supercilious git beside her.

When her eyes opened, she all but ignored Ivo, instead stretching out her hand.

'I wasn't sure if you'd forgotten our . . . date, Mal. Come on. You can give me a hand to move my bags, if that offer to . . . share your bed still stands?'

Malachy arched his brow but instead of replying turned back to Ivo.

'You heard the lady. If I ever find that you've accosted Marie again, not only will I ensure that you have a visit from the police I'll also have a little word with my father. You have heard of my father? Sir Nicholas Devine QC?'

'That was bloody genius. I can't thank you enough.' Marie gathered up her jacket and bag before turning to him, her voice full of laughter. '"Sir Nicholas Devine QC", although, knowing my husband he'll probably check.'

'And what if he does?'

Marie's laughter stopped as abruptly as her smile. 'You mean he's real. That your father really is . . .?'

'Of course he's real. Why would you think otherwise?'

'I'd no idea,' she said, her voice faltering.

'It's not important. What is important is that your husband doesn't know how to take no for an answer. Don't look now but that's his car parked about three behind. What did he want anyway, if it's not too inquisitive of me to ask?'

'He wants me back. He's decided after a month of moving his clerk in with her two kids that he doesn't want children after all.'

'And don't tell me. You're going to forgive him?'

'No, I'm bloody not,' she exploded. 'Not that it's any business of yours.'

'But it is my business, or at least until he gets the message.' He opened his door, walked around to the passenger side and helped

229

her out. 'Come on, let's get your bags or as many as I can squeeze in. That will give him something to think about and, before you ask, there's no room in my bed but a perfectly serviceable double in the guest bedroom.'

'That's just as well.' She tapped her briefcase. 'We have more than enough work to keep us busy.'

Chapter 45

Gaby

Thursday 23 July, 7 p.m. St Asaph Police Station

'I thought I'd find you in your office still hard at it.'

Gaby looked up from the Excel spreadsheet she'd been updating, pleased at the interruption even if it had to be Rusty. Lifting her hand from the keyboard, she massaged the bridge of her nose between her thumb and forefinger before starting to stand.

'No, stay where you are. No need to get up.' He settled in the chair opposite and, resting one foot across his knee, propped his elbow on his thigh. 'I take it Professor Ford has disappeared back to Liverpool?'

'Yes. Look, Rusty—'

But he interrupted her. 'There's no need to explain, Gabriella. I know how it is.' He pulled out a notebook from his pocket and removed a folded piece of paper. 'I've yet to type up my report from the Chivell autopsy but I thought you'd like the salient points.' He unfolded the paper and started speaking without waiting for a reply. 'Firstly it seems as if he tied plastic bags to her wrists so the prospect of any evidence from that source is unlikely. In addition, while sexual activity did take place, he used a condom so—'

'—there won't be any DNA. Bloody fantastic. Do you have anything that I can use?' she said, trying to keep the annoyance from her voice. 'I've been in touch with the CSIs and they didn't find anything.'

'Perhaps they weren't concentrating their efforts in the right place?'

'Excuse me?'

'I did find something – something, let's say, a little unusual.'

'How unusual?'

She was leaning forward, her arms propped on the desk, her gaze lingering on his face even as her thoughts diverted to Angus Ford and his departing comments.

Gaby had never been any good at reading men. If she had she'd have determined at one glance that Leigh Clark, the used car salesman she'd fallen for back in Cardiff, was a lying toad with a wife in the wings. She had only the opinion of Owen, Amy and Angus to lead her now – her gut instinct seemed to be on an extended break.

'Very.'

She blinked, immediately drawn back into the investigation while she waited for him to continue.

'She had a hair, just the one, secured around her small toe on her left foot, the foot nearest the door.' he clarified, his brows now almost meeting in the middle.

'And?'

He sat back, unfolding his legs. 'And if I didn't know any better, I'd swear in a court of law that it was left there deliberately.'

'Why?'

'God, Gabriella. You and your bloody whys! Because it screams of a plant, that's why. In all of the other crimes I've checked,

232

presumably attributed to our man, he's been assiduous in the absence of anything left that can be DNA tested. So much so that I can visualise him decked out in a full protective suit with shaved body hair to match. No, this is different. Our man doesn't make mistakes and this is a real doozy.'

'But – hold on a moment.' Gaby bit her thumb hard, her brow wrinkling. 'So this means that either he wants to be caught or . . .?'

'I'm sorry but I don't see it that way. Going back to what your friend Professor Ford said, the killer is on a power kick. He's carried out the most horrendous crimes for years without even a sliver of evidence. I can't buy that he only now decides to leave us a clue, no matter how many whys you strew in my path. I don't know why. I haven't a bloody clue why. That's your job.'

Her mind switched direction, landing on something Marie had said about that blasted button – something about the root and DNA extraction, her lips widening. 'I take it I'm going to get some useful DNA from this hair or . . .'

He nodded his head in affirmation, their eyes locking and staying locked until Gaby dropped hers to her desk and she started fiddling with her pen.

'Where's Conor?'

She knew she'd surprised him with her abrupt change of subject but she didn't care. She'd had a shit day and it looked like her evening was going to follow the same path unless she did something about it. It was time to make amends, not that she was admitting to being in the wrong. But he wasn't to know that.

Instead of the why she'd been expecting all he said was, 'He's on a sleepover.'

'In that case, what about joining me for a drink. No. Don't say anything, I know we've been here before just as I know that you're perfectly within your rights to decline but I do hope you won't.'

She could almost count the ticks of the clock while she waited for him to reply, hoping against hope that she hadn't made the hugest of miscalculations but, as the seconds stretched, fearing

233

exactly that. Maybe she'd left it too late. Maybe he had a girl-friend in tow. Maybe Owen and Amy in addition to Angus had been wrong.

'I'll let you buy me a drink but only if you'll let me take you out for a meal? And, to mirror your words, before you start objecting, I missed lunch. If I start pouring alcohol on this' – he patted his stomach – 'I'll be legless in no time.'

'Now that's something I must see. I'd like to pop home quickly to change if that's not too much of a problem?' She reached behind her chair for her jacket, dropped her mobile into her bag and picked up her briefcase.

'Fine by me. I was beginning to wonder if you'd taken up smoking?'

'Ha, that bad,' she said on a laugh. 'Come on. Knowing our luck they'll find another body for us.'

'Possible but unlikely. Chinese or Indian?'

'What about Italian?'

234

Chapter 46

Jax

Thursday 23 July, 7.30 p.m. St Asaph Police Station

Jax had another hour to waste before picking up Georgie from her late shift at the hospital and with empty pockets to match his empty bank account, he had two choices. Go home or stay in the office – and while he had the greatest regard for both his parents, sitting in front of the TV with a plate of food poised on his knee while they mulled over their day didn't do it for him anymore. His mum would do what she always did and keep something warm for him in the oven. He was quite happy with the incident room to himself while he used the high-speed broadband to stream music on his phone, all the time continuing to work on the puzzle that was Leo Hazeldine. He didn't mind staying late and, in this case, he felt he owed it to the department and to himself to try and piece together why Leo had been killed.

Reviewing the life of an unknown individual was very different to the celebrity-style obituaries that seemed to pop up within hours of the death of somebody famous. Leo hadn't been famous.

If anything he'd been a dropout. Whether that had been influenced by what had happened on the Great Orme all those years ago was difficult to say but Jax thought it likely. Within a year of Angelica's death he'd flunked veterinary college and fled to Australia, something that was easy to track through university and passport records. But Jax knew all that. He also knew exactly what Leo's mother had said when Malachy had travelled down to see her. What he didn't know was what kind of a man he'd been. While he'd dipped into the interviews after Angelica's death, of which there'd been six in total, there wasn't much to fill the gaps in his mind simply because DI Tipping had ruled him out in the end as being irrelevant.

It all came down to motive and opportunity. Why would Leo Hazeldine murder his girlfriend only to leave her untouched body on the Orme? A question that didn't change in importance now they knew he was gay. He'd have had the opportunity all right if someone had gone to collect him from his residential in Blaenau Ffestiniog, but who and why were currently unanswerable questions.

Jax was diligent to the core, liking nothing better than sifting through piles of documents for that one stray illusive fact. It was a skill he'd honed at school. Socially isolated by his peers because of his stutter, he'd quickly learnt that the quickest way to avoid the bullies was to stay out of their way. The school library became his refuge, the large catalogue of books in some way helping to alleviate his feelings of anxiety and inferiority. Speech therapy helped to improve his self-esteem but only up to a point. Joining the police force and asking Georgie out had done the rest. There were lots of better places to be other than sitting behind his desk doing a background search with Drake's latest album playing in the background – at that moment he couldn't think of a single one.

Leo Makepiece Martinez né Hazeldine, born on the 5th February 1976 to Elise Makepiece Hazeldine, spinster. He only glanced at the certificate. The blank space where his father's name was meant to be filled out in the same black spidery handwriting, told its own story.

The fact that Leo had been brought up in a one-parent family held no bearing on the case, but it directed Jax along a path he wouldn't ordinarily have followed. His next step, already pencilled down on his notepad, was to look into Leo's school records but instead he changed his mind, his fingers tapping on the desk even as his attention flickered to the tiny clock on the lower right-hand side of the screen and where time was fast running out if he didn't want to be late in picking up Georgie. He had time, just, to go through one last box file marked Leo Hazeldine. He'd gone through all the rest. And that's where he found it, nestling right at the top.

How could he ever have doubted that DI Tipping wouldn't be anything less than thorough? They'd sifted through all relevant portals, gathering acres of evidence. Their only downfall had been in not realising the importance of the marriage certificate in front of him. A marriage certificate that changed everything.

He grabbed his jacket and phone before making his way up the flight of stairs to Gaby's office only to realise that he must have missed her. Instead of hanging around he tore down to reception.

'DI Darin?'

'She left five minutes ago,' Clancy said with a frown.

'But I need to . . .' He stared down at his phone, starting to type.

'I suggest you wait until morning unless it's urgent, lad,' he said, his voice for once laced with steel. 'It looks like she has other things on her mind.'

237

Chapter 47

Gaby

Thursday 23 July, 10 p.m. La Dolce Vita, Rhos-on-Sea

Gaby and Rusty had finished their meal and were lingering over coffee when her mobile rang. They were both of a mind to continue the evening despite the empty tables and the waiter starting to set up for tomorrow. She couldn't remember when she'd enjoyed a meal more and that included the disastrous six months in Cardiff with Leigh. Then she'd been swayed by the breadth of his shoulders and his cheeky grin but bored to distraction with a conversation that only had two themes: football and sex.

Rusty, on the other hand, had an eager, enquiring mind, which matched her own, thought for thought. She'd been concerned that they'd have nothing to talk about outside of work but it was a subject they barely touched upon. Halfway through her plate of spaghetti marinara she couldn't remember why she hadn't liked him. By the end she was wondering if she should invite him back for a coffee. A decision she didn't have to make in the end.

238

She glanced at her screen before picking up, shooting an apologetic look in his direction.

'Jax, everything all right?' she said, when clearly it wasn't.

'I'm really sorry to interrupt your evening, ma'am.'

'Don't worry about it. What do you want to tell me?' She waited a moment, the phone cradled in her ear while she lifted up her bag and pulled out her wallet only to have it taken out of her hand and popped back inside. But apart from offering Rusty a gentle smile in acknowledgement, she barely noticed that he'd stepped away to the bar to pay.

'Okay, if you can hold the fort, I'll be along shortly.' She returned the phone to her bag and picked up her jacket but didn't bother to put it on.

'I take it there's been a development in the case?' Rusty said, his hand on her elbow.

'Yes. I'm afraid so. That was Jax. He found something earlier but was reluctant to phone. Instead he returned to the office after dropping off his girlfriend and did some more digging.'

She watched him pause, his hand still on her elbow as he stared down at her. 'And?'

'And it's a good job I'm well versed in the art of eking out a single glass of wine. I'm going to have to go back into the office. He's waiting for me. Sorry for having to end the evening like this.'

'And here was me thinking that the call was a ruse to ensure I didn't take advantage.'

'Would you have?' she said, her eyelashes flickering along with her pulse.

He lifted his hand and tapped the end of her nose with his knuckle before heading to his car. 'Definitely. Come on. Get in. I might as well drive you there, I'm not going to sleep as it is after—' he turned, his gaze hovering between her eyes and her lips '—all that garlic.'

239

Chapter 48

Owen

Friday 24 July, 7.15 a.m. Owen's House

'No, you stay there and have a lie-in. I might as well get Pip sorted. Won't be long, darling. I'll bring you back some of those croissants you like.' Kate gave him a quick kiss on the lips before slipping out of bed and heading for the door, clean clothes bundled under one arm.

Owen rested his head against the padded headboard and, arms above his head, stretched, relishing in having the bed to himself for once. When they'd bought the house one of the first things they'd saved for was a king-sized divan, complete with parachute-sized sheets and a duvet that needed an acrobat to change the cover. Now he wished he'd gone all the way and purchased a super king. With Kate taking up more than her fair share and Pip coming in every morning for a snuggle, he spent most of the time clinging to the edge. Of course the thing that would make it perfect would be to have Kate by his side and, as much as he loved his son, a morning without him bouncing between them.

240

The morning plan had been a quick breakfast before hauling himself back into the office, a plan upset by Kate's currently empty jar of pickled onions. So, instead of having to help with Pip he found himself dropping off again for an impromptu little snooze . . .

He jerked from sleeping to waking, his heart in his mouth at the sound of the phone ringing in his ear. He'd had no plans to nod off, but after the stress of recent days that's exactly what had happened. He scrubbed a hand across his beard before answering, his voice gravelly.

Owen was laidback to a fault. Nothing worried him and, most days, he was the voice of reason in the office. There was no trace of that Owen Bates as the phone slipped through his fingers and landed on the floor with a crash. And it was a very different Owen that grabbed a pile of clothes from his wardrobe without a thought for what went where – it was only luck that ensured he left the house within sixty seconds of dropping the phone, with his keys, mobile and a pair of shoes that actually matched. The drive to the supermarket was a short one, five minutes on a good day. He managed it in two with no loss of life but a few near misses along the way.

His car was abandoned, strewn across a multitude of spaces, the door left wide, the keys on the passenger seat. He tore across the strip of tarmac and to the police car that was waiting, his son, Pip, having the time of his life sitting on a PC's lap while he played with his walkie talkie.

Much to his son's annoyance, Owen bent down and lifted him out of the car, burying his head in his neck before lifting up his war-ravished face.

'Where is she? Where is my wife?'

241

Chapter 49

Kate

Friday 24 July, 7.55 a.m. Supermarket

Kate heard the words, not believing them at first.

'Come quietly and this will be just between you and me – or do you want to end up like your sister? One shout and I'll take the boy too.'

She had no choice after that. She'd always said she'd give up her life for her child, never for a moment thinking that she'd have to prove it.

He walked her towards his car and settled her in the passenger seat, even taking the time to fasten her belt for her. To the rest of the people in the car park it must have looked exactly what it wasn't, a happy couple out doing their morning shopping. But she knew differently, her gaze focused on Pip, still strapped into the shopping trolley, his little face starting to wrinkle up into a scream. She watched him until the car pulled out of the space and did a U-turn before following the one-way system out into the busy morning traffic. Then she closed her eyes and her mind to all thoughts bar one. The man that murdered her sister. Here. Now. What next?

242

Chapter 50

Gaby

Friday 24 July, 8.55 a.m. Supermarket

'Oh my God, Owen?'

Gaby flew across the now empty car park, her trainers making quick work of the distance. There was no trace of the smartly turned out detective in her old joggers and Def Leppard T-shirt but then she wasn't acting like a copper. She was acting like his friend. No. She was his friend. She'd been heading for the shower when she'd received his call and had literally dropped everything before running out of the house and jumping into her car.

'She's been kidnapped, Gaby. Oh God. What am I going to do?'

There were plenty of things Gaby could have done and probably should have. As his friend she could have dragged him into a hug but she didn't. She could even have tried to placate him with words of comfort but he'd know that's all they would be. Words with no substance. Instead she did the only thing possible. She took charge.

243

'Diane, isn't it?' she said, recognising PC Diane Carbone, recently transferred from the Llandudno station. 'Tell me what happened and, while she's doing that, Owen, I need you to round up the troops for an emergency meeting.' She softened her voice. 'Come on now, my friend, it's time to be strong, if not for you then for Kate. We're going to find her but we need the team to help us. I'm not going to stop you from joining us but there's your son to sort out too, remember,' she said, tilting her head in the direction of the officer who was currently breaking all the rules by letting Pip try on his helmet.

She watched him slope off, a broken man if ever there was one. She only managed to stop herself from following him by the sound of Diane's voice.

'Ma'am?'

'A quick low down, Diane. Only the significant points if you please.'

She nodded her head in reply. 'Katherine Bates apparently left her house at around 7.45 to go to the supermarket. At 8 a.m. the store was alerted by a customer to a child left abandoned in a trolley. He, the child that is, was able to point out his car. We did a quick check and—'

'Okay,' she interrupted. 'What about witnesses?'

'Only two. A couple. Mr and Mrs Torrence, but there's not much. A tall man, helping his heavily pregnant wife into the car. No make or model but something dark. I already have someone checking through the CCTV footage to see if we can get a number plate.'

'Good.' She removed her phone from her pocket and pressed the well-remembered number. 'I'm going to ask DCI Sherlock to coordinate the search from this end, Diane. I'm needed elsewhere.'

She pulled a frown, again putting herself in the mind of the perpetrator just like Angus had taught her, all those months ago in Liverpool, only now she wished she'd listened harder and taken more notes. There was too much to lose. The obvious answer was

244

that Kate had been taken by someone who knew her, and possibly even because of her relationship to Owen. But she pushed that aside for later, concentrating instead on the sequence of events in the car park. It was far too early to speculate as to the reason for the abduction. It could also have been a random attack, Gaby reminded herself, but she didn't think so. It all sounded too quick and easy for it not to have been planned – therefore it was likely that she'd been followed from the house.

'I also want a team over at Owen's ASAP. The neighbours all need to be interviewed in case they saw something suspicious. I doubt there'll be CCTV but who knows. Phone me if there's anything – even the smallest thing. I'll be at the station.'

She ran across to her car, barely registering that she'd left the engine running. But instead of shifting into gear, she paused a moment, unable to quite believe the horror story unfolding out in front of her. And along with thoughts of inadequacy came the thought of guilt. What if it was as she feared and related to Angelica's murder? What if, instead of flopping into bed at 2 a.m., she'd stayed in the office to carry on looking into Jax's lead? If they had, perhaps Kate would even now be off somewhere playing happy families with Owen instead of . . .

245

Chapter 51

Kate

Friday 24 July, 9.15 a.m. A55

Kate, like Owen, had been born in Llandudno, only moving to St Asaph when Owen had been promoted onto the MIT, so she guessed that was her abductor's destination, something that was confirmed when he turned onto the A55. Llandudno was where it had all started. It seemed fitting that's where it should end.

Hunched up in the corner as far away from him as possible, the other thing she realised was that she recognised him but she didn't have a clue where from. There was something in his steely blue eyes and build that tickled her memory banks. She'd seen him and recently but as to who he was . . . she didn't have a clue.

There was no point in speaking. She'd tried that only to be told to shut up. There was also no point in opening the door and throwing herself on the mercy of the Friday traffic smearing the roads. She might have tried it if she hadn't been pregnant or if he hadn't centrally locked the car. She remained still to the point of hardly breathing but her mind wasn't quiet. Her mind

246

was pooling all its resources in trying to find a way out of her current predicament. There had to be some reason for him taking her outside of the obvious because she was as sure as she could be that it wasn't for her body. So if not her body then what? Her mind? But she didn't know anything. Certainly not something that would be of any interest to him.

They were driving along the seafront past Colwyn Bay and then Penrhyn Side, the hill of the Little Orme stretching out in front of them. The sign at the brow, Welcome to Llandudno, was almost her undoing and it was only thoughts of what he might do to her and her baby that dried the hysterical laughter up at source. Instead she huddled back even further into the corner. If she had any wish now it would be to press herself so hard that she'd vanish into the black moulding that lined the interior. But knowing the futility of such thoughts, she did the only thing possible and disappeared into that place inside her head where images of Owen, Pip and an unlikely rescue flickered through the darkness behind her closed eyelids.

247

Chapter 52

Gaby

Friday 24 July, 9.30 a.m. St Asaph Police Station

It was still only 9.30 but it felt much later, almost as if a lifetime had passed since Gaby had received the call which had made her drop everything in her race to get to the supermarket. She'd guessed that it must be Rusty, who'd promised to phone her in the morning. But she hadn't thought of him even once since and she wasn't thinking of him now. Now she had a team to command in the largest search that North Wales had ever seen despite hope fading faster than the coffee machine's ability to keep up with demands for its evil brew. The Golden Hour had long since passed. If a missing person was going to be found, the odds were it was going to be within those first frantic few glossy minutes. They were well past the first hour and screaming through the second.

Gaby had spent years perfecting her abrupt persona and it was only this mask that protected her despite the team showing distinct signs of bending to snapping. They looked to her for direction and that's exactly what she intended to do until circumstances dictated otherwise. There would come a time when she'd

248

have to slope off back to her house and let the tide of emotion rip through her barricades, but that was a long way off.

Owen was leaning by the window, alternating his attention between the car park and his coffee mug. He hadn't said a word since arriving back in the incident room after dropping Pip off at his parents'. He didn't need to. The tilt of his head and the slump of his shoulders was testament to the personal crisis that was ravishing through his mind and body if the shake of his hand wasn't evidence enough. There was nothing Gaby could do for him except keep him busy and keep him away from the centre of the search. While she had a duty to her staff, her responsibility lay with Kate and her unborn child. She only hoped Owen would see it that way.

She walked over to him, placing a hand on his arm to gain his attention. 'We'll do everything we can, Owen, but I do need you to stay focused. You know the Great Orme better than anyone so I'd like you to track down the warden; what's his name again?'

'Dafydd Griffiths.'

'That's it. Give him a bell to get things moving. The mines are as good a place as any to hide someone.'

'But ma'am?'

'No, Owen.' She tightened her grip briefly before dropping her hand and shoving it into the pocket of her joggers. 'You know I can't have you here and that's nothing to do with anything other than your ability to be impartial. In all honesty, I should be sending you home with our Amy and I would if I thought that you'd actually stay there. So I want you to hunt down Dafydd from wherever it is he's hiding. All we're going to be doing here is background stuff – stuff that, if you're honest with yourself, you're not going to be able to concentrate on. I promise you with everything I have that as soon as I hear anything you'll be the first to know.'

She watched a gamut of expressions roll across his face: disbelief, anger and grief closely followed by a trace of fear. At the sight of the last one she had to school her features and relax her hands from where they were bunched up in her pockets. She knew the

249

same fear, an emotion every copper had to vanquish if there was to be any chance of success.

The team remained silent for a good ten seconds when the door closed behind his back, no one quite sure of what to say, their attention now fixed on Gaby and where she'd propped her hip in its usual position against the edge of the desk. There was nothing they could say. It was up to her now.

Gaby finally spoke. There was no point with a preamble. 'Either this is a random abduction or it's tied up with the work we've been doing on Angelica's murder. As time is limited, we're going to have to go with the likeliest which, sadly, is the latter.' She turned to Jax. 'Tell the rest of the team what you told me.' She lifted her head, her gaze capturing his look of embarrassment at being put in the spotlight.

'T-t-there's not a lot really,' he said, flushing scarlet. 'I had to hang around before picking up Georgie so I decided to do some more searching into Leo's background. I know that you and Marie went to see the mother, but a question came up that I needed to confirm. After I dropped Georgie home I returned to the station to do some fact-checking in case it was nothing. I even managed to speak to the care home and had a very one-sided conversation with Leo's mother.'

'And the news that prompted your call?' Gaby reminded him gently.

'Oh yes, s-s-sorry. Elise Makepiece Hazeldine was a single mum but she did eventually marry when Leo was six although the marriage broke down when he was seventeen. I've checked through the court transcript and the cause for the divorce is cited as unreasonable behaviour.' Jax rubbed his hand over the back of his neck and took a deep breath. 'The thing is there was another child involved, a boy a few years younger, which would make him Leo's stepbrother. She tried to get custody but the son's father wouldn't hear of it.'

'And the child's name?' said Marie, leaning forward in her chair.

'Samuel Eustace.'

250

Chapter 53

Kate

Friday 24 July, 9.20 a.m. The Butterworth House

All Kate could think of was the level of preparation he must have carried out, closely followed by the thought that there was no way anyone would think to look for her here. A house only fit for demolition. She'd heard of the tragedy, not from Owen but from an article on the front of the local newspaper. At first glance, the battle-scarred building was much worse than the photo, the hole puncturing the outer wall showing the dusky dark grey damage from the fire that had indiscriminately ripped through the house. She was still reeling from the sight when he swung into the garage and hopped out of the car, securing the up and over door closed behind him.

Time paused for a second, while she adjusted to the sudden darkness but, with no light from any source, she might as well have been blind.

'Come on.' He wrenched open the passenger door with a confidence which shouted that he knew where he was going and, tugging on her arm, half pulled, half dragged her out of the car.

251

'Where are you taking me?'

'You'll know soon enough,' was all he said, now pushing her through a doorway and into the main body of the house.

At least she could see with the light from the window, but it wasn't the house that now scared her, both of her hands cradling her belly, the skin taut under her fingers. It was the thick smell of damp, wet, charred remains that pervaded the air. It smelt of decay. No. It smelt of death.

'Down the stairs. Hold on to the bannister. Don't want anything to happen to you, yet.'

Downstairs was slightly better not that she had time to notice. He propelled her into what must have once been the lounge, the full-length patio doors leading out onto a small brick-paved walled seating area pierced with a wooden gate and the beach beyond. The walls, once white, now a dirty grey. The cream carpet squelched underfoot. The table and lamps were strewn across the floor.

He walked over to the window and closed the vertical blinds before picking up a couple of chairs.

'Sit. It's time for a little chat.'

Kate sat. There was nothing else she could do. Sit and pray to anyone that might be listening.

252

Chapter 54

Gaby

Friday 24 July, 9.35 a.m. St Asaph Police Station

Gaby ended the call and placed the mobile on the desk beside her. 'That was Diane. There's no answer from the Eustaces. She spoke to an elderly neighbour who hasn't seen the husband for a few days. The wife left first thing with a pile of carrier bags. Apparently, it's usual for her to do her weekly shop on a Friday. She even asked if there was anything she needed bringing back, which again is perfectly normal. We've tried contacting Eustace on his mobile but it's switched off – telling in itself. I've asked for an ANPR trace on both cars to be on the safe side.' She spread her hands, the drag of her T-shirt a sharp reminder of her appearance. She looked scruffy. She felt scruffy. She didn't care.

'So, what am I missing, lads? You need to help me here. Why a heavily pregnant woman? We know she's Angelica's sister and fits the profile but nowhere in any of this has a pregnant woman been targeted.'

253

'Unless he's taken her for a different reason altogether?' Marie said, her voice not as confident as her words.

Gaby scrutinised her, taking in her carefully styled hair although, like her, she must have left home dressed in whatever was close to hand when they'd phoned her. But instead of sloppy joggers, which Gaby was pretty sure Marie wouldn't give cupboard room to, she was dressed in jeans and a pretty summery top. She seemed better. More relaxed, something that was a huge relief for purely selfish reasons. Gaby needed her team at the top of their game if they were going to catch this maniac before it was too late.

'Explain?'

'I'm not sure if I can. All I'm saying is that we've had a whole pile of murders that appear to be loosely linked to the Penrhyn Yacht Club. Tony and Mary Butterworth were employed there as were Leo and Angelica. All of whom are now dead. But Samuel Eustace is younger, isn't he?' she said, tipping her head in Jax's direction.

'Four years, give or take.'

'So at fifteen he wouldn't have been of an age to work behind the bar but as the younger brother he'd have known the crowd Leo was hanging around with. What if he'd planned Angelica's abduction? As we all know, juvenile facilities are crawling with criminals still wet behind the ears.'

'That's all a bit far-fetched, isn't it? He wouldn't have been able to do it without help. And what hold would a kid have to force . . .' Gaby paused, her attention now fixed on Jax and the grin spreading across his cheeks. 'Okay, so Leo was gay,' she added, almost to herself. 'That might work. Younger brother bribing older brother to help him or he'll spill the beans. Leo probably didn't even know what it was about – some prank or other that went horribly wrong, leaving him with a lifetime of guilt. So, what's your theory on Tony and Mary then, Marie?'

'Well, he'd have needed Leo to drive, wouldn't he, as he didn't have a car . . .'

254

'So Samuel bribes Leo to help him or he'll squeal like a stuck pig but he still needs someone to pick him up from his residential placement,' Gaby said, thinking aloud even as she tilted her head at Malachy. 'Mal, get on to the DVLA and check to see when Tony and Mary passed their tests and whether either of them had cars or access to them? So, what we're thinking is a pact that lasted through the years. Four people irretrievably tied to that morning on the Great Orme and, in the meantime, he carries on with his killing spree, changing his modus operandi as he both ages and matures.' She jumped up from the desk and started to pace, her tight plait swinging behind her like a pendulum. 'That's all very well except for one thing. Why now? Something must have happened for him to suddenly start bumping them off – and why abduct Kate?' She swivelled on her heel, staring at each of them in turn, hope flickering like a fading candle about to run out of wax. What reason could Samuel Eustace have to change his MO and murder both Mary Butterworth and Leo Hazeldine? But there was more than that. A lot more because, of course, Tony Butterworth had died at his own hand, she thought, nibbling at her bottom lip. What could have happened for him to take his own life in such a spectacular fashion? And finally, what about poor Avril Eustace? She'd said herself that her parents didn't get on with her husband. Gaby wasn't a bit surprised but, with the hold he'd had over them, there was probably very little they were able to do to stop the wedding.

255

Chapter 55

Samuel

Friday 24 July, 9.45 a.m. The Butterworth House

'Tell me how you found out,' he finally said. 'Tell me before it's too late.'

'Tell you how I found out?' Kate repeated. 'Found out what?'

Samuel Eustace could see from the sheen on her skin and the way her eyes couldn't meet his that he had her exactly where he wanted. She was scared shitless that something was going to happen here in Mary and Tony's wreck of a house and in a way she was right. He couldn't let her live no matter what the outcome of his questioning. His gaze travelled down to rest on the tight bulge nearly bursting out of her thin sundress before returning to her blonde hair, any compassion he might have felt eradicated as he took in the almost white strands curling across her cheek. Even the barest glimpse and rage started to swell under his breastbone as memories flooded back.

The pitch-dark bedroom with posters from his favourite football team adorning the walls and his stomach still full of the shop-bought birthday cake instead of the handmade one he'd been used to. But all that had stopped when his stepmother had walked out a couple of weeks before his thirteenth birthday, leaving the faint trace of perfume and an old nightdress lost and forgotten in the bottom of the ironing pile. Instead of her chocolate gateau he'd been left to deal with the creak of the door and the sound of muffled slippers sliding across the floor. The feel of tight bony fingers grabbing onto his skinny frame. The dry scream in his throat as he stared up into the dead eyes of his father, his snowy white hair flowing around his shoulders, the putrid stench of his breath as he'd climbed on top of him.

Samuel had chosen Angelica as the answer to his redemption. He'd needed someone to go to, someone intelligent and kind that he could tell his secrets to but the one time he'd tried to talk to her she'd laughed in his face. She hadn't laughed that morning on the top of the Orme when he'd stripped her bare and dressed her in his stepmother's nightdress. She'd pleaded then, pleaded with everything she had. It had been almost too easy to subdue her with his words. Threats that if she didn't lie back and take what was coming to her then he'd look to her sister. The one thing he couldn't guard against was her death. He'd thought it a joke at first. Some joke as he'd watched the breath desert her body, leaving him to pick up the pieces. Four friends joined by one desperate act, an act constructed out of hate but shaped by silence and fear. He was as convinced as he'd ever been that Tony, Mary and Leo would never have acted against him. His stranglehold had been too tight. But that didn't change the reality of first Tony and then Leo's death. He didn't spare a thought for Mary and the carefully planned explosion. His lovely mother-in-law had only herself to blame when she'd started telling her secrets. No. Someone else must have known, he puzzled, scavenging back and forth through time before hovering on the person he'd only seen once in the inbetweening years. And yet he'd recognised her as Angelica's sister straight away that

257

day at the police station, his grip on the knife tight enough to weld tendon to bone.

In some part of Samuel's mind he knew that it wasn't just his father that was a monster but it wasn't a large enough part to make a difference. The only time he was able to gain any relief from his tortuous thoughts was when he was buried up to the hilt inside someone else's flesh, the sight of their fear the route to the peace he'd been denied. But that was all changing. His carefully planned lifestyle was being threatened and he needed to know why. He needed to know who was following his tracks and obliterating his history. It almost felt as if someone was wiping out his past with the deaths of both Tony and Leo. They were harmless, the pair of them. Innocent bystanders in the crock that was his life. People to be manipulated, just like his slut of a wife. He'd needed a cover, a high sheen of normality that would keep the ever-present threat of discovery at bay and what better way than a nonentity at home who could cook his meals and wash his clothes into the bargain.

'Really! You're going to play games,' he finally said, dragging his thoughts back to where they belonged. 'You don't seem to realise what a vulnerable position you're in, Katherine,' he said, purposefully looking at her stomach. 'So, what is it, a boy or a girl?'

'That's not relevant and I really have no idea what you're asking?' He watched her flick her tongue across dry lips, her hands two tight balls of anger. 'Tell me what you want to know?'

'I want to know who told you that it was me who took your sister. I want you to tell me what you're trying to gain from this. Leo wasn't a threat to anyone, for God's sake.' Samuel struggled to retain a grip on the conversation by pushing aside memories of those few glorious years when it had been just Elise and Leo. His father had been working then. Long months away ferrying goods up and down the length of the country. Life had been as good as it could be until the day they'd made him redundant.

Samuel's breath hitched in his throat and he blinked away the images. Life had changed in an instant and they'd had to watch his father descend into his own personal hell, trying to drag Elise and Leo with him. The image of his brother, lying on some slab, cold and solid, caused his hands to tremble and his mind to scatter.

'Leo was my brother and absolutely harmless. He'd never have turned against me.'

'No, he wouldn't.' They both turned to stare at the person walking towards them. 'But I would!'

Chapter 56

Gaby

Friday 24 July, 9.45 a.m. St Asaph Police Station

Clancy burst into the incident room, interrupting Gaby mid-sentence.

'Ma'am, we've had a call from Llandudno station. There's been a report of a possible break-in at the Butterworths'. They were all set to send out a couple of officers to investigate when some bright spark decided to phone us first.'

'What did they say?' Gaby had been thinking that they'd need a miracle. Perhaps this was it.

'The neighbours on the right, ma'am. They reported seeing a dark car slip into the garage, closing the door behind them. That was about thirty minutes ago.'

'For fuck's sake!'

'My thoughts exactly. But the neighbours wanted to make sure they hadn't got it wrong. They're just back from a walk around the property but there's nothing to see. All the curtains and blinds have been pulled.'

'But that's not right,' Gaby said with a start. 'I was around there yesterday and there was bright sunlight streaming in through the windows, before all that rain hit.' She hurried across the room, catching Malachy's eye. 'Mal, grab a car. I'll meet you out front. Marie and Jax, continue trying to work out what's going on and phone me with anything, no matter how small.'

'What about Sergeant Bates, ma'am?' Marie asked, lifting the lid on her laptop.

'What he doesn't know won't hurt him.'

Chapter 57

Kate

Friday 24 July, 10 a.m. The Butterworth House

Samuel jumped to his feet, his jaw slackening at the sight of the woman lunging at him, a black-handled kitchen knife clenched between her fist.

'What—?'

Kate watched the words die in his throat, never to be spoken, the thrust of the blade piercing through his skin and slicing through his flesh with a speed that defied logic. He took in a sharp intake of breath but whether this was in surprise, shock or pain it was difficult to tell, his hands now rounding on the handle of the knife. She wasn't sure what he was trying to do, but by the dimming of his gaze and slowness of his movements it was too little too late, his hands faltering. She stared, open-mouthed, as he swayed sideways and toppled to the floor, the spreading lake of blood almost black against the pale carpet.

He was dead but the thought brought no relief to Kate. Owen was always saying what a strong person she was to cope with everything that life kept hurling at her. What he really meant was that she had to be strong to stay married to a copper. That or stupid, she didn't know which. But it was easy to have strength and determination when she knew that she had to guard Pip. After all, losing a sister tended to sharpen the mind as to what the dangers were.

Now, with the first cramp-like pain shooting from her core and the first trickle of moisture pooling between her legs, she was scared, more scared than she'd ever been. Pip's birth had been difficult. They'd ended up having to agree to an emergency caesarean section in the end and she'd been warned of the risks involved in trying to give birth naturally, risks she was prepared to take with the support of a team of trained midwives and obstetricians only a shout away. But this wasn't hospital. This wasn't the clean, almost sterile environment with a call bell at hand and an expectant father gripping her fingers. This was the black hole of hell with the devil beckoning from the abyss.

She closed her eyes but not her mind to the trickle, blooming into a gush. The back of her dress was a mass of sodden cotton, her tightly gripped thighs unable to stem the flow. Now she wasn't scared. Now she was terrified.

'Well, well, see what we've got here. Little wifey looking fit to pop.'

Kate lifted her head, careful to avoid the mound of dead man in front of her. She'd made the mistake of glancing that way a few seconds ago and wouldn't be repeating it. She should feel safe at the thought that he was dead but she couldn't. She still didn't know his name or who he was, not that it mattered. The mad man had been replaced by the mad woman and this time there'd be no one to save her.

Heaving air into her lungs, her hands cradling her stomach, she knew she was within seconds of full panic mode – something she had to divert. There was no one here to save her bar herself. But pregnant, with the sharp stab of contractions starting to build, her options were limited.

The air was heavy and silent, the woman in front of her watchful, the long thin knife, now wiped clean, difficult to ignore. She could plead. She could beg. No. She needed to waste time, what little time she had left, and think up a plan. There must be something she could either say or do to distract her.

'Please. I don't understand?'

'You don't understand? And what? You want me to explain it to you like some toddler sitting on its mother's knee? There's not a lot to explain. There lies before you the man that murdered your sister. A man that has raped and murdered a plethora of women just because he could. He had to be stopped, Katherine, and I seemed to be the ideal choice.'

Kate lifted her eyebrows at the use of her name when she still had no idea who it was bouncing the blade of the knife off their legs. But her mind quickly lost its train, as an urgent need wiped away all sensible thought aside apart from one. The need to push.

Sweat poured and tears gathered but the strength that had first attracted Owen to her fragile blonde beauty remained in her next words – more of a gasp really, her body consumed by a force outside of her control.

'Why? Why you and – not the police?'

'Because he happens to be the man who murdered my mother. He also happens to be my husband. My man. My responsibility.'

264

Chapter 58

Gaby

Friday 24 July, 10.10 a.m. A55

The drive from St Asaph along the A55 usually took thirty minutes on a good day. But with the sun shimmering out of the heavens and everyone heading to the beach it was far from ideal driving weather. With Malachy behind the wheel of the squad car, sirens blazing, it took half that. He only slowed down at the top of the hill on the approach to the house, the sparkling sea along the length of Llandudno promenade dimmed by a light haze stretching out as far as the pier and the Great Orme rising up above it like some benevolent uncle.

'Right, Mal, you take the back. I'll go in through the garage being as I was only here yesterday and remember the layout.' Gaby pulled open the glove compartment, withdrawing a couple of powerful flashlights. 'Don't use this unless you need to. It's probably more than likely nothing but we can't be too careful.' She stepped out of the car, paused with her hand still on the doorframe, her look frank. 'I know you're built like the proverbial brick shitter but I don't want any fatalities on my watch so let's be extra cautious – radio Llandudno station for back-up, bearing in mind that technically this is their patch.'

The garage door lifted with barely a squeak and, after a cursory glance at the car to check that it was empty, she made use of the light coursing in to locate the arched entrance into the back of the hall, her trainers disguising the sound of her footsteps. She didn't bother with the stairs up to the bedrooms above because there was little point. That part of the house was barely standing and any thief would know better than to try to ransack it. The open-plan lounge, set on the middle floor with its panoramic beach-filled views, had taken the brunt of the blast and it was easy to see that there was no sign of any life amongst the blackened, charred remains. Instead she headed for the stairs and to the lower floor with its clutch of bedrooms and second lounge, her hand snaked over the bannister, her ears pinned for any sign of noise. She halted on the bottom step, breath paused at the tableau unfolding before her. Kate on her knees, her head stretched back by a hand that grasped onto a fistful of hair, reminiscent of an execution type pose as the blade started its descent across her neck. The lifeless body of Samuel Eustace slumped at her feet.

Time paused only to be broken by the sound of shattering glass behind her. But instead of beckoning Malachy in, she stopped him with a lift of her hand, all her attention on the woman in front of her.

'Please think this through, Avril. He's dead. He can't hurt you anymore.'

'Don't you see? It's too late for that. I'm damaged goods, damaged beyond redemption.'

'No one's too late to change. We know what he did. We know the kind of man you married. This isn't your fault.'

Avril Eustace stood back, stretching to her full height of five-foot-one or two, the knife now pointing in a very different direction. 'If you think that, you're as mad as he was. I told you

266

I killed my mother.' She laughed, a hollow sound. 'You didn't believe me then. But I did, as surely as if I'd been the one to turn on the gas and place her hand on the switch instead of my husband. And do you know the very best bit? If it hadn't been for her brain tumour, I'd never have known about him. I'd have perhaps remained married to the murdering bastard forever. It all came out, albeit in fits and starts. The whole unhappy story. Her infidelity with anything in trousers including Samuel, which he used like a gun to her head when he needed someone to collect Leo from that farm he was working on. Her forcing my father to help Leo bundle Angelica into the car. She signed her own death warrant and she didn't even know. It might have been all right if I hadn't asked him to pick me up from the house that one time. But one look at my mother, and the rubbish she was spouting, and he knew that his dirty little secret was about to be exposed.' She wiped the back of her hand across her eyes. 'If I tell you that I also murdered my father, will you believe me? No, probably not.' She shook her head. 'It wasn't intentional but that won't count. As soon as he realised that Samuel had been screwing his wife right up to her health failing it did the trick rather nicely. It was all there in the letters she'd hidden so carefully, letters he found me reading. The money she'd had to find for Samuel to start his little empire. The hold he had over her financially and emotionally.' She dropped to her knees, bending over the blade, her gaze switching between Gaby and Malachy. 'Samuel blew up my mother and as good as murdered my father so I decided to give him a taste of his own medicine and kill the only person he'd ever loved – other than himself, of course. His brother.'

Gaby walked across the room, her hand outstretched, her expression resolute. 'Avril, if you do this, he wins and we can't let that happen. They'll take Samuel's behaviour into account and the fact that, without your intervention, we'd probably still be scratching our heads at the unusual number of murders on our patch. Come on now. Let me help you.'

She could sense that Avril was wavering and, in that second, she walked that final distance and took the knife, which had already started to fall from her suddenly loose fingers.

'I'm going to have to take you into custody but I promise I'll do what I can,' Gaby said, placing the cuffs around her wrists.

'Ma'am! You need to—'

Gaby twisted her head, only now aware of what was happening on the other side of the room.

Kate.

Chapter 59

Gaby

Saturday 24 July, 9.50 a.m. The Butterworth House

'I can't. I'm sorry. I have to push.'

Gaby must have missed that part of her training because any thought that she knew how to deliver a baby flew from her brain. There was something about lots of hot water and towels – lots and lots of towels but . . . she stared around the remains of the house knowing all too well she'd find none of those things here.

'Kate. Let's get you onto the floor.' She grabbed her under the arms, gently lowering her onto a clear patch of carpet before finding a damp cushion for under her head.

'There. That's more comfortable isn't it,' she said, trying to hide her horror at the sight of Kate's knees, as if controlled by some hidden strings, bending up and opening wide. 'You need to hold on a little bit longer and breathe. That's it. In and out. In and out. I'm going to get Mal to radio for an . . .'

The sound of a loud crash had her turning her head, her mouth dropping open at Malachy Devine, one of the tallest, broadest men she'd ever met, stretched out in a dead faint. Nothing on

269

earth could have stemmed the expletive gathering momentum on her tongue except the suddenly scared look crossing Kate's face. Shifting her gaze, she glanced at Avril and where she was sitting staring at the floor. It was all down to her now.

'That's men for you. He has to go and collapse and just when I was starting to like the big lummox too. Okay. It's you and me, kid. You'd better believe that I've got this,' she said, her calm exterior making a strong attempt at hiding the terror within. 'I'm going to slip off your knickers and see what's . . . Ah. Okay. So we've got a head. A fine head of black hair.'

'Gaby, I need to push, now.'

'In one second, my sweet. I just need to find something to wrap junior in.'

But with nothing available, Gaby slipped off her T-shirt, turning it inside out before wrapping her hands in the fabric like a pair of gloves. 'Right then, my lovely. Take another big, deep breath and hold when I tell you. Junior is keen but remember I'm the novice here. On the count of three, push.'

Gaby guided the head out from its home for the last nine months, her hands supporting the baby's crown as if it were made from china, her mind dragging through the depths for the next bit. Now that she was here, she remembered the video they all had to watch on an annual basis, the bones of the talk coming back to her, a talk that had the women crossing their legs and the men cracking sick jokes.

'Panting next, I believe. Tell me when the next urge hits so I'm ready.'

Shoulders, arms, tummy, bottom, legs, toes . . . Gaby counted the parts out in the silence of her mind, not even realising that she'd stopped breathing until the weight of the baby in her arms prompted the need for air. With a quick sweep of her hand down the baby's face, she cleared the nose and mouth, a small smack to the bottom did the rest, the sound of the baby's cry the sweetest music she'd ever heard.

'Well, my dear, you and Owen have a beautiful daughter.'

270

Chapter 60

Gaby

Monday 27 July, 3 p.m. St Asaph Hospital

'Kate and I would like to ask you something important.'

Gaby had arrived on the maternity unit, her arms filled with a pile of pink baby clothing that she'd stopped to pick up along the way. She hadn't intended to stay long, only long enough to be sure that she hadn't done either Kate or the baby any irreparable damage. Now she paused at the sound of Owen's obviously pre-prepared speech, sparing a thought for the adorable little dot even now asleep in her dad's arms.

'I appreciate the sentiment but there's more than enough babies named after me and, while I don't mind Darren so much, Gabriella is such a mouthful for little tongues to get around.'

She watched the hasty look they exchanged and knew immediately she'd gotten it wrong, yet again.

'Well, actually, that wasn't what we'd like to ask you although there's nothing wrong with your name or anything. It's just that we've decided to call her—'

271

'What Owen is trying to say is that we're calling her Angelica,' Kate interrupted. 'No. What we'd like is for you to tear up Owen's letter of resignation, that is, if it's not too late?' She ran a hand down her daughter's plump cheek before dropping it on Owen's knee. 'I never realised before quite what it must mean to him, being a detective, that is. You saved my life, Gaby, and that of Angelica's. But in stopping Owen from doing the job he loves, I'd be ruining his.'

There was an unusual hush over the station, something that Gaby had experienced on a few other occasions. That day in Swansea when she'd returned to work following the death of one of her colleagues. Her first day back after being stabbed and now . . . the first recorded interview with Avril Eustace, married to a murderer and a murderer in her own right. But also a victim.

It had taken all weekend for them to get to this point. Gaby and her team had worked solid twelve-hour shifts gathering evidence and collecting statements while Avril, collapsed at the scene, had spent the last two nights under armed guard at the local hospital while the doctors assessed both her physical and mental health.

With a flick of her wrist, Gaby switched on the microphone and settled back in her chair, comforted by the sight of Amy by her side and Andy Parrish opposite. As a lawyer, he was one of the best. But as a man he was one of the kindest and that's what Avril Eustace needed right now.

Even after the passage of only a couple of days, Avril had diminished, retreating under the cover of her thoughts, thoughts which couldn't offer her any comfort. It didn't take an expert to see that she was at breaking point and plans were already in place to remove her to a secure hospital for further assessment before any decisions could be made about her future. Would she be fit enough to stand trial? Gaby might be in a better place to answer that after the interview.

With a glass of water pushed beside a large box of tissues, she started to speak, getting the formalities out of the way first.

'Mrs Eustace, you've told us already about your mother sharing her secrets about Angelica's death but what made you suspect that your husband had carried on with his killing spree?'

Avril lifted her head, her skin stretched over bone, her eyes deep pools of despair. There was no hope in their depths, only fear laced with self-loathing.

'I've known since just after our honeymoon what kind of a man I'd married but by then it was too late.' She laughed, but it was far from a humorous sound. 'A damaged man without honour, sympathy or the capacity for anything other than hatred in that black heart of his. He hated women. He hated men. But primarily I think he hated himself most of all. I knew he was screwing around right from the start.' She dropped her gaze, her hands tight balls of anger. 'He certainly wasn't sharing my bed, even on my wedding night.' She started picking at her nails, her attention focused on peeling back a piece of loose skin. 'After my mother let slip about Angelica I started following him. All those nights when he was meant to be working and instead he was wandering the streets picking his next victim.' She looked up then, her lips paper-dry, her cheeks damp. 'You have to believe me that I would have done something if I'd known what he was planning. The truth is he deserved to die and I'm pleased that I was the one to kill him.'

273

Chapter 61

Gaby

Monday 27 July, 4.10 p.m. St Asaph Station

Instead of returning to the incident room and the team of officers that had been brought in to unravel exactly how many rapes and murders could be linked to Samuel Eustace, Gaby headed for the quiet of her office and the pile of paperwork that had been silently growing ever since she'd returned from sick leave. Was it only four weeks ago? It felt like a lifetime. But the very first thing she did was to pull out the letter that had been haunting her top drawer and tear it to shreds without opening it. Owen had made the right decision for now. That might change in the future but she hoped not. She was delighted that he'd been allowed a second chance at trying to manage his work-life balance. It was something that she should perhaps think of doing for herself if only she knew how.

Gaby appreciated more than anyone the importance of being given a second chance. In her case she'd needed a third before finding both a place and a job that seemed to suit her. For Avril Eustace, currently being detained under caution at St Asaph's

274

Custodial Suite while they tried to untangle the layers of her involvement, at least her willingness to cooperate would go in her favour. Samuel had manipulated her right from the beginning and, with the psychiatrists involved, who knew what the outcome would be.

'Ah, Detective Darin, having a little rest, are we?'

Gaby glanced up to find Rusty Mulholland propping up the doorway and felt a smile break.

'Don't you think I deserve it after the weekend I've had?'

'Ah yes.' He placed a coffee in front of her and sat in the chair opposite, his own cup cradled between his fingers. 'I have a bone to pick with you for practising on my patch,' he said, his eyes twinkling. 'Delivering babies one minute. The next thing, you'll be taking an Open University course in forensic pathology.'

'Ha. Bloody. Ha. As if.' She rested her elbows on the table, balancing her chin in her hands. 'I'll have you know I've never been more scared of anything in all my life. Let's get one thing clear, Doctor. You stick to your job and I'll stick to mine. The baby part wasn't too bad but the umbilical—'

He held up his hand. 'You really don't have to go into details. I have delivered a couple of brats in my time. I do appreciate a woman who knows her place though. What are you like at washing the dishes?'

She stuck her tongue out before returning her attention to her coffee, suddenly at a loss as to what to say. 'So . . .'

'So, Gabriella. I do have news.'

'Oh really?' she said, unsure now whether the visit was as informal as she'd originally supposed and then annoyed with herself at the thought. 'Do tell.'

'We've had the DNA back and the hair wrapped around Tilly Chivell's little toe came from Samuel Eustace.'

'Yes, something confirmed by Avril. Did you know she admitted to having followed him that night? That was when the penny finally dropped.'

275

'That must have been difficult for her.'

'Almost impossible, I'm guessing. Between you and me I'm not unhappy that he's dead.' She lifted her cup only to settle it back down on the desk between them. It wasn't the only thing between them. 'Last time we met up it was good,' she finally managed, her attention now fully trained on the thick black liquid.

'It was more than good,' he said, tapping the back of her hand with his index finger. 'I'd go as far as to say we should repeat it very soon but—'

'But?'

'But Conor has broken up for the summer break and I'm not prepared to let him take second best even for you. He's been through enough with being pushed here, there and everywhere by his mother. Prepared to wait, Gabriella?'

'No.' She watched his grin fade. 'He'll just have to tag along. After all, you know we like the same foods. What about McDonald's and a movie later, if I can get off on time?'

He groaned. 'If that's your only suggestion . . .'

Gaby twisted her hand, capturing his fingers. 'It is for the moment. But I'm at work. Ask me later. I might be able to come up with something better.'

276

Acknowledgements

I'm writing this with the warm August sun streaming in through the window on what has turned out to be the most difficult of years, in the knowledge that *Fallen Angel* is going to be published within weeks of Christmas and hopefully a very different and happier 2021.

This is the third book in the Gaby Darin series and my third with HQ Digital. I know that some of you have been with me from the start of my long writing journey but for others this will be the first book of mine that you've picked up. A huge thank you for your support. Without you, the reader, no books.

A special thanks to my Dream Team – a very small bunch of ladies that have mostly been with me from the beginning. I'd also like to thank Valerie Keogh, my writing pal, for the daily chats and general encouragement. The same goes for Beverley Hopper, from The Book Lovers.

Abi Fenton from HQ Digital has been instrumental in turning Gaby Darin into who she is today. The work behind the scenes that goes into the final polished version is immense and I'm so thankful she saw something in my words that she could work with. So, thanks to you, Chris Sturtivant, Dushi Horti and the rest of the team.

As a nurse I'm far from an expert on police procedures. While I have sought help from both the Guernsey and the Welsh police in the past, any mistakes in this book are entirely my own. In the same way, I've only scratched the surface on the role criminal profiling plays in modern-day policing so thank you to Professor Louise Almond, Liverpool University, for both your help and advice.

Fallen Angel is primarily set in Llandudno, where I used to live. My sister, Caroline, still lives in the area and has been brilliant in helping me with the book research so thanks, Callie. Also thanks to Laura Fairbairn-Percival for the bus advice. When I was looking into buttons and how I could incorporate them into my book, Kit Ellis from The Button Queen, a business that really does exist both online and in Newport, was instrumental in telling me about memorial buttons, so thank you.

I do try to use real businesses in my books as added background so thanks to The Imperial Hotel, Llandudno and La Dolce Vita, Rhos-on-Sea, for allowing me to include you.

While the characters in the book are fictitious there are a few that aren't. Amy Potter is a dear friend and a smashing nurse while Kay Enderlin won a competition to be included as a character. Vanessa Mahy is a real-life bar steward at the Guernsey Yacht Club. The book dedication will be auctioned off in a couple of days to raise funds for a new pool pod for disabled swimmers at Beau Sejour, a local Guernsey sports complex. Thanks in advance to the successful bidder.

Finally, thanks as always to my family for all the support and encouragement, especially Freya for the plotting chats. Love you to the moon and back.

Jenny O'Brien 10th August, 2020

278

Dear Reader,

We hope you enjoyed reading this book. If you did, we'd be so appreciative if you left a review. It really helps us and the author to bring more books like this to you.

Here at HQ Digital we are dedicated to publishing fiction that will keep you turning the pages into the early hours. Don't want to miss a thing? To find out more about our books, promotions, discover exclusive content and enter competitions you can keep in touch in the following ways:

JOIN OUR COMMUNITY:

Sign up to our new email newsletter: hyperurl.co/hqnewsletter

Read our new blog www.hqstories.co.uk

https://twitter.com/HQStories

www.facebook.com/HQStories

BUDDING WRITER?

We're also looking for authors to join the HQ Digital family!
Find out more here:

https://www.hqstories.co.uk/want-to-write-for-us/

Thanks for reading, from the HQ Digital team

ONE PLACE. MANY STORIES

HQ

**If you enjoyed *Fallen Angel*,
then why not try another unputdownable
thriller from HQ Digital?**

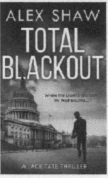